Talk to Me

Roseanne Beck

COPYRIGHT

TALK TO ME
Copyright © 2018 Roseanne Beck

Cover by Fresh Design

DEDICATION

This book is dedicated to my family and friends. Your support and encouragement have been nothing short of extraordinary.

A special thank you to Grammy A, who passed along the storytelling gene. I am ever so grateful

ACKNOWLEDGEMENTS

Thank you to everyone who has helped me in this most exciting journey.

I have an amazing group of critiquers and beta readers. Although there are too many of you to name, I couldn't have done this without you. Thank you for helping me shape Laura and Austin into what they are now.

A special shout out to the Marbles, who not only helped me get this story whipped into shape, but patiently answered my endless questions about the writing and publications processes and provided gentle nudges along the way.

And of course, I thank *you*, the reader. Thank you for taking a chance on my first book. I truly appreciate your time, your energy, and your open mind.

Talk to Me

ONE

Austin's hand searches the kitchen cabinet blindly, latching onto the bag of coffee for dear life. Carefully shifting his position, he balances between his crutches and the counter as he empties the bag into the coffee maker. The last remaining grounds tumble into the filter, forming a measly pile that comes nowhere close to being able to appease his caffeine demons.

"God dammit."

He digs through the cabinet again. *Nothing.* He works his way down the line of cabinets, then does a thorough inspection of his freezer. Finding little more than frozen dinners for one and bags of vegetables that double as ice packs, he slams the freezer door shut. *Crap.* Icy fingers of dread sweep away the early morning brain fog.

I'm completely out.

He glares at his leg, then does the same to the crutches holding him upright. Running out to the store is no longer a simple option. He huffs a bitter laugh. *Not gonna be doing anything in the same* universe *as running any more.* The coffee shop up the street would normally be a viable option, but the rain slanting sideways past the window makes it a very unappealing option.

Guess I could just give up coffee altogether. Austin snorts. *Yeah right. Already given up plenty since the accident. Not gonna give that up, too.*

His hands tighten around the handle of his crutches. *Come on. You wanted your independence. Figure it out.*

Calling for an emergency grocery delivery will likely cost an arm and a leg. *And I definitely don't have any of those to spare.* Not to mention the fact that there's a good chance it wouldn't arrive until the next day anyway.

Austin's head snaps up. *The neighbors.* He glances at the clock and drags himself through his apartment. He tries the neighbors on his right. No answer. He knocks at the apartment next to them and the two apartments across the hall. His desperation increases with each unopened door. *Okay, fifth time's the charm.* He raps on the door catty-corner from his own apartment. It swings open before his knuckles leave the wood, and he fights to keep his balance, wobbling on his good leg.

His relief at not landing in a heap at his new neighbor's feet is tempered by the fact that the older woman is standing in her bathrobe. The frilly monstrosity is gaping in all of the wrong places. *Keep your eyes up. Don't look down. Don't look down.* "Sorry to bother you…"

"Oh, no bother, dear." Her gaze travels from his face down to his crutches and back up again. "You must be my new neighbor. From across the hall."

"Uh, yeah. Austin."

"Mrs. Walters." She extends her right hand while her left struggles to keep her robe closed. "But please, call me Marge."

Austin forces a smile and returns her handshake. "Well, Marge, I'm having a bit of a rough morning." He barely contains a snort of derision. *Yeah, lot of rough mornings lately.* "I ran out of coffee. Would you happen to have some? I'll repay you."

"Oh, dear." Marge frowns and shakes her head. "I'm afraid not. No regular coffee for me. Not with my high blood pressure. But I can offer you a cup of decaf."

"Ummm, that's okay. Thanks anyway." *I'd rather poke my eyes out.* Austin gives her a weak smile and turns to leave.

"But my niece is coming over shortly," she adds. "I could have her pick something up for you if you'd like."

"That's okay. Don't want to trouble you."

"No trouble at all. That's what neighbors are for." She waves her hand, chasing away his protests like a swarm of gnats.

Austin keeps his eyes averted. Under normal circumstances, he'd be appalled to accept her offer. *Yeah, well, these aren't normal circumstances.* He sighs and plasters a smile onto his face. "That would be great. Thanks."

"Wonderful." She claps her hands together and allows the robe to gape dangerously. "I'll have Laura bring it over. Shouldn't be long now."

"Thanks." *God, I hope she gets here soon.*

"Would you like to come in and wait?"

Austin shakes his head. "No offense, but I think it's best if I wait at my place." Chit-chat before coffee is tantamount to torture, and despite Marge's friendly demeanor and willingness to help, he's in no mood to delve into the reason why he's in this mess in the first place. *And it always comes back to that.*

*
**

Laura hits the End button on her phone and tosses it into her messenger bag. She mumbles to herself as she shoves on her shoes and belts her raincoat. "Yeah, sure Aunt Marge. No problem. I'll be happy to pick up coffee for your neighbor in the middle of a monsoon." She sighs, unable to hold onto her indignation. Her aunt's description of Austin hits way too close to home. *Just like Marge knew it would.*

"Honestly, that woman…"

She shakes her head. That Woman is as caring as she is sneaky. As diabolical as she is entertaining. As free-spirited as she is matter-of-fact. *And one of the only things keeping me together.*

Flipping up her hood, she dashes to her car, half-way soaked by the time she reaches it. The dash into and out of the grocery store completes her drenching.

By the time she arrives at her aunt's apartment, she's managed to regain her annoyance. She glares at her aunt when she answers her staccato knocks. "Low blow, Aunt Marge."

Marge waves her inside and takes her dripping jacket, hanging it over a chair. She gives her niece a look of innocence. "What? You were coming over anyway. Just a little detour."

"Uh-huh." She pulls the coffee out of its plastic bag and holds it out to her aunt. "Here."

"Why don't you take it over to him?"

Laura's eyes narrow. "Why don't you?"

"I have a coffee cake in the oven. Just about ready to come out. Don't want it to burn."

"Yeah, 'cause *that* would be a shame," Laura mutters.

"What's that, dear?"

"What? Nothing." She eyes her aunt, her resolve crumbling once again. "Fine. Where is he?"

*
**

"Oh, for fuck's sake," Austin mumbles. The knocking on his front door continues. "Keep your pants on."

He's done his best to keep himself occupied until the arrival of the caffeine cavalry. Admittedly, the leg exercises probably weren't the best choice of activity. In addition to his raging caffeine withdrawal headache, the portions of his leg that he can still feel are grumbling their general displeasure. It's a toss-up whether his head or his leg bears the brunt of his ire.

Austin works his left leg under his body, then hauls himself upright with the help of the coffee table and sofa, wavering precariously until he gets his crutches tucked under his armpits. As he makes his way through his apartment, a snarl of frustration threatens to escape every time his right leg proves its inability to hold any decent amount of weight.

And this is me getting better.

"If you don't have coffee, get the hell out," Austin grumbles as he opens the door. He runs his gaze over the woman standing in the hallway. Half a head shorter than his six-foot-one frame, short spiky bleach blonde hair, somewhere in the ballpark of his own thirty-two years of age. Not usually what catches his attention, but not bad either. Her appearance is not nearly as interesting as what she's got in her hand, however.

"Coffee," he breathes, coming very close to sounding like a deranged caffeine-addicted zombie.

"Ummm, Austin?" The woman's pierced eyebrow raises in question.

"Hmmm?" he asks distractedly, still fixated on the bag of caffeinated goodness just out of his grasp. *Damn crutches.*

"You are Austin, right?" She glances up and down the hallway.

"Unfortunately."

"Laura. Marge's niece. She said you were looking for this?" Laura shakes the bag in her hand, releasing the aroma of coffee into the air.

"Oh, thank God." His brain cells cry out, practically begging him to do whatever's necessary to give them their first hit of the day. He reaches out to take the bag, his hand stilling in mid-air as he remembers his limitations. Like the fact that he needs both crutches to haul his sorry ass back into the kitchen. Which leaves him one hand and one coffee bag short of being able to appease his caffeine demons.

"Umm…" A flush creeps up his neck as he tries to figure out the logistics of carrying the coffee without landing in a heap on the floor. It's an oblong package and lacks the usual folded over edge at the top. *Crap.*

"Want me to —" Laura begins.

"I'm fine. I can get it."

"Okay then." Laura extends the bag again.

He studies the package for a few additional seconds, then heaves a sigh. Moving to the side of his door, he reluctantly gestures for her to enter his apartment. His need for coffee has greatly outstripped his pride. Yet another part of him injured in the accident.

Laura's eyes roam over the man in front of her. Despite his less than sparkling personality, he's not all that bad to look at. *Quite good, actually.* His chiseled jaw, disheveled light brown hair, slightly scruffy beard, and hazel eyes are definitely right up Laura's alley. *Dammit, Marge.* She shoots a suspicious glance toward her aunt's apartment, then turns her gaze back to Austin and sighs. He's staring at the bag of coffee like a lovesick teenager.

Her annoyance at her aunt's meddling nature drops several notches. *Poor guy.* She's well aware of the limitations of crutches, and her own love affair with caffeine nudges her enough that she steps into his apartment against her better judgement.

Following him into the kitchen, she tries not to stare. His steps are slow and measured, and he keeps his concentration locked on the floor. It looks like it takes significant effort to move his right leg. *Wonder what happened?*

Her brother used to hate it when he'd catch people watching him walk after his accident. So instead, she lets her gaze wander around the apartment. For someone who has some serious issues walking, his place is surprisingly clean. Although, on second glance, perhaps it's not so much clean as it is lacking any personal effects. The walls are devoid of anything other than a couple of generic pictures of country scenery. *I think Marge had that same meadow in her living room when she first moved in.* The living room contains a sofa and matching armchair arranged in the center of the room, and a TV and basic stereo system are set up along the far wall.

His kitchen is just as tidy. No dirty dishes cluttering the sink or surrounding countertops. None of the baked-on bubble-over that seems to be all too ubiquitous on her own stove. *Steven would have approved of this guy. At least his living habits, anyway.*

Laura swallows as the similarities between this stranger and her brother mount. She takes a deep breath and lets it out slowly. *You're fine. It's all going to be okay.* She rolls her eyes as the grief counselor's words ring in her ears. *Breathing techniques and mantras, my ass. What a rip-off.*

Spying the coffeemaker in the corner of the counter, she sets her caffeinated gift next to it. *Good deed for the day, done.* She turns to leave, then groans.

Austin balances against the counter and spares her a glance. "What?" He rips the bag open haphazardly, and a few grounds spill onto the counter.

"Nothing. Just trying to gear myself up to go back over to Marge's."

He punches the start button, his shoulders relaxing as the coffee machine grunts to life. "She seemed nice enough."

"Oh, yeah. She's great. It's just her coffee's decaf and there's a sugar-free coffee cake waiting for me over there."

Austin wrinkles his nose. "Ugh."

"Exactly."

He studies her, his hands clenching and unclenching the grips of his crutches. "You want a cup?" He nods toward the machine. "You know, as part of your payment?"

"Sure." *But only to avoid Marge's coffee.*

She can almost hear Steven calling her a liar.

Austin does his best Jedi mind-trick in an effort to get the coffee percolating faster. It doesn't work. He shifts his weight in twitchy anticipation, the gurgling of the machine filling the otherwise silent room. *Why the hell did I ask her to stay?* He's much less apt to strike up conversations with strangers these days. *The lack of caffeine must really be scrambling my brain. Either that, or it's the damn head injury.*

Laura flashes him a weak smile when the machine beeps its readiness. He fills two mugs and hands one to her, waving her into a seat at the small kitchen table while he remains standing, propped up against the counter. Movement and caffeine ingestion are mutually exclusive options for him.

"Oh God, how I've missed you," Austin murmurs into his mug. His eyes roll back in ecstasy as he lets out a low groan of pleasure.

"Want me to leave you two alone?" A smile twitches at the corner of Laura's mouth.

Austin huffs a laugh, quickly returning to the coffee mug glued to his hand. He reaches the bottom in record time, oblivious to the heat of the precious liquid.

"Wow, and I thought I was bad," Laura says. Her own mug is still three-quarters full.

"Yeah, well, desperate times…" Austin trails off as he refills his cup.

"So, I take it you won't be joining Aunt Marge for her decaf coffee hour, then?" Laura asks.

"Not if I can help it."

"Probably for the best. And don't let her fool you with her desserts either," Laura adds. "She's diabetic, but she doesn't have to take it out on the poor baked goods. They're all sugar-free."

"Thanks for the heads-up."

"Hey, no problem. Glad to help. Speaking of," Laura adds, "you need anything else?"

"You got another leg somewhere you could lend me?"

Laura chokes on her last sip of coffee, a strangled laugh escaping her mouth. She shakes her head and gestures to his leg. "Can I ask what happened?"

Dammit. Should've just kept my mouth shut. He really hates that question. Hates it because if he says "No, you can't," then it seems like he's trying to cover something up. Or embarrassed. If he says "Yes," then he's obligated to spill the beans. Which inevitably lends itself to yet another whole round of questions and pitying remarks like "Oh, you poor thing."

But unless his leg miraculously gets its act together and stops acting like such a bitch, he's going to have to get used to this little exchange. Even if it practically kills him to do so. Doesn't mean he has to spill *all* the beans, though.

"Car accident. A few months ago." Austin clenches his jaw and looks out the window over the kitchen sink.

Like Steven. Laura struggles to keep her emotions in check as the latest similarity punches her in the chest. The fist around her throat tightens, and she clamps her hands around her coffee mug, focusing on keeping her breathing even. "Sorry." She cringes as soon as the word leaves her mouth. *Steven always hated it.*

He flinches but remains silent.

Laura's hands tremble as she raises her coffee mug to her lips. *What the hell was Marge thinking?* Tears prick the corners of her eyes. She blinks rapidly to keep them from spilling onto her cheeks. *Gotta get out of here.* Her chair screeches as she stands up abruptly.

Austin's gaze swings back to Laura. "Want a refill?"

"No. Thanks. I've gotta go." She gives him a tight smile, rinses out her mug, and sets it in the sink.

"Here." Austin pulls a handful of dollar bills out of his pocket and holds them toward her. "For the coffee."

She's about to wave off his offer of repayment, then sees the look in his eye. That same look Steven used to have when he thought someone was taking pity on him. She takes the money and shoves it into her pocket, giving him a nod of thanks. *What Steven would've wanted.*

Clamping her lower lip between her teeth, she hustles out of his apartment. She's not sure how much longer she can keep it together. She'd rather not be in the company of a stranger when she falls apart.

TWO

Okay, Laura. You can do this. Nothing big. Just going into your office. Something you've been doing for years.

Despite her mini pep talk, she stays rooted to the spot just outside her closed door, staring at the sign.

L&S Consulting.

The small placard on the otherwise bare wall of the corridor is a stark reminder of their years of hard work. The years of studying and interning to become electrical engineers. To build their own business. *Me and Steven. Together. And now it's just me.*

Laura hasn't been inside for a couple of weeks. Not since the day she found him. She'd taken a few days off, barely managing to get out of bed. Marge had practically lived at her house during that time. *Don't know what I would've done without her.*

Nor does she know what she would have done without Theresa, their part-time receptionist. Theresa had been the one to place the calls to the clients. The one who made sure Laura still had a business to return to when the initial shock and grief faded. The one who brought her the necessary paperwork to enable her to work from home until she got it together enough to return to the office.

A sad smile plays at the corners of Laura's mouth as she imagines Steven questioning if she ever really had it together in the first place. She can still see the stupid smirk that had usually accompanied his teasing words. S*hit. This is gonna be harder than I thought.*

She rests her hand against the door and bows her head. Taking a few deep breaths, she braces herself against the emotions about to be thrown her way. Unlocking the door, she steps over the threshold of her office for the first time since Steven died.

Correction, since Steven killed himself. Right over there. Next to his desk.

Laura can't help but glance over to the spot where she'd found her brother, slumped against the wall, empty prescription bottles and a few rogue pills scattered around his body.

Her breath is stolen for a few seconds as she relives those hellish moments. She recalls rushing over to him, finding his body cold and stiff. Performing chest compressions on him anyway in the hope she'd somehow read the situation wrong. That she'd somehow be able to make his glassy eyes see her again and his blue-tinged lips take a gasp of air.

It wasn't until Theresa had come in shortly thereafter that she'd finally stopped. The petite mother of two had dragged her off of Steven's lifeless body. From there things went blurry. The haze of paramedics and police mixed together to cement the nightmare scenario of Steven's death. Of his suicide. *All because I couldn't figure out how to help him.*

Shaking herself out of her macabre reflection, Laura heads over to her desk and sinks into her chair. She pulls her laptop and a couple of client folders out of her messenger bag and arranges them on her desk, the top of which is lacking its usual clutter. *Must remember to thank Theresa for cleaning it up for me.* Her desk usually looks like a small tornado has touched down. Steven's had always been just inches away from immaculate.

Her throat constricts, and she closes her eyes against the threat of tears, trying valiantly to keep her mind on her work. She takes a few deep breaths and opens her eyes, gluing them to the spreadsheets on her desk in an attempt to keep her gaze from wandering over to where Steven had chosen to end his life.

She works on the calculations for the Richardson proposal for about an hour before she gets the feeling something isn't right. *And not just with these damn numbers.* Nothing she can put her finger on, just something that puts her senses on alert. Like the feeling that someone else is in the office with her.

Except there's not.

From her seat, Laura can clearly see the rest of the small office. She is definitely the only one in the room. As she casts her eyes around the space, she sees the same view she's seen for years. A few photos of her and Steven stand atop the filing cabinets along the wall to her right. There's a fern in the far corner of the room that only Theresa ever seems to water. Graduation diplomas and certifications hang on the walls. When her gaze falls on Steven's desk, her eyes narrow. *Wasn't that coffee mug sitting on the opposite side when I first came in?*

Frustrated by her inability to clearly recall the placement of the only item on Steven's otherwise bare desk, she heads to the restroom down the hall. She locks the office door behind her before making the short trek, grateful she doesn't come across any of the other occupants of the second floor. She's really not sure she'd be able to handle the inquiries or the empty words of comfort right now.

She washes her hands at the sink before splashing her face with cold water. Patting her face dry with one of the scratchy brown paper towels from the dispenser on the wall, she takes a hard look at herself in the mirror. She's not a fan of what she sees.

The haircut is no different from the one she's had for over a decade. The barbell piercing through her right eyebrow is as natural to her now as the earrings she wears. It's the pallor of her face and the puffiness under her eyes that are unnatural.

Dammit Steven.

She bites down on her lower lip in an effort to keep any additional tears at bay, relenting only when she tastes the coppery tang of blood. *Get it together.* Giving her head one final shake, she heads back to her office.

She manages to make some headway with the proposal and is in the midst of calculating the necessary load for the power distribution when that same sensation sneaks up on her again. The hairs on the back of her neck stand at attention as her ears prick at the feeling she's missing something just out of her range of hearing. *What the hell is going on?*

Laura gets out of her chair and scours the office, checking every corner in an effort to prove to herself that no one else is there. *Just my mind playing tricks on itself.*

Reassured but still a little on edge, she decides to give her aunt a call. Marge has been invaluable these past few weeks; her stories and anecdotes are always just enough to keep Laura grounded. She's sure Marge will be able to come up with something to help her through whatever the hell this is.

Laura's hopes of finding solace in her aunt are suspended when she can't find her phone. *That's weird.* She always keeps it in the same place—in the inside pocket of her messenger bag. She also knows she had it just a little while ago; she clearly recalls using it while she'd spoken to Theresa on her way in to work.

Laura rummages around in her bag a bit more, finally resorting to dumping its contents onto her desk. She thinks back, trying to retrace her steps that morning. Her blood runs cold when her gaze falls on a partially opened filing cabinet drawer behind Steven's desk.

Her eyes widen as she recalls several other instances of missing personal items. Once it had been her car keys. Another time it had been her eye drops for pink eye. Steven had always been the culprit. Used to love stealing her things and hiding them from her, delighting in her resultant frustration. *The filing cabinet had been one of his favorite hiding places.*

Heart beating wildly at the possible implications of that cabinet drawer, she peels herself out of her chair and crosses the room. Her hand hovers over the handle of the drawer for a few interminable seconds. *I'm just being paranoid.*

Her breath catches in her throat when she pulls the drawer fully open. Her phone is lying on the bottom. Where she most certainly did not leave it.

She snatches the phone from its resting place and casts a frantic glance around the rest of the room. Her eyes inevitably fall on that one spot she's been so desperately trying to avoid. Her heart hammers against her rib cage as she tries to make sense of it all. Of Steven's decision. Her phone's disappearance and inexplicable relocation. Her tenuous mental state.

She chokes back a small sob as the weight of Steven's actions come crashing down on her. Dangerously close to yet another breakdown, she gathers her belongings and shoves her laptop and a couple of files into her bag for perusal later on. When she's not in danger of completely freaking out.

Laura beats a hasty retreat, locking the office door behind her. She sags against it, trying to will her heart to slow down before it jumps right out of her chest. The mantras from the grief counselor run through her head on a continuous loop. *It will be okay. I'll be okay. This too, shall pass.*

She doesn't know if she's ever believed herself any   less.

THREE

Marge reaches across the corner of her dining room table and gives Laura's arm a squeeze. "Well, dear," she says, "you knew the first day back wasn't going to be an easy day. But you did it. You never have to do it again. It's behind you."

Laura runs her fork through the sauce on her plate, making abstract art out of the congealed remains of the takeout Chinese. "I know. It just... It just feels like he's still there."

Marge tilts her head and sighs. "I know, dear. It probably will for a while yet. You'll get through it."

Laura opens her mouth to protest, then shuts it. *That's not what I meant.* She's considered telling Marge about the phone on several occasions but has yet to divulge the events that led her to hide out in her aunt's apartment for the rest of the day. Instead, she's gone along with Marge's assumption that it was simply the stress of her first day back at her office that got to her.

Marge pushes herself up from the table. "What would you like for dessert? Oh, I know. I made a batch of cookies the other day."

Laura is careful to keep her features schooled. Her aunt's attempt at sugar-free cookies have been nowhere near successful. "No thanks. I'm feeling better now. I should probably be going."

Marge envelops her in a hug, and Laura inhales, taking comfort in the mingling scents of lavender and honey. *Thank God I've still got her.* "Thanks again, Aunt Marge." Laura gives her a final squeeze and steps away.

"Anytime, dear." Marge opens the door and looks down the hall, then back at Laura. "And thanks for helping Austin the other day."

"Yeah, sure. No problem."

A smirk plays at the corners of the older woman's mouth. "That is one good-looking man."

Laura narrows her eyes. "Yeah? I hadn't noticed."

"Bullshit." Marge gives her a pointed stare. "You know, one of these days someone's going to crack through that wall you put up."

"Not if I can help it." Laura gives Marge an exaggerated grin and pecks her on the cheek. "All right. See you later."

Marge places her hands on either side of Laura's face and locks her gaze with her niece's. "It *will* get easier. You *will* get through this."

The empathy in her aunt's eyes is almost more than Laura can take. She presses her lips together and nods, unwilling to let her emotions run roughshod over her yet again.

Marge gives her one last smile and closes the door.

Laura leans against it, taking measured breaths while she works to keep herself under control. *It damn well better get easier. I'm not sure it could get any worse.*

Her gaze rests on the door to Austin's apartment while she corrals her emotions. *Wonder how he's doing?* Her answer comes rather unexpectedly when she hears a loud thud from behind his door. The noise is initially accompanied by a string of rather colorful curses, followed by silence.

She heads to her car, her steps faltering halfway down the hallway as she engages in a lightning-quick debate with herself. *You are not obligated to check on him. But what if something happened? I would've wanted someone to check on Steven.*

Laura retraces her steps and stands outside Austin's apartment for several seconds, listening intently for any reassuring sounds. Hearing nothing but her own conflicting thoughts, she knocks on his door. "Austin? You in there?"

"Yep." His faint reply does little to reassure her.

"Are you okay?"

"Fan-fucking-tastic," comes the slightly slurred, overly-cheerful answer.

Laura tries once more to talk herself out of intervening, then lets out a weary sigh and drops her head in resignation. She knocks again but gets no response. She turns the doorknob, more than a little surprised to find it unlocked. Peeking around the door, her gaze sharpens when she finds Austin sprawled face up on the floor.

"Umm, you sure you're all right?" Laura steps into the apartment and looks around. The only clues she can find to explain his current situation are the empty beer bottles and a half-empty bottle of whiskey on the coffee table.

"Laura?" Austin raises his head slightly. "What are you doing up there?"

"Trying to figure out what you're doing *down there*."

"Oh. Nothing. Just lying here. Enjoying the view," he says, his words slurred.

"All right." *Three sheets to the wind, but he seems fine otherwise.* "Looks like you're having a party. I'll just leave you to it then."

"Aww, come on. Stay. Have a drink with me," he says, waving his hand toward the bottles littering the table. "I'm celebrating."

"Oh?" Her eyebrow lifts slightly, well aware of what kind of "celebrations" inspire a drinking party for one.

"Saw the doctor today." Austin's forehead creases in concentration as he tries to haul himself into an upright position.

"Did he give you some good news?"

"Something like that. Told me I should probably switch over to the other crutches." He gestures to a pair of forearm crutches leaning against the sofa.

"Okay…" Laura drawls. *Not quite sure what that has to do with anything.*

"Those are the ones they give to people when they're gonna be using them for a long time. When it's permanent."

"Oh. You sure you're okay?" she asks again, a little more weight behind her words.

"Never better," Austin says, working himself into a seated position against the sofa. He fists the jeans of his right leg in an effort to get it repositioned. "Shit," he breathes out, letting his head fall back against the couch.

Austin's weary gesture has Laura's senses on high alert. His obvious dejection and attempts at self-medication are sending her back to a couple of months ago. Back to when Steven had been having one of his low moments. One of the many her brother just couldn't seem to shake. *No matter how much I tried to help.*

"Want to talk about it?" Laura deposits her bag on the floor and lowers herself into the armchair. It looks like it's seen better days but turns out to be quite comfortable.

"Not really." Austin rolls his head toward Laura. "Besides, nothing much to say except my leg's screwed to hell, I think I'm going crazy, and my life sucks. But enough about me," he adds, squinting one eye shut. "How was your day?"

Laura snorts, completely taken off guard by Austin's change in conversational direction. Her initial amusement takes a sudden downward turn as his question reminds her of the day's events. "Sucky," she finally says, huffing out a sad little laugh at their respective situations.

"Want to talk about it?" Austin asks.

"Not really."

"Okay then." He reaches out his hand, carefully scooting the bottle of Jack toward Laura in a show of solidarity. "Liquor it is."

Laura eyeballs the offering, weighing her need for escape against the need for sobriety. *If today's events don't call for a drink, I don't know what does.* She takes a quick swig from the bottle, hissing as the burn hits the back of her throat.

"Atta girl."

A sad smile tugs at her mouth. *Drinking to forget about Steven with a stranger who kind of reminds me of him. Definitely screwed up.* She tilts the bottle to her lips again, taking a longer pull.

"Gimme." Austin flaps his hand toward Laura, then takes another sip when she hands him the bottle. "Ah, refreshing." He hands the bottle back to her, his expression turning to one of contemplation. "Hey. You ever wonder what the color black tastes like? Like, is it everything rolled together in one giant burrito? Or maybe like nothing; like the opposite of an all-you-can eat buffet."

"Huh. Never thought about it." Laura takes another drink, feeling the edges of her sadness dull as the 80-proof liquid floats through her bloodstream. "But I'll bet it sounds like the low moan of a thousand souls slowly being tortured."

Austin bobs his head. "Yep. Or maybe it's like after you're at a concert and there's still stuff echoing in your head but you can't really hear it anymore. Maybe it's like that." He stares into the distance for several seconds, then meanders his gaze back to Laura. "You ever hear stuff you're not supposed to hear?"

Laura scrunches up her nose. "You mean like hearing your neighbors having sex?" She tilts the bottle to her lips again.

Austin shakes his head, then grabs the coffee table when he starts to tilt to the side. "No. I mean like voices in your head that aren't yours."

Laura looks closer at Austin. *I really hope he's just drunk and not crazy.* She huffs a laugh as the earlier events of the day replay in her mind. *Although I might be crazy, too.* "Hey. Do you believe in ghosts?"

Austin adjusts his position against the sofa. "Yeah. I think so. Sometimes I wonder if they're in my head."

"If who's in your head?"

"What?" Austin's face crinkles in confusion.

"You wonder if who's in your head?"

Austin scoffs. "You're drunk."

"Umm, pretty sure you're drunk."

A grin spreads across Austin's face. "Yeah. I think you're right." His head bobs slightly as his eyelids fight gravity; he finally succumbs, and his head drifts downward until his chin rests on his chest.

Laura lays her head back against the chair as she studies her host. *Dammit, Marge is right. He is one good-looking man. One good-looking, very drunk, man.* Long dark lashes rest against his cheeks, and his breaths come in a steady rhythm through slightly parted full lips. The dimple in the middle of his lower lip looks especially inviting.

Austin's left leg twitches, and his breathing speeds up. "No." His eyes remain closed but his forehead scrunches as he mumbles. "No."

Austin's panicked mutterings bring Laura back from the edge of drunken carelessness and serve as an anchor. She rises from her chair, holding onto it for a moment while the room undulates. Squatting down beside him, she gives his shoulder a gentle shake. "Hey."

He startles under her touch; his head jerks up, and he blinks rapidly until his eyes focus on her. "Oh, hey." His lips curl into a lazy smile. "You're still here."

"Yep."

Austin's eyes drift closed again.

She shakes him. "You think maybe you should go to bed?"

His eyelids flutter open. "Are you prepositioning me?"

She slides him a bland glance, the corners of her lip twitching in amusement. "No. I am neither prepositioning nor propositioning you."

"Oh," Austin says with an air of disappointment. "Bummer."

"All right, come on," Laura says, trying to coerce him into moving from his spot on the floor. "Unless you're just going to sleep down there?"

"Yeah, that'll feel great in the morning." He winces as he tries to shift his position.

"Need some help?"

Austin glares at the hands Laura's holding out to him. He makes a couple of false starts, managing to do little more than get his left leg under himself before he lets out a growl of frustration. "Shit. Fine." He takes Laura's hands and hangs on as she hauls him upright, clinging tightly to her as he wobbles.

"Think you can manage?" Laura nods toward his new crutches.

"I'm pretty sure I can manage to fall flat on my ass, if that's what you mean," Austin slurs, a self-deprecating smile accompanying his sarcastic retort.

"Okay, wanna help me out here?" Laura asks. *How the hell am I gonna get him to his bedroom without both of us ending up on the ground?*

Austin nods her over to his side and slings an arm around her neck. She takes his weight and lets out an involuntary "oof". He's got several inches on her, more than a few pounds, and has the added benefit of drunken uncoordination. His right leg really isn't doing anything to keep him upright and his left doesn't seem to be faring much better.

Austin punctuates each of his limping steps with a muttered curse as they proceed to the back of his apartment. "Fucking leg. God damn cat. Fucking tree."

"What's the poor cat got to do with it?"

"What?" he asks, a confused look on his face. "How'd you know about the cat?"

"Because you just told me."

"Oh," he says, falling silent once again as he concentrates on his proper footing. "Hey," Austin says after another few seconds of intense silence, "can we take a little detour? Bathroom," he adds with a sheepish smile of apology.

"Yeah, sure. Think you'll be okay?" While Laura's willing to help him get to bed, she draws the line at anything bathroom-related.

"Oh God. If I can't figure out how to take a piss in my own bathroom, just kill me now."

Laura flinches, his words far too on point for her liking. She gets him into the bathroom and makes sure he has a firm grip on the grab bar next to the toilet before she lets go. "All right. Can I trust you not to fall over or drown in the toilet?"

Austin manages a small nod, although the pallor of his face cancels out his reassurance.

Laura gives him his privacy and waits on the other side of the door, her senses on high alert. *Please don't make me have to call 911 tonight.*

"All right. I'm good." Austin's voice is accompanied by the flush of the toilet.

When Laura opens the door, she finds Austin upright, no worse for wear, propped against the sink as he washes his hands. He dries them haphazardly on a nearby hand towel, then shuffles around so she can resume her previous position.

The two continue their trek, finally arriving in Austin's bedroom out of breath from the effort. Dumping her charge rather unceremoniously onto his double bed, she helps him get his leg up onto it, taking note of the brace around the lower portion of his leg. "You want to take this off?"

"What?" Austin cracks open an eyelid. Catching sight of the brace in question, he rolls his eyes, lets out a groan, and slams his eyes shut. "No," he ekes out, "just leave it."

"Okay." The greenish tinge of his face prompts Laura to cast a quick glance around the room. She spies a metal trash can in the corner and sets it within easy reach in case Austin feels the need to empty his stomach sometime during the night. "You good here?" she asks, backing away just in case that necessity comes a little sooner than later.

"Yep. Awesome." He gives her a rather weak thumbs-up in confirmation, his eyes remaining tightly closed.

"All right then. Good luck. Don't fall overboard," she says as she backs out of the room.

Her parting words elicit a soft laugh followed by a longer moan as Austin clutches his bed.

Poor guy. Hate to be him in the morning.

Laura halts her progress to the front door, her own level of inebriation giving her pause. *I should definitely not be driving.* She thinks about crashing at her aunt's, then reconsiders when she thinks about explaining to Marge that she'd been drinking with Austin. *Don't want to give her the satisfaction.* She eyeballs the oversized couch. *Maybe I can just sleep it off and then drive home.* She curls up and wraps herself in the crocheted blanket draped over the back. *Yeah. Just a few hours.*

FOUR

"Why can't I move my leg?"

A hand on his shoulder. "Austin, listen to me. You were in an accident. They flew you to the hospital. You had surgery."

"Am I okay?"

The hand squeezes his shoulder. "You're alive. That's all that matters."

Austin tosses and turns, the memories creeping past the waning haze of alcohol. His mind flips through a rolodex of images. *Driving. Cat. Swerving. Tree.*

"No!"

A gigantic oak tree approaching at supersonic speed jolts him awake. Sunlight hits his retinas. He hisses and slams his eyes shut. His brain pulsates in time with his heartbeat, and his stomach churns in a slow mixture of dread and displeasure. *Fuuuck. As if the nightmares aren't enough. Looks like I get to deal with a hangover today, too.*

He lies still, caught between the desire to try to fall asleep again and the knowledge that sleep will only delay the inevitable. *Need some water. And ibuprofen.* Not to mention the fact that if he stays in bed too long there's a good chance his leg will punish him for it.

Peeling his eyes open once again, he slowly pushes himself into a seated position, wincing against the increased pounding in his head. The room sways, and he braces himself, breathing deeply through the nausea roiling in his gut.

When he's no longer in danger of emptying his stomach into the trashcan next to his bed, several details raise questions. *Why is the trashcan over here next to the bed when it's normally across the room? Why the hell am I still wearing my shoes and brace? And where the hell are my crutches?*

Carefully sliding off the bed, he works his way around his room in an awkward combination of shuffles and hops, a maneuver he'd perfected during his stay at the rehab facility. Using first his bed and then the nightstand next to it to hold himself upright, he makes it to the door of his bedroom. He surveys his apartment, clinging to the doorframe for dear life; his forearm crutches are propped up against the sofa.

Dammit.

As he looks closer, he can make out a lump underneath the blanket on his sofa. *What the hell?* He racks his brain, trying to recall the previous evening's events. *Not really sure about anything after the Jack.*

He wobbles as his concentration strays, and he clings tighter to the doorframe. "Shit." He eyeballs the empty space between himself and his crutches. *Really don't want to have to scoot over there on my ass.*

The lump on the sofa stirs, and a spiky blonde head appears from beneath the blanket.

"Laura?"

Laura yawns and rubs her eyes. She looks around the room, the confusion on her face mirroring his own. "What time is it?"

"Seven-thirty."

"Ugh. Sorry." Laura sits up, then massages her temples. "I was just gonna sleep the whiskey off for a couple of hours, then head home." She stands up and stretches, then slings her bag across her body. "Thanks for the Jack. And the couch. I should get going."

His leg buckles and he shifts more of his weight against the doorframe. "Uh…" *Shit. You are* not *gonna fall down in front of her.* "Can I get a little help here?" He nods toward his crutches.

Laura's eyes widen. "Oh, yeah. Sorry." She crosses the room with the requested items, then studies him. "How's it going this morning? You were in rough shape last night."

Austin slides his crutches into place. "Super. Haven't had this good of a hangover in a couple years."

"Need anything before I go?"

"If you could get the lights to stop hurting, that'd be great."

Laura cracks a smile. "I'll see what I can do."

"And about last night. Thanks."

"For?"

Austin nods toward his bedroom. "I'm guessing you helped haul my sorry ass to bed."

Laura shrugs. "No problem. Looked like you were gonna camp out on the floor otherwise."

"Yeah, I really don't think my leg would've been happy with that."

"Plus it was educational. Although I'm still not quite sure what the poor cat had to do with anything."

"Cat? What cat?"

"Last night. You kept talking about a cat." Laura tilts her head, a confused look on her face. "And a tree?"

Dammit, Austin. Can't keep your drunken mouth shut. He drops his head, his hands tightening around his crutches. Sighing, he catches her eye and tilts his chin toward the kitchen. "I don't know about you, but I really need some coffee. Especially if I'm gonna tell you about the damn cat. You want a cup?"

Laura studies him, her fingers tightening around the strap of her messenger bag. "Sure."

Austin heads into the kitchen while Laura makes a pit-stop in the bathroom. He downs a couple ibuprofen, gets the coffee percolating, then lowers himself gently into a chair at his kitchen table. He lays his head on the table in the hopes that it will give him relief from the raging jackhammer in his brain. *Nope.*

"That good, huh?"

"Awesome." Austin doesn't look up at Laura's question, just keeps his head still against the cool wood. He winces as her chair scrapes across the floor, then again as the machine beeps.

"Stay," she says, "I'll get it." She fills the mugs he'd set beside the machine, then places one next to his hand and sits down.

"Thanks." *Wonder if she'd mind if I just snorted the coffee grounds? Get the end result quicker?* They sit quietly, allowing the caffeine to slowly kickstart their brains.

He finally speaks once he feels like conversation isn't quite such a chore. "Damn cat. Came out of nowhere. Late at night, no one else on the road but me. And the cat of course. It just darted across the road in front of me like it had a death wish. I slammed on the brakes, wasn't even thinking. Just a reflex. Practically stood on the brake pedal as I swerved to avoid it. And I did. Although the tree, not so much." He glances up at Laura and gives her a wry smile. "Dislocated hip, broken femur, head injury, along with a lot of other bumps and bruises. But at least the cat's okay."

"Well, thank God for that."

Austin snorts at her bland retort, then winces at the resultant icepick through his skull. "Yeah. It took a couple of surgeries to get my leg and hip put back together again. But I was also lucky enough to damage a couple of important nerves." His gaze travels down to his outstretched leg and his lip curls in disgust at the sight of the brace peeking out below the bottom of his jeans. "Because of the injuries and the nerve damage, my leg's really weak and unstable. Doesn't hold my weight. Need the crutches to walk, and the brace keeps me from tripping over myself."

"Is it getting any better?"

Austin clenches his jaw as he plays with the handle of his mug. "I wasn't allowed to put any weight on it for the first two and a half months. Did inpatient rehab before moving here; now I'm doing intensive outpatient rehab. Still can't really walk." Austin swallows past the fear clogging his throat. *What if this is as good as it gets?* "But on the upside, the nerve damage keeps me from feeling the majority of the pain. So at least there's that," he says with a huff of a laugh. "So, I'm guessing I win the prize for Most Likely to Bring Down a Party right now."

While Laura can tell Austin's making a concerted effort to gloss over the emotions of his story, she can also see the pain lingering just behind the façade. *Something Steven tried so hard to fight.*

She's not quite sure why she feels pulled to share her own story, especially given the parallels between Austin and her brother. But something about his openness nudges her to divulge her own current level of hell.

"Don't be so sure about that."

Austin raises an eyebrow as he sips his coffee.

She closes her eyes and inhales, blowing it out slowly before she speaks again. "So, I'm kind of a mess right now. My brother died a couple of weeks ago. Killed himself." She bites down on her lip to keep the trembling under control. "Sorry," she says, hating the way her voice wavers.

Austin holds up a hand. "No apologies. You got an earful from me. Least I can do is return the favor."

She gives him a weak smile. "We were always so close growing up. Only a year apart, we might as well have been twins. Most people thought we were. But we weren't like, *creepy* close or anything," she hastily adds. "We had our own friends, went to different colleges. Started out in different jobs before we decided to join our Wonder Twin powers and go into business together." Her face softens as she recalls their jokes over what particular powers they would each actually have. Steven had always chosen super strength while she'd always wished for the ability to fly.

"He was in a motorcycle accident a little over a year ago." Laura's lashes dampen and she blinks in an effort to avoid a display of waterworks. "Lost his leg, went into a depression. All stuff that was kind of normal for his situation, you know?" She glances up at Austin, who bobs his head slightly. *Oh, right. Guess he really would know.* "And then he was better. Got a prosthetic, got his life back on track. We thought he was doing fine. And then all of a sudden… he wasn't."

The tears gather force, and she finally resorts to a rapid swipe of her eyes with the heel of her hand. "I tried to talk to him. Had Aunt Marge try. Dragged him to the doctor. No matter what we did, we just couldn't seem to pull him out of it." Her voice drops to a whisper. "*I* couldn't pull him out of it. I found him on the floor of our office one morning. He overdosed on medications."

Silence stifles the room for several heartbeats.

"Hey." Austin reaches across the table and lays his hand on Laura's arm. "I'm sorry."

"No apologies, remember?"

Austin leans back in his seat, his lips forming a half-smile. "Well then, how about co-ownership of the Debbie Downer award?"

Laura gives him a wobbly smile in return. "You sure you want to relinquish full possession? I hear that's a pretty hot commodity."

"Hey, that's just the kind of guy I am. Willing to share."

"Well, thanks. I guess."

"My pleasure."

Laura's a little surprised to find she feels a bit lighter after her discussion with Austin. Like maybe the weight of Steven's decision won't continue to crush her soul into a thousand pieces. After the weeks of hell she's endured, the lightening of that load is a pleasure unto itself.

She drains her mug, glances at the coffee machine, then back at Austin. "You a good enough guy to let me have the last cup of coffee?"

"Don't push your luck."

FIVE

Laura rolls her head and shoulders, trying to keep the tension from sinking its claws into her muscles. She's been staring at the same drawing for half an hour and there's something about the calculations that still isn't making sense. *Dammit Steven, I could really use your help with this.*

Goosebumps materialize on her arms. She looks up and glances around the room.

Theresa's on the phone, discussing something about construction hang-ups and labor disputes. Steven's desk is completely empty; the coffee cup that had been sitting there is no longer in sight.

Her eyes stray over to the filing cabinet. *Thank God it's still closed.*

Theresa places the phone back in its cradle and studies Laura from across the room. "You okay over there?"

Laura works a smile onto her face. "Yeah, I'm fine." She sighs and rolls her shoulders again. "Just trying to get back in the swing of things."

Theresa tilts her head to the side. "Don't try to bullshit me." Her face softens as she continues.

"You're allowed to grieve, you know. You've been through a traumatic experience."

"Yeah, well, so have you." Laura clears her throat. *No crying.* "Thanks for sticking around. I don't know what I would've done without you."

"Not gonna lie to you," Theresa says. "That was one of the toughest days of my life. Thought about quitting right then and there. Rob told me I should."

"Maybe your husband's right."

Theresa stands up and shakes her head, then walks over to the filing cabinets. "Not gonna happen." She rifles through a drawer and pulls out a file, then turns to face Laura. "That family of mine's liable to drive me crazy. I need this job to get me out of the house." Her playful grin falters. "Besides, I couldn't do that to you."

"Well, thanks. I appreciate it. Really, I do." She stares down at her desk, swallowing against the threat of tears, then darts her glance back to Theresa. "And thanks for cleaning up my desk. I almost didn't recognize it when I came back to work the other day."

Theresa holds her hands up in a defensive gesture. "I didn't touch that disaster area of a desk. You've threatened me with physical harm enough times that I just kind of pretend I can't even see it." She waves her hand in Laura's general direction. "It's like a big black hole over there as far as I'm concerned."

Laura forces out a weak laugh. *Then who the hell straightened up my desk?* A puff of cold air sends a shiver racing down her spine and she swivels around in her chair. The window behind her is closed. She holds her hand out and runs it around the edges, searching for any leaks which could have accounted for a gust of chilly fall air. *Nothing.*

She turns back to face the room and sees Theresa packing up her bags. "You heading out?"

Her receptionist nods. "Yeah. Gotta take Kaylee to the dentist. You should be good for the rest of today. You've got that meeting over at the new building site this afternoon, but your schedule's otherwise clear. Let me know if you need anything."

"All right. See you tomorrow."

Laura tries to focus on the drawing still lying in the middle of her desk. Ten minutes later, the frustration levels begin to build again. No matter how many times she runs the numbers, the estimations just don't add up. She props her elbows on the table and drops her head into her hands. "Dammit. What am I missing?"

A sudden thud causes Laura to glance up. The same filing cabinet that held her phone is again partially opened.

Heart beating wildly, she springs out of her seat, the wheeled armchair skidding away. Her eyes dart around the room. *What the hell?*

The air is heavy and still. Her ears strain for the sound of anything other than her own blood pulsating in her ears. Body tense, she lets one word slip out of her desert-dry mouth. "Steven?"

The filing cabinet closes with a squeaky groan.

Oh, hell no.

Laura grabs her bag, leaving her papers and laptop lying on her desk. She double-times it out of her office, barely stopping long enough to lock the door behind her. Her feet carry her down the stairs and out the front door of the building, one thought on her mind.

I need a drink.

Austin pauses on the sidewalk and readjusts his grip on his forearm crutches. *Come on, man. Just a little farther.* The aroma of freshly-brewed coffee wafts toward him, reminding him of the pot of liquid gold at the end of the rainbow. He shakes out his arms one at a time, then continues toward the coffee shop, eyes on the ground. *Crutches forward, right leg up to the crutches, left leg forward.*

He pauses outside the entrance, getting himself balanced to open the door. A young woman pushes through the door on her way out, coffee in one hand, her eyes glued to the phone in the other. He tries to step out of her way, but his movements aren't fast enough. *Shit.* She brushes against him and his balance wavers. His hand darts out and clasps her forearm to keep from falling, her phone clattering to the ground.

"Hey, watch it…" She looks up, her expression morphing from outrage to apology. "Oh my God. I am so sorry!"

He drops his hand from her arm, heat creeping up his neck. *Would've rather had the outrage.* "It's fine."

She picks up her phone and drops it in her bag. "Do you need any help?"

"No. I've got it." His hands tighten around his crutches.

"Here." She opens the door for him. "Least I can do."

Austin's pride takes a direct hit. *I'm supposed to be holding doors open for women. Not the other way around.* He clenches his jaw and gives her a tight smile. *Keep it together.*

Pre-accident, he probably would have snagged her number. Might have made an effort to actually get in her way in the first place. But these days... *Not really sure who'd want to get involved with this now.*

He makes his molasses-like way to the counter and places his order.

The barista slides his coffee across the counter. "You need help with that?"

"What? Oh." Austin looks at the cup, then down at his crutches. *Crap. How did I not think about that?* He tamps down additional disgust at his situation and sighs. "Yeah. Thanks." *God, this sucks.*

"No problem." The man comes around the counter. "Where would you like to sit?"

Austin looks around the room, his eyes stopping when he sees Laura sitting at a table in the corner. He nods toward her. "Over there." He leads the barista toward her table. "Mind if I join you?"

She startles at his words and her eyes jump to his. "What? Austin? What are you doing here?"

"Thanks," Austin says to the barista as he sits down across from her. "Need to practice with my new crutches. Figured I'd give myself a reward at the end." He sips his special dark roast as he studies her. "How about you?"

"Couldn't find any open bars." Her accompanying laugh sounds slightly off-kilter.

"It's ten-thirty in the morning."

"And?"

He looks closer. Her eyes are so wide he can see the whites around her irises, her hands have a fine tremor, and her leg is jiggling like she's trying to shake something loose. "Uh, do you think you should be drinking that?"

"Why?"

"Because any more caffeine and you're liable to blast off."

She takes another sip, then places the mug on the table but keeps her hands wrapped around it.

"Do you come here often?" Austin cringes. *That sounded like a bad pick-up line.*

Laura nods. "My office is a couple blocks away." Her face blanches. She pries one hand away from her mug and squeezes the bridge of her nose. "Just had to get out of there."

He leans forward, resting his arms on the table. "Any special reason?"

Laura gnaws on her lip as she stares at her coffee, then locks eyes with him. "Do you remember anything about our conversation a couple nights ago?"

Austin scours his memory but comes up short of anything resembling a meaningful discussion. "Unless it was about burritos and hearing your neighbors having sex, then no."

She's quiet for a little while, her coffee holding her attention, and he waits to see if she'll shed additional light on the subject.

The ring on her middle finger beats out an uneven rhythm as she taps it against her mug. She swings her gaze back to his. "Do you ever get the feeling you're not alone?"

"Um, yeah. When I'm not alone."

"No, I mean like you're being watched. Or maybe something's there but you just can't see it."

He eyes her warily, sifting through the muddled memories of the other night. *Crap. Did I tell her about the voices in my head?*

"Forget it, never mind." She slides her gaze away, a look of dejection on her face. "Maybe I'm just imagining it."

Austin tenses. *That's exactly what they said to me in the hospital.* "What if you're not?"

Laura swallows, her knuckles white around her mug. "What if I'm going crazy?"

He leans closer and drops his voice. "Do you hear things? Like, voices you can't quite figure out who they belong to?"

Her eyes snap back to his and she shakes her head vigorously.

Crap. Now she's gonna think I'm *crazy. Or she's gonna think I think* she's *crazy...*

"But I think my office might be haunted." She focuses all her effort on the empty coffee mug clasped between her hands. "I think Steven might still be there."

Austin's shoulders relax and he lets out a relieved breath. *Thank God. At least she doesn't think I'm crazy. Wait...* "What?"

"I can feel him there sometimes. His presence. And there's these little bursts of cold air. Sometimes things move, get hidden; stuff he used to do to try to piss me off."

"You sure? Going through trauma sometimes does funny things to you." *Something else they kept telling me in the hospital.*

Laura shrugs. "The only thing I'm sure about is how messed up this is."

"Yeah, join the club," Austin mutters. He shifts in his seat, adjusting his leg under the table. "Do you need to go back today?"

"Yeah. Left my laptop there. Need some of the files for a meeting this afternoon."

"Are you there by yourself?"

"Yeah. My receptionist won't be back until tomorrow."

Austin chews on the inside of his cheek. *Might not be able to do much these days, but I could at least keep her company.* "I could come. If you want."

"No. That's okay. You don't have to do that. I'll be fine."

"I don't mind. Really, you'd be doing me a favor. I could use the practice." He gestures toward his crutches.

Laura takes several deep breaths, and the tension lines on her face relax. "Okay. I'm ready if you are."

Austin nods and drains his cup, then pulls himself to his feet as Laura returns their mugs.

"So," she says, once they're outside. She darts her eyes around and keeps her voice low. "You seem pretty calm about the whole 'I'm either having a mental breakdown or being haunted by my brother' thing."

He waits to answer her until they're stopped at the crosswalk waiting for the pedestrian light. Walking and talking aren't a great combination for him anymore. "Let's just say my accident gave me a new perspective on things." He bites back a sarcastic laugh. *Yeah. Understatement of the century.*

SIX

"Aw, crap." *This is not what I meant when I said I needed the practice.* Austin lets out a heavy sigh at the sight in front of him. A daunting flight of stairs are the only means to get up to Laura's second-floor office. There's an elevator in the corner, but the 'Out of Order' sign taped to the front of the closed metal door may as well be a flashing neon sign screaming 'Austin's screwed.'

"Sorry." Laura gives him a sympathetic wince. "I forgot about the elevator."

"It's fine," Austin says. *If she thinks you're awkward and slow on flat surfaces, wait until she gets a load of you on stairs.*

"Do you want some help?"

Austin bristles. "No. I've got it." *Yeah, right.*

"Okay." Laura puts a hand on the railing but doesn't move otherwise.

"Meet you up there?"

She nods and heads up, glancing back at him when she's half-way up. The tension in her shoulders is back, and her lips are pressed together in a tight line.

It's not until the door at the top of the steps closes behind her that he realizes why she'd been so reluctant to go up without him. He'd been so busy thinking about the stairs and his leg that he'd forgotten the reason he's there in the first place. *Her office. Shit.* He sighs in disgust. *Idiot.*

Narrowing his eyes, he stares down the demon in front of him. *All right. You can do this. Just a couple of stairs. Nothing to it.*

Several steps later and his reactions aren't quite as optimistic.

"God dammit. Come on. Get up there, you motherfucker." Austin's concentration is locked on his right leg while he tries to coerce it up another step. The weakness in his thigh makes lifting his leg a serious workout in its own right, and the difficulty he has extending his knee only makes it worse.

He makes it just over halfway up the flight before he has to take a break, sweat already beading on his forehead and trickling down between his shoulder blades. The searing fire he tries to avoid at all costs threatens to erupt down the side of his leg at any moment. He gets a firm grip on the railing and reaches down to massage the twitching muscles in his thigh.

Before his accident, he would've taken the stairs two at a time. Wouldn't have even given it a second thought. Now he has second thoughts all the time, not to mention third and fourths. Simple things aren't so simple anymore. Walking requires concentration so he doesn't end up kissing the ground, and stairs are practically an Olympic sport. Showering requires the use of a handrail and a shower seat in addition to a few prayers; he'd really rather not be found naked by the paramedics should a mishap occur. And sex, well. As much as he hopes that's still one of his areas of excellence, he hasn't yet given it a try like this.

Pushing away the self-doubts that continue to creep into his head, he turns his attention back to the task at hand. His therapist's words, *up with the good leg/down with the bad*, ring in his ears as he slowly ascends.

"Oh, thank God," Austin mutters once he's reached the top. He props himself against the wall to catch his breath and give his limbs a much-needed rest. He glances down, and his face wrinkles in disgust when he sees the patches of sweat on his T-shirt. *Ugh. That's a turn on.* He swipes the bottom of his shirt over his face, toweling off the sheen of sweat. *Great. You're a grown man who just got your ass handed to you by a flight of stairs. What a catch.*

"Nice place."

Laura's head snaps up at Austin's words. Relief washes over her, and she sags back against her chair. "Thanks."

She'd wanted to fight harder to wait for him, but the look in his eyes reminded her too much of Steven. Needing his independence. Not wanting to have to rely on others. So, she'd waited on the other side of the door at the top of the stairs for a while, finally heading into her office when she'd heard Austin's curses in the stairwell. *He probably doesn't want me hearing that.*

Gluing herself to her desk chair, she's kept her eyes on the same drawing that's been giving her fits. While she hasn't had any luck with making sense of the calculations, at least she hasn't witnessed any further unexplainable activities. *Thank God for small favors.*

Her gaze sharpens on Austin, a slight frown marring her face as she takes in the flush on his cheeks, his sweat-stained T-shirt, and the weary set of his shoulders. She gestures toward Steven's side of the office. "You wanna sit down?"

"Nah. I'm fine."

"Don't be an idiot. Sit." Laura points forcefully toward Steven's chair and raises her eyebrow.

"Yeah, yeah." Austin makes his way over to the offered chair and sinks into it. The groan that escapes his lips is somewhere between pleasure and pain.

"That good, huh?"

"Oh yeah." Austin winces as he shifts his right leg around with his hands. "That was fantastic. Can't wait to do it again." He holds up his hand when she begins to apologize, shaking his head slightly as he shoots her a warning look. He leans his head against the back of the rolling armchair, closes his eyes, and massages his thigh.

Laura doesn't miss the clenching of Austin's jaw or the look in his eyes before he closes them. She knows all too well that look of doubt and frustration. She'd seen it on Steven's face frequently over the past year. *Shit.*

Clamping her lips together to prevent making the situation worse, she turns her attention back to the drawing and wills herself to make some sense of the damn thing. She palms her face in her hand and lets out a prolonged sigh. In times like this, she'd usually call on her brother to take a look; more often than not, he'd figure it out in seconds. *Used to drive me nuts. God, I really miss him.*

The stillness hanging over the room is broken by the squeak of Steven's chair. "Hey. Does the name Sasspants mean anything to you?" Austin works to sit upright and throws a questioning glance toward Laura.

Her eyes widen, and her mouth flaps like a fish. "What did you say?" she asks when she finally manages to find her voice.

"Sasspants?" Austin tilts his head to the side, an expression of confused concentration on his face.

"Where'd you hear that?" The calm in her voice belies the rest of her body; her hands clench the armrests of her chair, and her body coils in tense anticipation.

"In here." Austin taps the side of his head, and his eyes rove across her face. "I heard a voice say, 'I miss you too, Sasspants'."

"Are you fucking with me?" Her voice is deadly calm even though her heart beats wildly, and her palms break out in a cold sweat.

"Um, no?"

"Cause if you are, I will beat you to a bloody pulp, gimpy leg or no." Laura fights the wavering in her voice and the trembling of her lower lip. *Don't fall apart now.*

Her gaze travels wildly around the room, searching for anything to keep her grounded. Her eyes alight on the picture sitting on top of the filing cabinet where her phone had been hidden. The sight of her and Steven grinning like idiots on the day they'd opened their business finally breaks her resolve.

"Oh God, oh God, oh God." Laura's soft mumblings are accompanied by a gentle rocking motion, her head cradled in her hands.

"Hey, hey, hey... What's going on?"

Laura takes several stuttering deep breaths in an attempt to get herself under control. She wipes away a rogue tear, finally meeting his eyes with her own wide-eyed stare. "Sasspants was Steven's nickname for me. And I was just thinking about how much I miss him," she adds, her voice barely above a whisper.

"Oh shit!"

"So you wanna explain to me how you knew about it? Marge didn't tell you, did she?" Laura's heart races while she awaits Austin's answer.

"No." He lifts a hand in oath. "I swear to you I'm not crazy."

"That's usually what crazy people say."

"I started hearing things after my accident. In the hospital. Usually only little phrases, little snippets of conversation." Austin winces and adjusts his leg. "The first couple of times it happened, I thought maybe it was my roommate. Or one of the nurses I was too drugged up to notice. Then they weaned me off the really heavy-duty pain meds. I was with it enough to know when there was someone else in the room and when there wasn't. Still heard the voices, even when the room was empty."

"Did you tell anyone about it?"

Austin bobs his head. "At first. They did some scans, told me everything looked okay."

Laura gives him a bland look. "Yeah, hearing voices after a car accident is totally normal."

Austin shrugs and continues. "Didn't want to end up in the psych ward so I stopped mentioning it. Besides, it's not like there was ever anything interesting being said. The occasional 'Where am I?' 'What happened?' 'Where's so and so?'"

"Different voices?"

"Yeah. Not like I was having actual conversations with anyone." A wry smile crosses his face. "Although that might have helped. Might have made those weeks after my surgeries pass a little quicker."

Laura doodles in the corner of the desk calendar, her focus on her hands as she says her next words. "Well, is he saying anything else?" Austin's silence causes her eyes to dart over to him, her gaze then sweeping the room in search of anything out of the ordinary. *Besides a potentially crazy person who may or may not be able to hear dead people.*

The ticking of the wall clock across the room and the honking of car horns from the street below are the only noises in the otherwise quiet room. Austin's eyes are closed, his brow furrowed in concentration. After a few moments of tense anticipation, he opens his eyes and shakes his head, his expression offering Laura a silent apology.

"Oh, okay." Laura slowly exhales. *What did you expect?* "I just need a minute." *Really don't want to fall apart in front of him. Again.*

In the bathroom, she soaks a couple of the grainy brown paper towels and wrings them out. She presses them firmly over her eyelids and hopes it's enough to stem another deluge of tears. Laura moves the towel to the back of her neck and takes a few deep breaths. "Is he crazy?" she mutters at the reflection in the mirror. "Am I?" She laughs softly, a sad smile on her face. Steven had told her on many occasions she'd crossed that bridge long ago.

She reaches out to open the bathroom door, but her hand freezes on the handle. The possible implication of Austin's words tumble over her. *Steven's still here. Communicating with Austin.*

She's not sure if that makes her feel better or worse.

"Oh shit." Austin stands stock-still at the top of the stairs. *Thought those steps were bad coming up; they look even worse from up here.*

The echo of Laura's footfalls halt when she stops a quarter of the way down the stairs. She turns around and glances up. "You okay?"

Austin's knuckles whiten as he tightens his grip on his crutches. His breath comes in short, shallow little puffs and his Adam's apple bobs convulsively. *Don't pass out. Don't pass out.*

They'd decided to call it a day when Austin had confirmed he hadn't heard any further whisperings in her absence. That all had been quiet as far as he was concerned. He'd assured her he was ready to head home. That his leg was up to the task. Seems like the rest of his body might have other plans.

"Crap," Laura mutters while she double-times it to the top of the stairs. "Whoa, whoa, whoa." She plants herself directly in his line of vision and places a hand on his shoulder. "Just breathe. In and out." She takes a deep breath, holds it for a count of two, and repeats the process several times until they're breathing in sync. "Good; you're fine." She nods her encouragement as he continues his own deep breathing.

"Okay." Austin gives her a nod and lets out one final prolonged breath. "I'm okay."

"You sure?" Laura's stance relaxes slightly, but her steadying hand remains on his shoulder.

"Yeah, thanks." Austin offers her a small smile with a hint of apology. "It's just..." He pauses, swallowing again as the panic bubbles up inside his chest. *Oh God, what if I trip on a step? Lean too far forward? Lose my balance?*

Laura runs her eyes over his body; her gaze stutters on his trembling arms. "Think maybe I could help?"

Austin slides her a glance and manages to eke out a husky "yeah" through the threat of impending hyperventilation. *It's either that or have a heart attack right here on the stairs.*

"Okay. Here's what we're gonna do." Laura guides his hand over to the railing and wedges herself under his shoulder. She wraps her hand around his waist and takes his crutches in her opposite hand. "All right, you're fine. I've gotcha."

Austin nods and tightens his grip on the railing. He adjusts the positioning of his left arm and swallows while he stares down the steep set of stairs in front of him. *This sucks.*

Laura clears her throat. When she gets no response from him she hits his left hand with the crutches she's holding, moving her head to avoid hitting her face.

"What?"

Laura pointedly directs Austin's gaze to his left hand. Which is resting on top of her breast. She quirks an eyebrow at him and says, "As long as you keep your hands to yourself, Mr. Grabby, you'll be fine. Otherwise you'll be down a hand as well."

"Oh, right. Sorry." Austin shifts his hand and readjusts his positioning. *Great. That's the most action I've gotten since my accident, and I practically assaulted her.* He lets out another long breath, clenches his teeth, and gives Laura a nod.

"All right, remember. If you fall, I fall," she says. "So don't fall."

"Right." *Easy for you to say.*

They begin their slow descent. Austin's right hand has a death grip on the railing while his left arm remains clamped around Laura's shoulder. His focus is divided on keeping himself from any further inadvertent groping and on getting his leg to cooperate as fully as possible.

While he easily accomplishes the first, the second is much more complicated. Hauling himself up the stairs had been a bitch. Coming down is even worse. The weakness in his leg is compounded by the sensation his knee is going to buckle, sending both of them crashing to the ground in a tangle of limbs that would be both humiliating and painful. Not to mention the fact that he's not entirely convinced he won't pass out right there in the stairwell.

"Easy, that's it. We're fine." Laura keeps up a steady stream of murmured encouragements, allowing Austin to set the pace.

He focuses on his proper footing while they make their way down the stairs. His breathing hitches and his arm tightens around her every time his balance falters, which is far more frequent than he cares to admit.

Laura takes it in stride and continues her one-sided conversation. "I used to have long hair."

Austin stops their procession and swivels his head toward Laura. She glances at him out of the corner of her eye, readjusts her grip around his waist and gently nudges him forward before continuing.

"Dirty blonde. To my shoulders. Cut it about ten years ago." She laughs softly before she continues. "First time Steven saw it he didn't even recognize me. Then, when he finally realized what I'd done, he couldn't stop laughing. Jerk laughed until he got the hiccups. He used to do that. Laugh so hard he'd start to hiccup. Of course, then I'd start laughing. Marge used to call us a couple of laughing hyenas."

Austin pauses again and tightens his grip on Laura as he reaches down and rubs his thigh. "Sorry," he says, unable to keep the wince off his face. "My leg's really not happy right now." He works to breathe through the fireball racing up and down his leg. *Not sure which is worse – the leg or the fear of falling.*

Laura holds herself rigid, taking Austin's weight while she waits for the signal that he's ready to continue. "It's okay. Take your time."

Nodding his readiness, they continue the rest of their journey in silence. He breathes a sigh of relief when they reach the ground floor and sags against the side wall, keeping a hand on Laura's arm until he gets the cuffs of his crutches positioned.

"Oh God," he mumbles. He leans his head back and thumps it lightly against the wall, rolling it back and forth. "That sucked."

"What? My story?"

Austin huffs a laugh. "No. Story was great. Took my mind off the stairs." He takes several slow, deep breaths in an effort to calm his racing heart and closes his eyes. The panic slowly drains from his body and he opens his eyes, giving Laura a lopsided grin. "Thanks."

"No problem," she says with a shrug. "I'm just glad we made it down in one piece."

"Me too." Austin straightens up and shifts his position, then he nods toward the stairs. "You, uh, think maybe we can forget about that?"

"What? You groping my breast?"

Austin winces in apology. "Yeah. Sorry about that. But I actually meant more like the whole last fifteen minutes of my life."

Laura narrows her eyes, a smile playing at her lips. "Maybe. But it'll cost you."

"I believe that's called blackmail."

Laura shrugs. "Perhaps."

"And here I thought I actually liked you."

"You do." Amusement dances in her eyes.

He does his best to give her a level stare, biting back his own reluctant smile. *Dammit. She's right.*

She glances at her watch. "I have a meeting across town in about twenty minutes. Are you okay to get home?"

Austin gives her a reassuring smile. "Yeah. I'm fine." *Already needed enough help today. Not gonna ask for more.*

Concern crosses her face and she runs her eyes from his face to his leg and back up again. "Uh-huh."

"Seriously. I'm fine." The burning in his leg says otherwise.

She scrutinizes him for a few additional seconds, then nods. "Okay." She holds the door open and waits until he passes through, then walks with him until they reach the parking lot. "Hey, thanks again. For coming."

"No problem."

"Any chance you want to get dinner tonight?"

Holy crap. Is she asking me out? "Uh..." He shuffles his feet and rolls his lip between his teeth. "Like a date?"

"Oh, God. No." Laura shakes her head. "I just meant, maybe we could talk about what happened up there." She points to her office.

"Right." *What the hell, man? Why would she ask you out?*

"Forget it. Never mind." She turns and takes several steps toward the parking lot.

As she walks away, he feels something fading. Despite the embarrassment and frustration of his morning, he actually kind of enjoyed it. At least his time with her. *Definitely not the stairs.* "Hey. If you

59

want to talk, I'll make dinner." He's not sure which of them is more surprised by his words.

She stops and turns back to him, a look of uncertainty on her face.

"I actually enjoy cooking." *Used to, anyway.* "And it'll keep me occupied. Keep my mind off the fact you had to haul my ass down the stairs."

"Seems like I'm having to haul your ass around a lot, huh?" Her lips quirk in amusement.

"Ha, ha."

She heaves an exaggerated sigh. "All right. I guess if it'll keep you out of trouble."

"Gee, thanks."

"I have to stop in at a job site after my meeting. Should be done by six."

"Sounds good. If you can pick up some bread and salad, I'll handle the rest."

Laura grins. "Great. It's *not* a date."

"Can't wait."

Austin kicks himself the majority of his way home. Half the time, it's for refusing a ride from her, the other half is because of his fumbling over the discussion about dinner. *Seriously, man. What the hell?*

He's been a ladies' man since high school. Never had trouble getting their attention. Definitely never had any trouble talking to them. But now, he feels like he's back in junior high. Awkward, no confidence, unsure of himself.

He lets himself into his apartment, hissing as he sinks down on his couch. *Come on. Calm down already.* His thigh continues to jump and he spends the next several minutes alternately massaging and cursing it.

When his leg feels like it's no longer in danger of locking up, he hauls himself back to his feet and heads into the kitchen. He peruses the contents in his refrigerator, then does the same with his cabinets, pulling out the necessary ingredients for supper.

What used to be a mindless action now takes careful planning. Crutches make the process much more laborious than it used to be. *Hell, they make everything difficult.* He'd had to be careful when he was looking for apartments, checking for grab bars and safety features in the bathroom as well as accessibility in the kitchen. Even though he's gotten the hang of crutches overall, there are still significant limitations to what he can do while using them.

But at least I'm doing it on my own.

While his friends' offers of help were always well-meaning, Austin fought to keep his independence. Sometimes to the detriment of his friendships.

He cringes. *Like that last blow-up with Matt.* When he'd screamed at his best friend to leave him the hell alone. *Well, he did. Haven't heard from him since I moved into this apartment.* Austin huffs a sarcastic laugh. *Guess I showed him.*

As he dices the tomatoes, green peppers, and onions, he can feel the tension in his body unwind. The easy rhythm soothes him. *Always has.* Keeps his hands busy while calming his mind. He's able to shift his focus from the useless thoughts of "what ifs" to solving more important problems. *Like what the hell's going on in Laura's office and my head.*

SEVEN

Laura traces the grid outlines of the newest spreadsheet, her mind trying to make sense of what's happening in *her* office, while tuning out the ramblings taking place in *this* one.

She looks across the table and catches the eye of Richardson's secretary, who glances at her boss, then rolls her eyes.

Laura sends her a quick smile. *He does love to hear himself talk.* She doodles a tree in the corner of the page. *At least I don't have to listen to him all day like she does.*

"Laura!"

Her tree grows an unintended branch as her hand jumps, and her eyes snap to the front of the room.

The beefy man standing at the head of the table crosses his arms, a challenging look on his face. "Are you going to be able to get us the new estimations on schedule or not?"

"Absolutely." *As soon as I figure out those damn calculations.* She gives him the sweetest smile she can muster.

"I've given you a lot of leeway, what with your brother and all…" He scratches his beard, beady eyes narrowed as he continues to stare her down. "But don't think I won't hesitate to put the bid out again."

Jackass. She clenches her jaw to keep her opinion to herself. She can almost hear Steven whispering in her ear to keep her shit together. That he may be a prick, but at least he pays the bills. "Got it." Her fingers curl the page in her hands, and she fights to keep her middle fingers from making any further comments.

Richardson switches gears and launches into a diatribe against one of his potential rivals, and Laura tunes him out again. Her thoughts return to her office and the mornings' events.

And Austin.

The tracing of the tree trunk thickens as she tries to work through the newest wrench in her life. He could clearly use someone right now, but she's reluctant to let anyone else get close to her. *Not with my track record.* Especially given the fact that his situation is so similar to Steven's.

But his potential ability to help her communicate with Steven is a huge bonus. Not to mention the fact that he's easy on the eyes. And funny. She shakes her head, trying to dislodge the last thoughts from her head. *Nope. Not gonna go there.*

On her way out the door, she catches up with Richardson's secretary. "Hey, thanks for the flowers. That was very thoughtful."

"You're welcome. You know you don't have to worry, right? He's not going to re-bid the project."

"If you say so." Laura glances over her shoulder to make sure no one's in hearing distance. "How do you put up with him?"

"Eh. He's fine. Just a bunch of hot air." She pulls Laura closer and drops her voice. "Besides, when he gets too uppity, I switch out his Lactaid creamer for regular dairy. A couple hours of diarrhea and we're square."

After a brief check-in with another project job site, she heads to pick up the groceries Austin requested. Aerosmith's "Crazy" plays from within her messenger bag on her way into the store and she bites back a laugh. *Marge's ring tone.* Steven had surreptitiously programmed it into her phone several months ago. She about died laughing the first time it went off.

"Hey, Aunt Marge. What's up?"

"Hello, dear. I just wanted to see if you have plans for dinner tonight. If not, come on over. I'm fixing Herbed chicken and risotto."

"Oh, thanks. But I can't. I have plans."

"Hmmm. Something exciting, I hope?"

Laura peruses the vegetable section. "Nope. Just dinner."

"With a man?" Laura can almost hear the smile in her aunt's voice.

"Maybe."

"Ohh, do tell."

"It's nothing, Marge. Just dinner."

"It wouldn't happen to be with Austin, would it?"

Laura snatches a bag of salad from the refrigerated case. *Dammit.*

"Good for you."

"No. Not good for me. It's just dinner." Laura stalks toward the bakery section. "And keep your nose out of it." *Yeah right. Fat chance of that happening.*

Marge chuckles. "Whatever you say, dear. You and Austin have a lovely dinner."

Laura grunts.

"And don't do anything I wouldn't do."

"Pfft. That's not saying much."

"I know."

Laura rolls her eyes and disconnects the call. *Honestly.* She grabs a loaf of Artisan bread, checks out, and drives to Austin's. She stops at his apartment, shoots her aunt's door a dirty look, then knocks on his.

"Hold on." His muffled words are accompanied by the thump of his crutches. He opens the door and steps aside. "Hey. Come on in."

She marches into his kitchen and sets her grocery bag on the table as she runs a curious glance around the rest of the room. Neat piles of vegetables are lined up in bowls along the counter, and a few jars of spices are sitting next to the stove. "What the hell is that?"

"Uh, dinner?" Austin gives her a curious glance and props himself against the counter next to the stove, setting his crutches aside within easy reach.

"Thanks, Captain Obvious. I meant, what you making?"

"*We* are making pasta. With homemade sauce." He pulls the ingredients toward the stove with one hand while he keeps the other planted firmly on the counter.

Laura scoffs. "I don't think so."

Austin looks over his shoulder. "What? You scared of a little work?"

"Scared? No. *You're* the one who should be scared. The smoke detector usually goes off when *I* try to cook."

"You'll be fine. Besides, I'm a pretty damn good cook. Just need some help these days." He glances down at his leg. "Have to get creative with carrying things. I don't really want to end up in the Burn Unit because I scalded myself with boiling pasta water."

"All right. I can handle the lifting and carrying. Bread and salad too." She gives the stove a wary glance. "Not sure about anything else."

"Oh come on." Austin repositions himself against the counter. "It'll be fun."

"Yeah, fun like chiseling charred hard boiled eggs off of the bottom of the pot."

"How the hell did you manage to burn hard boiled eggs?"

Laura shrugs. "It's a gift."

Austin whistles. "Yeah, well, we're gonna keep that gift far away from here. Just follow my instructions and we'll be fine."

"All right. But don't say I didn't warn you."

Austin makes short work of sautéing the onions and peppers while Laura fills a large pot with water. She sets it on the stove to boil, then divvies up the prepackaged salad into two bowls. Her eyes stray to him far more frequently than she'd like. *Stop it.*

"How about spilling a couple more beans?" she asks while she sprinkles a handful of croutons atop each of their salads. *Focus on Steven.*

"What?" Austin lays down his wooden spoon and adds the bowl of tomatoes. "Oh, crap, the basil," he mutters. "Hey. Can you grab the basil?"

"Ummm..." *Basil, basil...*

"Basil. Green leafy plant. Looks like...basil. It's in... Forget it. Just stir this. I'll get it." Austin holds the spoon out to Laura.

She approaches the stove cautiously. Her mouth waters at the smell of the sauce bubbling happily on the burner. *Really hope I don't mess this up.* "Okay. And I just...?"

"Stir it." Austin makes a vague stirring motion with his right hand while he gets his crutch situated on his left. "You'll be fine."

Laura copies his stirring motion until he returns and pulls a handful of leaves out of his jeans pocket. He gives her a shrug and settles himself against the counter next to her. "Keep it on the windowsill in the living room." He pulls a cutting board from behind the knife block in front of him and finely chops the leaves, then sprinkles the basil into the mixture. "Look at you. No smoke detectors."

"Don't get too cocky. The night's still young."

Austin chuckles and adds salt and pepper to the sauce as Laura continues to stir. "Okay. That just sits there and simmers now while the pasta boils." He reaches over and turns down the burner, then stirs a package of spaghetti into the boiling water. "All right. Now we wait."

"No." Laura crosses her arms across her chest. "Now you spill."

"What?"

"Talking to dead people. Spill it."

Austin gives his sauce another stir, then sets down the spoon. "Don't know that I can. Talk to them. No more than you or anyone else. I think maybe I can listen, is all."

"Well thanks. That clears things right up."

"Look, I don't know what the hell is wrong with me." Austin gives the pasta a quick stir before continuing. "Never had anything like it happen before my accident. Thought it was the drugs at first. Then maybe something having to do with the head trauma. Then I thought maybe I was going crazy."

"Don't rule out that last one just yet."

"Don't worry, I won't," he says with a laugh. "I'd just hear little bits and pieces here and there. Different voices. Things that didn't make any sense. Until Steven." Austin pauses and narrows his eyes as they roam over Laura's face. "Then it was kind of like a lightbulb went on in my head. His words only made sense when I knew what you'd been thinking. Because he'd been responding to you. But I'm the one who heard it."

"What, so you've got some kind of freaky superpowers now?" Laura wiggles her fingers toward Austin's head.

"Ummm, I don't think they're superpowers."

"Sure they are. Or they might be. Just nothing cool like flying or x-ray vision or spider webs shooting out of your wrists."

"Great," Austin says with a derisive snort. "Supergimp. I can't walk, but I can listen in on the supernatural frequency. I think I'd rather have the use of my leg back, thanks."

"Well, good luck with that, Supergimp." Laura grins.

"Shit," Austin mutters, shaking his head. "You're never gonna call me by my real name again, are you?"

"Nope!" She cackles in glee. "Supergimp it is."

"Well, all right then, Sasspants. If that's the way you want to play it…" He tries to give her an intimidating stare but can't keep the corner of his mouth from twitching.

"Sasspants and Supergimp," Laura says, wrinkling her nose. "Sounds like the worst superhero team ever."

"Well," Austin says, giving her a look of mock challenge. "At least I can hear voices that may or may not be ghosts. What can you do?"

"Snark my way out of any situation?"

"Yep," Austin says with an exaggerated sigh. "Worst dynamic duo ever."

The stove timer interrupts further conversation, and Austin pulls out a few strands of spaghetti. He tests its readiness, then nods. "Okay, we're good. Strainers are in that cabinet down there."

Laura strains the pasta, then dumps it into a bowl Austin nudges her way. Austin pours the sauce into a bowl and pulls out a couple of serving spoons while Laura shuttles the bowls and silverware over to the table.

"Smells great," she says as Austin scoops spaghetti onto their plates.

"Yeah. And no smoke detectors."

They eat in silence until Laura speaks again. "So what the hell was the other part all about?"

"What other part?" Austin twirls his spaghetti onto his fork and flicks his gaze across the table.

"The stairs part."

"Thought we weren't going to talk about that."

"No. Maybe *you* decided not to talk about it." Laura points at him with the remainder of her bread slice. "I thought we agreed I was blackmailing you. Besides, I'd kind of like to know when I have to check to see if you're about to pass out."

Austin scoffs. "I did not pass out."

"Yeah, well, you were about to."

Austin gives her a steely look and jabs at his plate. "Yeah, well, you freaked out over hearing your childhood nickname."

She glowers, then smirks in triumph. "Yeah, well, I freaked out over my dead brother's spirit telling you my childhood nickname. You freaked out over a set of stairs. Pretty sure I win."

Austin returns her glower, then heaves a sigh.

"So what happened anyway?" Laura asks. "Has that ever happened before?"

"What, you mean turning into a whimpering mess?"

"Panic attacks."

He closes his eyes and flinches slightly. "No."

Laura continues to eat while she waits for further explanation.

"Not even close." Austin twirls his pasta and gives a half-hearted laugh. "I've skied double black diamond trails. Gone bungee jumping. Been skydiving. Pretty sure if there was ever a time for a panic attack, it would've been while I was hurtling toward the ground at over a hundred miles an hour."

"Huh."

"Yeah."

"So, what are you going to do about it?" Laura asks around a mouthful of pasta.

"Umm, besides boycotting anything with more than five steps?" He sighs when Laura continues her studied silence. "What's your bright idea, Sasspants?"

"Tell you what," she says after a few thoughtful chews. "I'll help you with the stairs if you help me with Steven."

"Help you how?"

"I don't know. Figure out why he's still here. Or there. Or whatever," she says, flapping her hand around.

Austin leans back in his chair, the corners of his lips turning down into a slight frown. "All right, I guess we can try. But I have absolutely no idea what I'm doing."

Laura snorts. "That makes two of us."

EIGHT

"Oh, thank God." Austin's shoulders sag in relief when the door to the elevator in Laura's office building slides open. *I hate those stairs.* He crutches his way inside and jabs the Up button, leaning against the wall to steady himself when the car lurches into motion. He makes his way down the hall and raps his knuckles lightly against the partially opened door, then pushes it open.

Laura sits at her desk; she waves him in with one hand while the other holds a corded office phone to her ear. "Yes, Mr. Richardson. I'm working on it. Sure. Right away." She drops the phone back into its cradle and lowers her head into her hands.

"Everything okay?"

Laura glances up at Austin and points toward the phone. "Client. Kind of an ass, but he pays well. Got along better with Steven."

Austin slowly walks around Laura's office. Not much had registered during his first visit a couple of days ago; he'd been too busy trying to get himself together after his epic battle with the stairs and then too preoccupied with the whole "Sasspants" incident.

His lips curve into a smile at the thought of her nickname; they take a sudden downturn when he recalls his own. *Supergimp? Seriously?*

He picks up one of the framed photos on top of the filing cabinets. Laura and a guy around her age holding up a couple of champagne glasses, brilliant smiles on each of their faces. "Is this Steven?"

Laura looks over and nods. "The day we opened this place."

Placing the picture back on the cabinet, he glances at the other photos. Steven in a graduation gown holding a diploma while Laura makes rabbit ears behind his head. Laura giving Steven a noogie while he tries to twist out of her reach.

"All right, so what is it you want me to do?" Austin turns his attention back to Laura, a thousand-yard stare on her face.

"Oh, yeah. Right." Laura shakes her head. "So, you're supposed to talk to Steven." She gets up from her chair and paces behind her desk. "Find out what he wants. Why he's still hanging around here."

"Oh, well then. Let me just call him up and ask him. You got his number?" He gives her a bland stare.

"Don't look at me. I don't know how your freaky superpowers work." She wiggles her fingers in his general direction with her last sentence.

"They're not superpowers."

"Well, whatever. Just talk to him."

"Fine, *whatever*." He heaves a sigh. He has absolutely no idea how it is he can hear the things he hears. Has no idea if it's all the time or just in certain circumstances. If he has to do anything special to gain access to the supernatural frequency he'd referenced earlier. *Guess there's only one way to find out.*

He settles himself in Steven's chair, leans back, and closes his eyes. Gets himself into the same position he was in when he heard Steven's voice the first time. He takes a couple of deep breaths and tries to empty his mind. Works on some of the relaxation techniques his therapists taught him after surgery; focuses on feeling his muscle groups relax one by one.

"Anything?"

He keeps his eyes closed and shakes his head, then returns his focus to his shoulders. They're finally softening when Laura interrupts again.

"How about now?"

"Shhh." Austin glares at her, then closes his eyes again.

"Sorry."

The steady tick of the wall clock and the occasional muted voice on the other side of the closed office door are the only sounds for several minutes. Austin manages to relax all the muscles to his toes without another interruption from Laura or a word from Steven. He glances to his left and sees her nibbling her thumbnail while she watches him. "Are you thinking anything?"

She drops her hand and squinches her face in disbelief. "Of course I'm thinking."

"About Steven?"

"No. About the calculus test I failed in high school. Of course about Steven." She shakes her head in exasperation.

Austin cocks an eyebrow and waits. "You done?" When she glares but fails to say anything else, he continues. "Fine. Then maybe try saying something out loud."

"You're an ass."

"You talking to me or your brother?"

Laura tilts her head to the side. "Both?"

Austin bites the insides of his cheeks to keep from smiling. *Dammit, she is kind of cute when she gets all sassy. The way her eyes spark, the way she juts out her lower lip... Crap. What the hell?* He clears his throat and shifts in his seat. "How about you try something a little more Steven-specific?"

She holds his gaze for a few moments before abruptly standing up and resuming her pacing and thumbnail chewing. After five passes behind her desk, she stops, braces herself on the back of her desk chair, and drops her head. "Hey. It's me. I know you're still here. Just trying to figure out why. If you could let me know, that would be great. Just tell Austin. Or write it in steam on a mirror or something."

Austin settles back in his chair and again works on clearing his head. He flinches when he hears the squeak of Laura's chair but keeps his eyes closed, his focus on listening for anything out of the ordinary. *Come on man, give me something.*

*
**

"Seriously?" Laura raises her eyebrows to her hairline. "You've been meditating over there for half an hour and you've got nothing?"

"What do you want me to say?" Austin hauls himself upright with the aid of the desk and his crutches. "I listened. He's not talking."

"Yeah, well listen harder. Or better. Or something." Laura sighs and rubs her forehead. *Come on, Steven. Where are you?*

"Hey," he says in a gentler tone. "So he's not Chatty Cathy today. Doesn't mean we can't try again later."

Laura looks up, dropping her hand from her head. His expression has softened and his green eyes seem to be offering empathy instead of irritation. She swallows around the lump in her throat and nods. She releases a slow breath, equal parts disappointment at not hearing any further whisperings from Steven and relief that at least he didn't tell her anything she didn't want to hear. *Not sure I could handle that.* "I think I'm done here for the day. Go on down. I'll be right behind you."

"You sure?"

"Yeah." She forces a smile until Austin leaves the office. She shoves a couple of files into her bag, slings it across her body, then locks the filing cabinets. Her eyes linger on the photos Austin had studied earlier, and she gently traces her finger around the frame of Steven's graduation picture. *Love you, you big jerk.*

She blinks rapidly to keep her tears at bay and beats a hasty retreat before another round of emotions can take hold. Her heartbeat quickens when she sees Austin standing at the top of the stairs. His gaze is locked on something toward the bottom of the steps and she can see the rapid rise and fall of his chest.

She approaches cautiously. *What the hell is he doing?* "Hey, you know the elevator's fixed, right?"

"Yeah." He doesn't move. Doesn't change the fixation point of his wide-eyed stare.

"So, you don't have to take the stairs now if you don't want to."

He shifts his position on his crutches and clenches his jaw, then swallows a couple of times. "Yeah, I do."

"Okay." Laura stands still and waits for Austin to make a move. *Preferably not a nosedive down the stairs.*

The only movements he makes are the tightening of his hands around his crutches, a few adjustments to the position of his left leg, and the bobbing of his Adam's apple.

Laura wills him to move. *Any day now.*

Austin's breathing hitches and his face loses several shades of color.

Uh-oh. Laura scurries over, plants herself on the step below him and places her hand on his chest. "Hey. Austin."

The jackhammering of his heart underneath her hand is his only response.

Oh, man. If he passes out he will squash me like a bug. "Hey, Supergimp!"

Austin blinks and shakes his head. His gaze loses the thousand-yard stare and sharpens on her face. He matches his breathing with hers, and she feels his heartrate gradually slow.

"You back with me now?" Laura keeps her eyes locked on his while she continues to take slow deep breaths with him. *Oh God, those eyes. Gorgeous.*

Austin nods. "Yeah. I'm good."

Laura removes her hand from his chest and crosses her arms as she studies him. "What exactly is it that has you so worked up?"

Austin huffs a strangled laugh. "You mean besides the fact that I'm a grown man having a panic attack because of a set of stairs?" He chews on his lower lip and adjusts his stance.

Laura nods and waits for him to continue.

He flicks his gaze to her, then darts it away again. "I'm afraid I'm gonna fall."

"So it's got nothing to do with heights?"

Austin frowns. "No."

"Oh, well then." Laura waves her hand in a dismissive gesture. "That's easy. Nothing to it." *I can work with that.*

"Easy for you to say," Austin mutters. "Not your leg that won't hold your weight."

"But you've got your crutches and a railing. You're fine."

Austin rolls his eyes and one corner of his mouth curves upwards. "You sound like my physical therapist." He tightens his grip around the handles of his crutches several times and clenches his jaw. "Shit. Okay." He takes a few hobbled steps to his right to position himself next to the metal railing. The knuckles of his right hand whiten around it, and his bicep bulges as he holds himself upright while his left takes possession of both crutches. He fumbles, then gets them properly situated, forming a T.

Laura descends two steps and stops, her body tensed and her right hand raised in case she needs to help stabilize Austin. "Okay. One at a time."

Austin takes a deep breath and slowly blows it out between pursed lips. He carefully places his crutch on the next step down and looks up at her before returning his focus to his feet. His expression is one of intense concentration as he works to get his right leg onto the same step as the crutch. Shoulders tensing as his arms take the weight, he moves his left leg down to meet his right.

He repeats the process several times; Laura moves with him, staying two steps in front of him. Pausing a third of the way down the stairs, he sends her a half-hearted smile. "Fun, huh? This is why I got a first-floor apartment."

"You're doing great." She's not sure if she's more impressed with his initiative to take the stairs in the first place or his progress on his first try.

Austin's snort echoes through the empty stairwell. "Yeah. If you consider making it down seven steps the highlight of your day."

"Then you'll be super great, because you've still got a dozen more to go." *Come on, you can do this.*

Austin releases a soft laugh. "Fantastic." He keeps a slow but steady pace for the remainder of his descent while she does little but offer the occasional encouragement. "Hallelujah." His sarcastic comment coincides with his arrival at the bottom of the stairs. He props himself against the wall while he shakes out his hands.

"That was super great, Supergimp."

Austin rubs his right thigh. "Yeah. I'm a real daredevil."

"No, really. Good job." Her serious tone causes him to glance up from his leg. Before he can say anything, she continues. "I worked on stuff like this with Steven. Stupid stuff we take for granted. Everyday stuff. You did good."

Austin nods once as a slow grin slides over his face. "Thanks, Sasspants. So did you."

NINE

Austin steps into the hallway and pulls his apartment door shut, surprised to see Laura walking toward him. "What are you doing here?"

"Heading to Marge's."

"Oh, good. Me, too." Relief washes over him. He'd been a little wary when Marge invited him over for dinner. Wondered if it was a welcoming party or more of a pity invitation. *Shouldn't have doubted her.*

Laura's eyes narrow and her lips flatten. "Yeah. Super." She passes him and pounds on her aunt's door. "Marge!"

The door swings open and Marge raises a finger to her lips. "Shh. You'll disturb the neighbors." She gives her niece a disapproving look as Laura brushes past, then waves Austin inside with a smile. "Come in, come in."

"Seriously?" Laura taps her foot, arms crossed over her chest, glaring at her aunt.

Marge closes the door behind Austin and ushers them to the table in corner, already laid with three place settings. "I just thought I should probably get to know Austin. You know, since you two have been spending so much time together."

"Uh-huh." Laura sits down, the look of suspicion still on her face.

Austin looks between the two women. *What the hell is going on?* He gives the older woman a reassuring smile. "Thanks for the invitation. Smells great."

"Comfort foods. I hope you like them." Marge dishes meatloaf, mashed potatoes, and carrots onto three plates. "Oh, would you like anything to drink? I have beer, vodka, wine…"

Austin carefully lowers himself into the chair, then sets his crutches on the floor. "I'll take a beer."

"I might need all of the above," Laura mutters.

Marge brings them each a drink, then settles in her chair, an expression of innocence on her face. "So. Are you two dating yet? Friends with benefits?"

"Aunt Marge!" Laura's hiss is accompanied by a look that could wither a lesser person.

"Oh, come on, dear," Marge replies, disregarding her niece's protest. "You're both young, attractive people. And I know you're unattached." She points toward Laura. "Perpetually."

Austin fights down a grin when Laura growls at her aunt. *Yep. Cute when she's fired up.* A slight flush highlights her cheekbones and the set of her mouth makes him want to reach over and smooth out her lips. *Come on, man. Get a hold of yourself.*

"And how about you, Austin? Are you single as well?"

Austin pauses, the beer in his hand mid-air to his mouth. *Uh-oh.* "Yes?"

"And I suppose even though that leg of yours isn't working all that well, the rest of you is?" Marge gestures toward parts of Austin he'd rather not have questioned.

"Aunt Marge!" Laura barks, her eyes wide as she tersely shakes her head.

"What, dear?" Marge takes a sip of her lemon-lime vodka and gives her niece a bland smile. "You weren't telling me anything. So I figured I'd just go straight to the source." The corners of her mouth turn down slightly, and she sends her two guests another penetrating look. "Although, you haven't actually answered my questions, now, have you?"

Laura breathes out an exasperated huff. "No, we are *not* dating. We're *not* sleeping together. We're just friends. Without benefits." Laura raises her eyebrow in challenge. "Okay?"

"Fine." Marge sits back in her chair and raises her hand in placation. "Just be sure to invite me to the wedding."

Austin coughs and thumps his chest to dislodge the beer that's taken a wrong turn, while Laura's fork screeches across her plate.

"Now," Marge continues. "Austin. Why don't you tell me a little bit about yourself?"

Austin shoves a forkful of meatloaf into his mouth to give himself a few seconds to think. As he chews, he runs his eyes around her apartment. Similar layout as his, but hers actually has some personality. Black and white photos of Paris are scattered across her walls. A large oil painting of a field of poppies and a windmill hang over her sofa. *Much better than the crap I've got hanging up.* The sideboard against the back wall is littered with candles, framed photos, and various knickknacks.

He swallows and returns his gaze to his hostess. "This is delicious, Mrs. Walters."

"Marge. Please," says the older woman.

"Marge." He glances toward Laura, who's busy stabbing her meatloaf. "What do you want to know?"

Marge narrows her eyes. "Where are you from?"

"Small town a couple of hours away."

"What brought you here?"

"Good rehab program. And fewer steps." He looks over and catches Laura's eye. "I was fixing up an old house. Three stories." He pats his leg and smiles half-heartedly at Marge. "This place is much easier."

"Job?"

Austin flushes and takes a gulp of his beer. *Holy Hell. Didn't know I was coming over for the Spanish Inquisition.* "Well, I used to have my own landscaping business. Started mowing lawns when I was in high school; just sort of grew from there." He shifts in his chair and repositions his leg with his hand. "Sold it after the accident. No way I could keep the business going like this. And it helped pay off some of the medical bills." He swallows around the lump forming in his throat at the thought of losing what he'd worked so hard to build. *All because of a stupid cat.*

Marge's face softens. "And what about now?"

The concern in Marge's question threatens to unleash the emotions Austin's trying to keep at bay. Because that's the same thing he asks himself every damn day. *What the hell am I going to do now?* So far, he hasn't come up with an answer. Just a whole lot of questions. What he's going to do for a job once his nest egg and insurance money run out. What he's good for. Who he is now.

Ask her about the panties.

An unfamiliar male voice overrides the litany of worries and concerns tumbling through his mind. He straightens up and glances around the room, searching for a physical body to account for the voice. "What? Who?"

Ask her.

"Who, what, dear?" Marge asks, her gaze traveling around her apartment.

"Uhhh."

Ask her about the frilly pink panties.

"You okay, Austin?" Laura's eyes search his face.

The voice continues its endless loop, pressure building inside his head until he can't hold back any longer. *Dammit.* "Do you still have those frilly pink panties?" He slumps in his chair while the other two inhabitants of the room stare at him in round-eyed surprise.

Marge recovers quickly. She chuckles and runs an appraising eye over Austin. "And just what inspired that question?"

Austin rubs his forehead. *How the hell am I supposed to explain that? The usual ramblings are bad enough. But that?*

"Austin can hear things," Laura blurts out. She gives him a shrug of apology.

"Things?" Marge leans forward and rests her chin on her folded hands.

Austin glares at Laura, a growl rumbling in his throat.

"What?" Laura shrugs and sends him an exasperated look in return. "Not my freaky superpower."

"It's not a… Oh, never mind," Austin says.

"You were saying?" Marge prompts.

"People," Austin says. His eyes dart between Laura and her aunt. "I think I can sometimes hear dead people."

"Ah." Marge leans back in her chair, a sly smile working its way across her face.

"Ah?" Laura's incredulous gaze focuses on her aunt. "Is that all you've got to say? 'Ah?'"

"Well, what would you have me say instead, dear? 'That's impossible?' When you reach my age, nothing is that surprising anymore." Marge runs an appraising eye over Austin. "Interesting," she murmurs.

Austin chokes out a laugh. "Interesting" isn't quite the word he would have used. More like "crazy," "insane," or "just plain weird."

Ask her about the frilly pink panties. Ask her. Ask her. Ask her.

The voice builds in his head again and he winces against its increasing forcefulness. "Look. I don't know what he's talking about, but can someone please answer the question about the damn panties?"

"George?" Marge cocks her head to the side and stares intently at Austin.

The voice suddenly cuts off and Austin nods.

Marge chuckles. "He always did like to wear my underwear."

Laura groans and slaps her hands to her ears. "The guy was as wide as he was tall," Laura whispers to Austin. "Probably took a shoe horn to get them on."

Austin wrinkles his nose and shakes his head to rid himself of that mental picture.

"Yes, George," Marge says. "I still have them. Wouldn't dream of getting rid of them."

I miss you.

Austin angles his head when the voice speaks again. "He says he misses you."

"Oh George," Marge breathes out, a hand over her heart. You were a good one. I miss you, too."

The room is silent for the span of a about half a minute while an air of peaceful reverie emanates from Marge.

A cacophony of new, distinct voices invade his head.

She was the best I ever had.

Never done it in that position before.

Had some good times on this table.

Hope those video tapes don't fall into the wrong hands.

Austin clutches the table. "Holy shit! How many dead guys you got hanging around here?" His brain is overloaded with multiple voices proclaiming their love and lust for the older woman sitting demurely at the table.

Austin's eyes widen as the words run roughshod through his brain. He's had his fair share of wild bachelor days. If the spirits' words are to be believed, however, he has nothing on Marge. *I can't say this crap out loud!* He clamps his lips together, trying to keep his newfound knowledge to himself.

It doesn't work.

Despite his pleas for hysterical deafness, the voices persist. *Shit. Here goes.* He squeezes his eyes shut and lets the words fly in rapid-fire succession. "Marge, you were the best some guy ever had, some other dude never did it in that position before, another guy has fond memories of this table, and some other guy really doesn't want you to lose those videos."

He opens one eye when the room remains quiet, thankful that the chaos in his head has dissolved as well. Marge looks like the cat that's eaten several canarie,s and Laura is practically curled up in the fetal position. Austin works to scrub his brain of the mental images he'd rather not be subjected to ever again.

"Well that was entertaining." Marge runs an appraising eye over Austin.

Laura snorts. "More like lobotomy-inducing."

"So," the older woman says, ignoring her niece's muttered remark, "how long have you been able to do that?"

"Not long." Austin swirls the remainder of his beer around the bottom of his glass. "A couple of months maybe. Ever since my accident."

"Well, that's quite the party trick," Marge says as she continues to study him.

Austin huffs a derisive laugh.

"Does it happen often?"

Austin leans forward, crossing his arms on the table. He chews on the inside of his cheek and shakes his head.

Marge narrows her eyes and turns her attention to Laura. "Yet you clearly know about it, so it's happened before."

Laura plays with the stem of her wineglass and keeps her eyes averted from her aunt. "Yes."

Marge looks back at Austin and gives him a questioning look.

"Steven," he says.

Laura flinches. "I think he's still in my office."

"Come again?" Marge's forehead furrows, and she bounces her glance between her guests.

Laura downs the remainder of her wine in one long gulp, then launches into her explanation. "That day I came over a couple of weeks ago? When we watched movies and had Chinese for dinner?" Marge nods and Laura casts a furtive glance at Austin. "I got freaked out because it felt like someone was in there with me. And then somehow my phone ended up in the filing cabinet. And then Austin was there last week and heard Steven." Laura blows out a breath and sags back against her chair.

"Hmmm. Anything since then?"

"No," Austin says. "We tried again a couple of days ago but I didn't hear anything."

"The stubborn bastard," Laura mutters.

"Ha!" Marge barks out as she stands up and clears the dishes from the table. "That's a bit of the pot calling the kettle black now, isn't it?" Austin smiles when Marge sends him a wink, and Laura scowls at her aunt. The older woman waves Laura back into her seat when the younger makes a move to help her. "Sit dear. Keep Austin company."

The rattle of dishes and silverware can be heard from the adjoining kitchen; the grandfather clock in the corner of the room chimes the quarter hour. Laura's face is still locked in a scowl, although as Austin looks closer, he can see a sheen of tears in her eyes and an occasional tremble of her lower lip.

"Hey." Austin nudges Laura's foot with his. "We'll try again. Figure out what he's still doing here. Maybe it takes a lot of effort to talk from the other side. Or maybe I'm just not very good at it."

Laura stops picking at the frayed end of the tablecloth and flicks her gaze to Austin. "Yeah, maybe we need to get you into superpower training camp."

"Oh for…" Austin rolls his eyes. "Forget it."

"Okay you two. I have something special for dessert tonight." Marge sets a plate of lumpy brownies in the middle of the table.

Laura shoots Austin a panicked look and shakes her head in an almost imperceptible motion. "Uh, thanks Aunt Marge. You shouldn't have."

"No problem, dear. I've been wanting to try this new sugar-free brownie recipe for a while now. Thought this was as good a time as any. Oh, I forgot the dessert plates."

"Save yourself," Laura stage whispers when Marge leaves to retrieve the forgotten items.

"Oh, come on. They can't be that bad."

A look of disbelief crosses Laura's face. "Okay, but don't say I didn't warn you."

TEN

"Oh my God," Austin groans as he unlocks the door to his apartment. "That was the worst excuse for a brownie I've ever tasted."

"Told you." Laura runs her tongue around her mouth in a fruitless effort to dislodge the lingering taste of dessert. "Ugh."

"You wanna come in for a beer? Or some mouthwash?"

"Or we could go out. Night's still young."

Austin looks around his apartment. "Sure. Why not? Not like I've got anything going on. What'd you have in mind?"

"There's a brewery a couple of blocks from here. Good stuff, low key." *No Marge.* "Couple of pool tables. You play?"

"Yeah. Used to. Haven't played since this, so…" He nods toward his leg and gives her a half-hearted smile. "Guess we'll see."

"Well then, consider this part of your rehab." She waits while he relocks his door. "Therapy for me, too. Need something to get the image of George in Marge's panties out of my head."

Austin's mouth turns downward as his nose wrinkles. "Ugh. Is there enough alcohol for that?"

"Probably not. But I'm willing to give it a try. You okay to walk? Or I can drive."

"Nah. Couple of blocks? I'll be fine. We might not get there until midnight, but…" Austin shrugs.

"I don't turn into a pumpkin until sunrise, so I think we're good." His answering grin makes her pulse jump. *Stop it. Just friends.*

The night air is crisp, and Laura wraps her coat around herself. She reins herself in, her usual purposeful stride turned down several notches to match steps with Austin. Small clusters of people huddle outside restaurants. Couples pass by, strolling hand in hand. *Suckers.*

"Not a good conversationalist while I'm walking." He keeps his eyes locked on the sidewalk. "Sorry."

"No problem. It took Steven a couple of months to really trust his prosthetic." She glances over at him. "Is it getting any easier? Walking, I mean?" She grimaces. "Sorry, you don't have to answer that if you don't want to."

"No, it's fine." They stop at a light to wait for the pedestrian crossing sign, and he repositions his grip on his crutches. "It's a little better than right after the accident, yeah. Still a bitch, though. Frustrating. Slow."

The light changes, and they continue walking. Laura shivers and glances over at Austin. His lightweight jacket isn't nearly as heavy as hers. "You warm enough?"

"Yeah. It actually feels good. Doesn't take much to work up a sweat these days."

"You know, they've done studies. Energy expenditure increases two to three times when using crutches."

Austin huffs a laugh. "Great. Best exercise program ever. My arms get a workout and I don't have to worry about my figure."

She casts another glance in his direction. *Wonder what else those arms are good for... Dammit!*

The remaining half a block is traversed in silence. Laura works on keeping her thoughts about Austin squarely in the friend zone, while Austin focuses on his footing.

She's relieved to see that although the brewery is doing a decent business, there are several open tables. "What do you want? First round's on me." She has to raise her voice to be heard over the raucous laughter and Bon Jovi playing in the background.

"Surprise me."

Laura chats with the bartender about the current selection and new releases while Austin takes a seat at a table along the side of the room.

"Here, try this." She sets a pint glass of amber liquid in front of him, then slides into a chair across the table. "One of their new releases. It's their Golden Sour Ale. Cheers." She raises her glass and clinks it with his.

"Hmm, that's pretty good." Austin nods his approval.

"How many of these do you think it'll take to wipe out any memory of what happened at Marge's?"

Austin laughs. "Yeah. That was quite the interesting dinner. Don't know which part was the best. Playing Twenty Questions, your aunt's inquiry into the working parts of my body, or putting on an after-dinner show."

"Yeah, you were kind of busy tonight."

Austin leans back and gives Laura a smile that puts her on high alert. "Exactly what I was thinking," he says. "I think it's *your* turn on the hot seat."

"But I just bought you a beer."

"So?"

"Isn't that repayment enough?"

"Not even close."

Laura gives him a narrow-eyed stare.

He matches her stare with one of his own. "Your aunt basically asked me if I was still capable of having sex. I do believe it's now *your* turn to answer some questions."

She bites the inside of her cheek, but can't conceal her amusement. "Yeah, she was on a roll tonight. Okay, fine." She heaves an exaggerated sigh. "What do you want to know?"

Austin's lips curl in a satisfied smile.

Shit. That smile.

He gestures toward her head. "What's the deal with the eyebrow piercing?"

Laura runs her finger over the barbell-shaped piercing. "Got it during spring break my junior year of college. One of my friends bet me I wouldn't do it." She grins. "I won."

"Hope you won something good. Besides a metal bar in your head."

"Free margaritas the rest of the trip. Of course, there were only two days left by the time I did it." She fingers the piercing again and twists it several times. "Steven hated it. Told me I'd better be glad it wasn't a ring because he would've put a chain on it while I was sleeping and used it as a leash."

"What about your parents? What did they think?" Austin's eyes linger on the piercing.

Laura's good mood takes a sudden detour. She studies her beer for a few seconds, then raises her eyes to Austin and takes a deep breath. *Just say it.* "Mom left when we were little. Went out for groceries one day and never came back." *Breathe.* "When Dad saw this," she points to her eyebrow, "he said 'One of these days you're going to give me a heart attack.'" She bites down on her lip and concentrates on the bubbles floating lazily in her glass. "He died five years ago. Heart attack."

Austin reaches across the table and lays his hand on hers. It's warm and reassuring, the accompanying tingling sensation a pleasant distraction from the grief lodged in her throat. She takes a deep breath and gives him a wobbly smile. "That's when Steven and I moved out here. To be closer to Marge."

"And Marge is…?"

"You mean besides crazy?" Laura laughs softly and leans back, breaking contact with Austin. "Dad's older sister. We grew up hearing stories about her. Nothing like what we heard tonight though. Thank God."

Austin crosses his arms and leans on the table. "She seems like a good person to have in your corner."

"Yeah. She is." *I don't know what I'll do when I lose her too.* Laura presses her lips together, takes a few ragged breaths, and closes her eyes. *She may be maddening, but she's all I've got left.*

When she opens them again, her heart does a little stutter step under Austin's intense stare. In the gentle lighting of the brewery, his eyes take on a dark moss-like hue. His lashes frame them perfectly, holding her riveted. *Oh God—those eyes. I could fall into them and never come back.*

"Hey." He nods his head over to the side of the room with the pool tables. "Ready to play?"

Laura blinks. "What? Yeah. Sure." *Focus on something else.* She downs the remainder of her beer in a few quick swallows, pushes herself away from the table, and stands up. "Want another one?" She gestures to his half-filled glass.

"No thanks. I'm good for now. Meet you over there?"

"Sure."

"Way to go, genius," Austin mutters as Laura walks up to the bar. He can see the tension in her shoulders. If he's lucky, a game of pool will act as a distraction and allow her to forget his line of questioning.

Pushing himself up from the table, he lets his eyes wander around the room while he gets his crutches positioned. Several people shift their eyes away when they meet his gaze, and he feels the weight of others staring as he walks over to one of the empty pool tables. While he's always tended to garner attention, the type of looks he gets these days is of a much different variety. Something else that has become only slightly easier since his accident.

He shoves the thoughts aside and slowly circles the pool table, trying to figure out the mechanics of holding onto the pool cue without falling over. *This should be interesting.*

"You ready?" Laura flashes him a grin that doesn't quite reach her eyes and sets her beer down on a ledge along the back wall.

Austin chews on the inside of his cheek, then nods. *Ready as I'm gonna get.* Balancing against the table while he racks the balls, he gestures for Laura to break. She sinks a stripe, then misses her next shot.

He stays rooted to his spot and takes stock of the ball layout. He's pretty sure there are several shots he could've made before his accident. Now, however, is an entirely different matter. "Maybe that one," he mumbles to himself as he hobbles around to the other side of the table. He leans against the table and picks up a cue Laura hands him, then shoots his crutches a disgusted look when they dangle from his arms and clatter against the table. He shakes his arms out of the cuffs and places them nearby, repositioning himself against the table with his hands. He wobbles as he tries to maneuver the cue into position and grabs onto the table in an effort to keep himself upright. *Dammit.*

Heat creeps up his neck. He drops his head and takes a deep breath, then blows it out slowly. *Come on. Get it together.* Irritation morphs into concern when he glances at Laura and sees her staring off into the distance.

"Hey." He waits a couple of seconds and tries again when he gets no response. "Laura."

She blinks several times and swivels her gaze over to him.

"You think maybe you could help me out?" He gives her a sheepish grin and a shrug.

"Sure. What do you need?"

"You mean besides a fully functioning right leg?"

"Yeah. I'll get right on that for you."

He grins at the bland expression that accompanies Laura's retort. *At least she doesn't look so lost anymore.* He nods her over to his side of the table. "Got any bright ideas?" He keeps his left hand planted on the edge of the table and uses the cue in his right hand to show her his intended shot. "I think I should be able to bank that one into the side pocket over there. Assuming I can manage to keep myself upright."

Her eyes narrow while she inspects the table. "Hmmm."

"I think I can keep most of my weight over on my left side." He tries to shift his position while he's talking. "Just need a little extra support when I take the shot."

"Yeah, that should work. How about this?" Laura positions herself against Austin's left side and wraps an arm around his waist, leaving his right side free to use the cue.

He leans into her and makes a few adjustments to his stance, then takes the shot. A wide grin emerges when he sinks his intended target. "Don't know if that'll be allowed when I go out on the professional pool circuit, but it worked. Thanks."

"No sweat. It's all about problem solving."

"Uh-huh." *And the art of distraction.* Although if he's being honest with himself, he likes the feeling of her arm around his waist. More than just its added stability. He likes the warmth of her, the way she fits against him, the curve of her hip against his.

"You okay if I let go?"

Austin clears his throat and nods as he plants his hands back on the table. He's not sure he could put his thoughts into words right now. Not only has his mouth gone dry, but his blood flow has been diverted from his brain to parts farther south.

Laura clears her throat. "Any day now."

"What?"

She nods toward the table. "You made the shot. It's still your turn."

"Oh. Right." *Focus, Austin. You'd think you've never been around a woman before.* He re-evaluates the layout of the balls, then uses the table to move a few steps to his right. He shoots Laura a questioning look. "You think maybe we could try that again?" *But only because I need help with the shot. Definitely not for anything else.*

"Yeah. Sure." She once again tucks herself against his side. "Is that okay?"

Oh yeah. Austin nods, afraid of what might emerge if he opens his mouth. He shifts against her, her arm tightening around his waist in response. It feels comforting. Makes him remember what it's like to be touched in something other than in the sterile medical setting. Makes him wish for more.

He lines up his shot, not at all shocked when he misses.

Making sure he's balanced against the table, Laura lets go and takes her turn, sinking three balls in quick succession. She grins before taking another swallow of her beer. "Your turn, Supergimp."

"All right, Sasspants. Come on." He jerks his head in a directive for her to come back over and works to reposition himself for his next shot.

Laura's grin slides into a frown and her eyebrows lower as she approaches.

"Hey," he says. "Don't get mad at me for using your nickname in public. You started it."

"Jackass Steven started it," she mumbles while she gets into position.

Austin takes his time lining up his shot. *Wonder how long I can stall before she gets suspicious?*

"Geez," Laura says after several more moments of inactivity. "What the hell are you doing? Just go already. My beer's getting warm."

"Sorry." Austin shakes his head and tries to focus on the game, snarling in disgust when his ball ricochets off the side of the table. The bigger disappointment, however, is when she lets go.

Laura takes a swallow of her beer and peruses the options left her on the table. She makes two shots this time before her third misses its target by a few inches. "Aww, come on."

Austin bites back a smile as he watches her. His enjoyment takes a sudden downswing, however, with her next actions.

"Here," she says, dragging over a wooden chair. "Try this."

Dammit. He glares at the object while she positions it to the side of the table and carefully checks the angles and trajectory necessary for his shot.

Laura smiles at him and moves back over to her beer. She raises her glass in the air in a mock toast. "Problem solving."

"Yeah. Problem solving." Austin's echo holds much less enthusiasm.

ELEVEN

"Here." Laura holds a scarf out to Marge. "It was in my spare bedroom."

Marge takes the pashmina rectangle, caressing it gently. "Oh, thank goodness. Thought I'd lost it."

"Yeah, you've lost it, all right," Laura mutters. "You know I'm scarred for life now, right?"

"What, last night? That was nothing. There was this one time—"

"Stop!" Laura holds up her hand. "My brain can't handle any more mentally disturbing images right now."

Marge sighs. "Such a prude."

Laura bites back a smile. *Crazy, but I love her.* She glances at her watch. "I've gotta run. Heading across town. I'll be near that spice store you like. You need anything?"

"Hold on. Let me check." Marge disappears, then reappears with a foil-wrapped plate in one hand and a piece of paper in the other. "If you could pick these up for me, that would be great. And on your way out, could you see if Austin's in? They're the leftover brownies from last night. Thought he'd like them."

Laura stuffs the paper in her pocket. "Yeah. I'm sure he'll love them." *Or his trash can will.* "But why don't *you* take them over to him?"

"I tried earlier. Nobody answered."

Yeah. He probably saw what was in your hand and pretended not to be home.

Marge narrows her eyes. "Why? Is there a reason *you* don't want to give them to him?"

"What? No." *Yes.* She works to keep herself from giving anything away.

Last night had been way more than she'd bargained for. Not so much having to relive the pain of her parents—that's pretty much second-nature. No. It had been the pool that had thrown her for a loop. The fleeting thoughts about his eyes and smile are one thing. The feel of him against her is quite another.

Even now, the memory of his hip against hers makes her skin tingle and her heartbeat quicken. She'd had to practically shove the chair at him so she wouldn't make a fool of herself.

She snatches the plate out of Marge's hands. "Fine. See you later." Crossing the hall, she knocks on Austin's door. *Just be cool. Maybe he's not home.*

The thump of his crutches and the faint "coming" says otherwise.

Just friends. Just friends. Just friends.

Austin opens the door. "Oh. Hey! What are you doing here?"

Laura tamps down the excited flutter. *That smile should be illegal.* She takes a deep breath, trying to steel herself, but gets derailed by the scent of Old Spice. *Dammit!* Her hands tighten around the plate, the crinkling of the foil reminding her why she's there in the first place.

"Here," she says. "These are from Marge."

His smile dies as he eyes the plate. "Please tell me that's not what I think it is."

"Yep. Marge's brownies." She sets them on the table just inside the door and shoves her hands in her pockets. "They're yours now. No take backs."

Austin wrinkles his nose.

"Well, that's what you get for telling her you liked 'em. You get to eat the rest."

"You know you're evil, right?"

Laura shrugs. "It's been said."

He slides a backpack over his shoulders, then gets his crutches repositioned. "Not that I wouldn't love to invite you in and make you choke down one of those brownies, but I was just on my way out."

"Oh? Hot date?"

"Yeah. His name's Jack. Hairy little guy. Looks like an Ewok if I squint just right. My physical therapist."

"Well, I hope you two will be very happy together."

Austin shudders. "I like my dates with a little less body hair, thanks."

Laura balls her hands in her pockets. She's had more than a few thoughts about running them through *his* hair. She waits for him to lock his door, then falls into step beside him. "I didn't think there were any therapy places near here."

"There's not. It's across town. Over by the hospital."

"Oh."

He continues talking when they reach the building's front door. "I usually take the bus. Or a cab. Car was totaled in the accident and there's no telling when I'll be cleared to drive. One of the reasons I chose this apartment. Same bus route as the therapists and my doctors."

As they make their way into the parking lot, the bus pulls away from the stop down the street, a cloud of exhaust trailing behind it.

"Aw, crap." Austin hangs his head.

Laura winces. "Sorry. I think that was my fault."

He gives her a half-hearted smile. "If anything, it was the brownies' fault."

"Come on." Laura nods to her car. "Hop in."

"Nah, I'm okay. I'll call a cab."

Laura rolls her eyes. "I'm heading across town anyway. Get in."

A smile plays at the corners of his mouth. "Geez, fine, Bossypants."

"It's Sasspants, thank you very much."

*
**

"Okay, Austin. Go again. Push." Jack holds his hand against Austin's leg.

"I am." Austin drops his head back onto the cushioned table in the tiny exam cubicle. *Come on, come on, come on.* He concentrates on trying to lift his leg off the table; he can feel his leg shaking after only a few seconds. *Shit.*

"All right. Good job."

Something about the look in his therapist's eyes causes the churning in Austin's gut to pick up its pace. He's been trying not to freak out over the fact that he hasn't made any progress over the last few weeks. He can still barely lift his leg off the table, and it doesn't seem like he's gained any strength in his weakened leg muscles. The loss of sensation along the outer portion of his leg hasn't changed either.

He works himself into a seated position while Jack takes a seat on the rolling stool across from him and types a few notes into his laptop.

"It's not good, is it?" Austin chews on his lower lip while he searches his therapist's face for any feedback that won't signal yet another death knell to his former life.

Jack swivels around on his stool and leans forward, planting his elbows on his thighs, and locks eyes with Austin. "I think we need to have that discussion about bracing your entire leg again." He holds up his hand when Austin opens his mouth. "Hear me out. I know you wanted to give it a while longer, to see what function comes back. Just because you get another brace doesn't mean things won't still continue to get better. It simply means you need more stability for the time being." He points to the brace on Austin's lower leg. "That one's been helpful, right?"

Austin clears his throat and barely manages to work the "yeah" out of his mouth. He'd agreed to it only after having learned the hard way, several times, that he couldn't fully control his foot and ankle after his accident.

"The one I think would work best for you would be a KAFO. Knee, ankle, foot orthotic. It would take the place of your AFO and give your knee some stability too."

Austin dips his head and digs his fingers into the exam table. The tightness around his chest is suffocating, and he takes several deep breaths in an effort to overcome it. He stares at his right leg, another few ounces of hope draining away. *Not sure how much more I have left.*

"Hey, I can go see if Greg's free. See if he has a minute to go over the options with you."

Austin nods at Jack's offer to bring in the orthotics specialist. *Shit.* He knew this was a very real possibility. He's had the discussion with his surgeons, rehab specialists, and therapists. He's just been hoping his leg would figure it out eventually. *What the hell am I gonna do if it doesn't improve?*

The squeak of sneakers in the hallway alerts Austin to the approach of his therapist and the orthotics specialist. He pushes his emotions down as Greg enters the room, Jack close behind him.

"Hey Austin. Good to see you again."

"Wish I could say the same." Austin plasters a smile onto his face and shakes Greg's hand while the other man chuckles.

"Yeah, I get that a lot." Greg pulls up a chair while Jack sits back down on the stool and continues typing. "So, I hear you might be in the market for a KAFO?" The older man pushes his glasses up on his nose and peers at Austin.

"Unfortunately."

"Hey man, don't knock it 'til you've tried it." Greg takes a few quick measurements and moves Austin's leg through several range of motion tests. "What say we head over to the parallel bars and do a little before and after? I have an off-the-shelf brace you can try, just so we can get an idea of what might work for you."

"Super. Lead the way."

Greg and Jack follow Austin out into the main therapy room. He's been here long enough to recognize the other therapists, as well as a few of the patients who typically share his appointment times. He gives a tight smile to Tom, the fit older man who had his hip replaced, and his therapist Nancy, as well as Beth and her patient Leslie, who's rehabbing a torn ACL. While they're all in the same therapy boat, Tom and Leslie actually seem to be making progress. *Lucky bastards.*

Austin positions himself between the despised parallel bars, carefully walking up and back while Greg and Jack monitor him closely, conferring on several occasions. Greg disappears, returning moments later with a large brace in one hand and a few brochures in the other.

Austin's stomach flips, and he fights down the accompanying nausea. His hands tighten around the parallel bars, and he swallows several times. *Crutches and a big-ass leg brace at thirty-two. Not what I had planned for my life.* He blinks and bites down hard on his lower lip to keep his emotions in check.

Tell Janie it's behind the cabinet.

Austin slams his eyes shut as the soft-spoken female voice echoes through his head. *Oh shit. Not again. Not now.*

"Austin? You okay?" Greg asks. "You're looking a little pale."

Austin opens his eyes and forces a smile onto his face. "Yeah, I'm good."

"Well come on over here and sit down." Greg uses the brace to point to a chair next to the bars. "Let's see if this is a good option."

Austin uses the bars to walk over to the chair, then leans on Greg for support, taking off his sneaker and brace after he's seated. He works on keeping himself under control while Greg slides the new brace into place over his track pants and the extra voice in his head rambles on about Janie and the cabinet.

The brace Greg chose has two separate carbon fiber shells, one that fits the back of his thigh, and another for his calf. Metal bars connect the two and run along the sides of his knee, and it's held in place by two straps around his thigh and two around his lower leg. A foot plate similar to his AFO keeps his toes from dragging.

"Okay, now try the bars again."

Greg holds out his hands and Austin hoists himself upright with his help. He holds onto Greg on one side and Jack on the other, then repositions himself between the parallel bars.

"How's that feel?" Greg asks.

"You mean besides weird?"

Greg nods. "Yeah, that's par for the course right now. As you get used to it, you should notice that it lets you bend your knee a little when you need to, but keeps it stable otherwise."

"Let's start with some balance work," Jack says.

Austin clenches his jaw and slowly shifts some of his weight to his right side. *Huh, doesn't feel like my knee's gonna buckle.* He lets a little more weight shift, his hands keeping a white-knuckled grip on the bars should the brace fail to hold him upright. *So far, so good.* Color gradually returns to his knuckles as he lets his hands relax.

"Good." Greg checks the straps again, then crouches down at the other end of the bars. "Now try taking a few steps."

Austin inhales and blows a deep breath past pursed lips. He takes a tentative step, swinging his braced leg forward in an awkward stiff-legged gait. A smile tugs at the corner of his mouth as his right leg helps hold him upright for the first time since his accident.

As he continues to work with Greg and Jack, he doesn't notice the voice in his head fading into nothingness.

TWELVE

Laura stares at the sign over the entrance of the one-story brick building. *The Rehab Group.* She checks the clock on the dashboard of her car. *Austin should be done soon.*

She'd been a little surprised when she'd received the text from Austin, asking if she was still in the area. His follow-up text asking if she wanted to get coffee makes her think something's up. When she'd dropped him off, he'd insisted he was fine to get back home. *Wonder what changed?*

Rummaging through her messenger bag, she pulls out her phone, checking to make sure Austin didn't text again. *Nothing.* She dials the number for the office; Theresa picks up on the second ring.

"L and S Consulting. How may I help you?"

"Hey. It's me. Just calling to check in."

"Oh, hi. Just a sec." The sound of Theresa shuffling papers around on her desk filters through Laura's cell phone. "You got the new specs on the Cliffton proposal you've been waiting for. McGarvey finally paid his bill. And that Marcus guy from the Renfro job called to see if you'd changed your mind."

"No," Laura says, shaking her head for emphasis. "Changed your mind about what?"

Theresa's tone is the epitome of innocent. Laura doesn't buy it. "Nothing. None of your business. Anything else?" she adds, hoping Theresa will somehow drop the subject of Marcus.

She has no such luck.

"Is he that cute one? The architect?" Theresa pauses, then continues when she gets nothing but silence from Laura. "You know, if I wasn't happily married to a man who usually remembers my birthday and our anniversary, I'd be all over him."

"Great, you can have him."

Theresa's sigh echoes through the phone. "Look, I know you haven't had the best track record with men. But you know they're not *all* bastards, right?"

Laura tips her head back and presses it against her headrest. "Seriously? We're having this discussion now?"

"We will have this discussion until you get it through your thick skull that there are good guys out there. Or until I'm dead."

"Yeah, well, I'll be sure to come to your funeral. Single." Laura smiles at Theresa's grunt of frustration. *Thank God she hasn't met Austin. Pretty sure I'd never hear the end of it.* Her smile falters as she envisions Theresa and Marge joining forces. "All right. Gotta go. Talk to you later." She hangs up as her receptionist sputters in the background.

Laura slouches down in her seat, the grin sliding off her face as her thoughts veer away from Theresa and her office and back toward her current location. *Another physical therapy office.* She spent more than enough time in a similar setting with Steven after his accident. Hours spent making sure he could transfer and get around okay after his amputation, followed by the hours of training to get him walking again with his prosthetic.

All for nothing. Because he threw it away. The selfish bastard.

While at first Laura's thoughts regarding her dead brother had been solely within the realm of denial, guilt, and excruciating pain, she's been finding herself more recently crossing over into anger. Angry that he couldn't pull himself out of it. Angry that he took the easy way out. Angry that he's not here for her to throttle anymore. *Because I would.* Some days she's so angry she thinks that if he weren't already dead, she'd kill him.

At least the anger keeps the waterworks at bay. Keeps her from drowning in her own sorrow. She knows what to do with anger. It's the helplessness of the grief and despair she's not quite sure how to handle. Laura is used to being anything but helpless. She's used to tackling problems head on. Sometimes to the detriment of having actually thought things through. *That was Steven's strength. Not mine.*

Her anger dissolves when Austin emerges through the front doors.

He pauses and looks around the parking lot. His face is tight, his shoulders are tense, and he adjusts his stance repeatedly.

Uh-oh. He looks upset.

She taps the horn to let him know where she's parked, then waves when he looks her way. Her concern grows as he gets closer, his lips set in a thin line and worry marring his forehead.

He opens the door and maneuvers himself into the passenger seat, then deposits his crutches in the back seat. "Sorry to bother you again."

"No bother. I was still over this way. Plus, I do believe you promised coffee…"

His attempt at a smile falls short. He stays quiet except to give directions, and ten minutes later they're seated at a table by the window, steaming coffee in hand.

"So, who called this meeting, anyway?" Laura keeps her tone light.

He swallows, then rolls his lower lip between his teeth. "I think I'm getting a new leg brace."

Laura's gaze snaps from Austin's lips to his eyes. Emotion lingers just below the surface, and the huskiness in his voice puts her on alert. "Oh?"

He takes a couple sips of coffee and sets it on the table, rotating the cup between his hands. "It goes all the way from my foot to my thigh. Keeps my knee from buckling. Gives me more stability." He takes another swallow of his drink and glances out the window. "I have another appointment next week for a fitting."

"That's good, right?" She searches his face.

Austin keeps his eyes on his coffee. "I haven't made any progress recently. Don't know if I'll get any more function back. I think this might be it." His breathing hitches and he clasps his cup between his hands.

Laura reaches across the table and lays her hand on his arm, giving it a squeeze. "Hey. I'm sorry. But you have to keep fighting. Don't give up."

Austin leans his elbows on the table and drops his head into his hands, breaking contact. His shoulders rise and fall as he takes deep, rhythmic breaths; he gives his eyes a quick rub before raising his head. He clears his throat but his voice is raw when he replies. "It's just not what I had planned for my life, you know?"

"Yeah. I know."

"I just…" He takes another deep breath and slowly blows it out. "The brace I have right now isn't really obvious." He tilts his head toward the crutches propped next to him. "Those kind of give it away that this isn't just a run-of-the-mill injury. But this brace…" He clutches his coffee cup, the tendons in his hands becoming prominent. "The new brace pretty much screams 'disabled'." His voice cracks over the last word.

Laura's gut twists, Austin's words so raw and vulnerable. *And so like Steven.*

"I mean, I guess I should be happy," he continues, his focus on his coffee. "I tried one on today. Seems like it'll help keep my leg stable." He shifts in his seat and repositions his leg with his hands.

"Does that mean I won't have to help drag your sorry ass around anymore?"

He looks up, locking eyes with her. "Guess not."

"Thank God. Almost threw my back out."

"Shut up." A smile teases his lips. "Oh, hey. I heard another voice. During my PT session. Kept telling me to tell Janie it's behind the cabinet."

"Who's Janie?"

"No clue."

"Do you still hear it?"

"No" He pauses and chews on the corner of his lower lip. "It was kind of fading in and out this time. Had a couple of random phrases pop into my head while we were sitting here, but nothing coherent."

"Huh." Laura frowns as she contemplates his words. "Any idea what's triggering it?"

"Not yet."

Silence hangs over the pair. Laura traces a scratch on the table with her thumbnail while Austin looks out the window and rubs his thigh.

He clears his throat again, shifts in his chair, and leans forward on the table. "Have you sensed Steven recently?"

Laura exhales forcefully when her thoughts about her brother turn to his most recent shenanigans. A reluctant smile works its way onto her face. *Shenanigans. Steven loved that word.*

"Yeah, I think my jackass of a brother is still there." She shakes her head. "You know the rolling chairs in our office?" She waits for Austin's nod, then continues. "Well, they lock in certain positions, so you can either lean back or stay upright. We used to unlock the other person's chair to see if we could catch them off guard. The other day I was sitting in my chair and it was locked. Then all of a sudden it wasn't. Jackass almost made me fall out of my chair while I was on the phone."

Austin bobs his head. "You know, I think I would have liked that brother of yours."

Laura sighs. "Yeah. I think so, too."

THIRTEEN

Austin lowers himself onto his sofa and places his crutches on the floor as Laura flops into the armchair. "Sorry I wasn't able to get anything from Steven today. We'll keep trying."

Laura sighs, props her elbow on the arm of the chair, and rests her head on her fist. "Yeah. I guess that's all we can do, right?" A smile tugs at the corners of her lips. "Unless we enroll you in one of those superpower training courses."

"You know you're not funny, right?"

"Shut up. I'm hilarious."

Austin bites back a smile. He's more than a little surprised at how much he's enjoying trying to contact Steven. Not so much the frustration of trying to figure out what he's missing or why he can only seem to hear things at certain times, but the part that enables him to spend more time with Laura. Because she really *is* hilarious. And snarky. And intriguing. Traits not usually found in the women he's used to hanging out with.

The vibration of the phone in his pocket diverts Austin's attention. He pulls it out and glances at the screen. *Matt.* He swipes the phone to ignore the call and sets it on the sofa next to him.

Laura leans forward and cranes her neck. "Your phone's been going nuts. You hook up with someone? Avoiding her calls?"

"Yeah. In the two days since I last saw you I've gone on a dating spree."

"What?" Laura shrugs. "It could happen."

He repositions his leg with his hands. *Not anymore.*

His phone vibrates again; he scowls when Matt's name makes another appearance. *Take the hint, man. Stop calling.* He tosses his phone onto the coffee table and lets it go to voicemail. A knock at his apartment door has him breathing a sigh of relief. "Thank God. That's probably the grocery delivery."

Laura bounces up from her seat. "I'll get it. You remembered to order coffee this time, right?"

"Uh, do I have the right place?" a familiar male voice asks.

Austin's retort to Laura's question dies on his lips. *Oh crap.*

Laura pulls her head back and glances around the door at Austin. She gives him a questioning look, then turns her attention back to the man on the other side of the door. "Depends on what you're looking for."

Austin heaves a sigh and gets himself upright.

"Is this Austin's apartment?"

Austin positions himself next to Laura and nudges the door open wider. He runs his eyes down the man standing in front of him. The same grungy baseball cap he always wears, the jacket he's had for years, the cargo pants that drive Monica nuts because he leaves things in the pockets and forgets to empty them when she does laundry. "Matt. What are you doing here?"

A little blonde head peeks around the large man standing in front of him in the doorway. "Uncle Austin!"

Despite his annoyance at his best friend's unexpected arrival, he can't keep his face from splitting into a wide grin when he sees Kelli.

Her pigtails bounce as she hops from one foot to the other, a smile lighting up her face. A concerned look takes its place, and she stills as she looks at Austin. "Are you still hurt?"

Her words punch him in the gut, stealing the breath from his lungs. He clenches his jaw and swallows. He doesn't think his smile is all that convincing. "Yeah kiddo. Afraid so."

"But you're getting better, right? Cause you promised to take me ice skating this year."

He tightens his grip on his crutches and bites down on the inside of his cheek. *Come on. Keep it together.*

"Okay, Kelli, that's enough." Matt places a hand on the girl's head. "Can we come in?"

Austin drops his head and takes a couple of deep breaths.

Laura clears her throat. "Umm, I think I'm going to head home."

Austin's head snaps up. "No—stay. Please." He shoots her a pleading look; he's not sure he can handle Matt and Kelli on his own. When she nods, he lets out a breath of relief and gestures his guests inside with a tilt of his head.

"We can't stay long," Matt says as he enters the living room. He turns to Laura and shakes her hand. "Matt."

"Laura."

"And I'm Kelli. With an 'I'." Kelli peers up at Laura. "Why do you have an earring through your face? Did it hurt? It looks weird."

Austin chuckles and relaxes his grip on his crutches as Matt tries to shush the little girl.

"Woman who speaks her mind," Laura says. "I like her."

"Yeah, me too." Austin's smile fades as his gaze travels from Kelli to Matt. "Although her father, not so much."

Matt sends him one of the looks of exasperation he's seen on numerous occasions. "Come on, man. If you would answer your phone, I wouldn't have to resort to this."

"Yeah, well, next time, take the hint." Austin hobbles over to the sofa and eases himself down. He keeps his eyes locked on his leg while he repositions it, then looks up at Matt. "Why are you here?"

Kelli answers before her father can get a word out. "It's my birthday. And I'm having a party. Will you come?" She skips over to Austin and gently places her hand on his right leg. "Please?"

Austin exhales forcefully through his nose as he stares at the placement of her hand. He knows it's there. He can plainly see it resting on the outer portion of his thigh. *But I can't feel it.* He clenches his teeth against another threat of emotions and lays his hand over hers. He swings his glance from Kelli to Matt. "Are you having your kid do your dirty work for you?"

"She misses you, man. We all do."

Austin tilts his head back and looks up at the ceiling. He swallows several times and closes his eyes. *Shit.* When he lowers his head, he has a smile plastered on his face. "When's the party?"

"Next Saturday," Matt replies.

"And who's coming?"

"Rena, Mikey, Taylor," Kelli ticks off the names of her friends on her fingers.

"A few people from the neighborhood," adds Matt.

Shit. Austin sighs and huffs a soft laugh. "There's no way you can just skip your birthday this year, is there Kiddo? Maybe go from six to eight and forget about seven?" Austin tugs on one of Kelli's pigtails.

She giggles and shakes her head. "No."

"Then I'll be there. Can I at least bring a guest?" Austin glances over to Laura.

"Hey, if it'll get you there, I don't care if you bring the entire offensive line of the New York Jets." Matt's gaze darts between Austin and Laura. "But you'd better not wuss out."

"Yeah," Kelli echoes. "Don't wuss out." She pokes Austin's leg for emphasis and then looks up at him. "What's a wuss?"

Austin chuckles and Matt clears his throat. "Come on, Kelli. We've gotta get back home."

"Yeah, your dad can tell you all about wussing out on the ride back." Austin gives Kelli's pigtail another tug and then looks up at Matt. "Have fun with that. And good luck explaining it to Monica, too." He laughs again when Matt cringes.

"Yeah, yeah. Nice to meet you." He nods at Laura and then turns back to Austin. "Next Saturday. 4:00 pm." He stares at Austin. "Right?"

Austin clenches his jaw and nods. "Yeah. See you then."

"Bye, Uncle Austin! Bye, Laura!" Kelli yells while Matt ushers her out the door.

The apartment is silent for all of five seconds before Laura unleashes a series of rapid-fire questions. "What the hell? Why didn't you tell me you had a brother? And a niece? What's going on between you and Matt? And did you just invite me to her birthday party?"

Austin waits for her to take a breath and then cocks an eyebrow. "Are you done?"

Laura narrows her eyes but doesn't ask any additional questions.

"Matt's not my brother. He's my best friend. At least he was. Not sure about that anymore."

Laura raises an eyebrow but remains silent.

"I was kind of an ass to him after my accident," Austin says. "What can I say? He was an easy target."

"Seems like he's over it from what I just saw."

Austin shrugs. "Yeah. I guess."

"So Kelli's not your niece."

A genuine smile works its way across his face. "No. But she calls me Uncle Austin anyway. Love that kid. Sure keeps her parents on their toes." He flicks his eyes to Laura, who has once again taken up residence on the armchair. "You know how they say paybacks are a bitch? Well, let's just say Kelli comes by her troublemaking tendencies naturally."

Austin's smile fades. "She came to visit me regularly in the hospital. Kept bringing me drawings of all the things we were gonna do together when I got better. Hiking, fishing, skating." He swallows convulsively, fighting against the lump forming in his throat.

Laura waits silently while Austin gets himself under control.

He takes several deep breaths and then continues. "Then when I was transferred down here to the rehab facility, it was farther from home, so I didn't see them as often. And it kind of made it easier in a way. Made it just a little bit easier to forget what I'd lost, you know?"

Laura nods, sadness evident in her eyes.

"So then after the inpatient rehab, I decided to stay down here. To continue with the same therapists and rehab specialists."

"To stay away from your friends," she adds.

Austin picks at a loose thread on the arm of the sofa and shrugs. "Maybe." He pulls the thread and watches it float to the floor. "So what do you think? Will you come to the party with me? I could use a buffer; I think there's gonna be a bunch of people I haven't seen since the accident." He pats his right leg. "Not to mention, I kind of need a chauffeur."

"Do I have to dress up and wear one of those chauffeur hats?"

The corners of Austin's mouth pull into a smile. *Bet she'd look good in one of those uniforms.* "Hey. Whatever floats your boat."

Laura taps her finger against her mouth. "All right. I'll come. *But…*" Austin groans when she holds up her finger at her emphasized word. "You have to help me out."

"I'm already helping you out."

Laura quirks her eyebrow to the ceiling but remains silent.

"With Steven," he adds.

She barks out a laugh. "Yeah. Once. Not doing so hot on that front there, Supergimp."

"Not like I haven't been trying," Austin mutters. He sighs and sends her a bland look. "Fine. What do I have to do to get you to drive me and run interference?"

A grin works its way across her face. "Come over and keep me company on Friday."

"What's Friday?"

"Halloween."

"What's the catch?" Austin eyeballs her warily.

"No catch. Just don't really want to be alone." She scuffs the toe of her shoe against the floor. "Steven and I used to dress up and hand out Halloween candy. I love it, but I'm not sure I can handle it by myself this year, you know?"

Yeah, I do. Austin lets out an exaggerated sigh. "Dammit. Does that mean *I* have to dress up?"

Laura shakes her head as the grin reappears on her face. "But it'd be much more fun if you did."

FOURTEEN

Laura bounds down her steps, one hand clasped around the chains hanging from her neck while she scurries to answer the buzzing of her doorbell.

An exasperated huff crosses her lips as she pulls the curtains aside and peeks out of the window beside her door. She opens the door and steps to the side, inspecting Austin's buttoned-up jacket and jeans as he enters. "Seriously man? No costume?"

Austin glances around her living room and crutches over to her sofa. He leans against it, slides off his backpack, and takes off his jacket.

Laura raises an eyebrow at the blue T-shirt with the Superman "S" in the middle.

"Wait for it," he says, holding up his index finger. He digs through his backpack and pulls out a piece of green fabric which he shakes out and ties around his neck. He repositions himself against the sofa, running his hands from his chest to his hips. "What do you think?" The grin on his face makes it clear he's impressed with himself.

"I think that's a tablecloth," Laura says, her eyebrows furrowing while she fingers the piece of cloth trailing down his back. "Is that Marge's?"

He smacks the cloth out of her hand and shoots her a look of exasperation.

The corners of her mouth twitch as she stifles a laugh. "Fine. I'll give you partial credit." She flicks her glance from his cape to his jeans. "But Superman's cape was red. And he wore tights. You got tights on under those?"

Austin rolls his eyes. "I'm not Superman." He stares at her pointedly for a few seconds and then grumbles under his breath. Louder, he says, "Supergimp. Duh."

Laura can't contain the smile that breaks out on her face, both at his exasperation and his costume choice.

Austin studies her, moving his gaze from her head to her feet. "What the hell are you supposed to be, anyway?"

Laura fingers the hoop that's replaced her usual barbell eyebrow piercing and looks down at herself. The idea involving the knee-length blue dress with a white apron, white tights, and black Mary Janes has been in the back of her mind for years. The addition of the chain running from her eyebrow piercing to her right earring and the mixture of necklaces and heavier chains she got from the hardware store complete her ensemble for the evening. "If you can guess, you get an extra piece of candy."

Austin gives her a questioning look but remains silent.

"That's what Steven and I used to do. Dress up as word play or puns and give extra candy to the kids or their parents if they could guess what we were." Laura tries to contain her amusement at Austin's blank expression. "Don't strain yourself."

"Shaddup."

"So. You want the tour?"

He glances around her living room. "Yeah, sure. Although I have to say I'm surprised. Didn't take you for the Townhouse type."

Laura shrugs. "What can I say? It was a good price. And a house is a house, right?" She glances over at Austin and catches the quick flash of sadness in his eyes before he sees her looking at him.

He clears his throat. "Yeah. Right."

Laura leads him through the living room toward the back of the house. "So obviously this is the kitchen." She waves her hand in a Vanna White-type gesture.

"So, the room you spend the least amount of time in."

Laura sends him a bland look, then continues around the downstairs circuit. "Half bath over here," she says, gesturing to a door to her right, "and dining room."

"You have a lot of dinner parties? This table looks like it could seat eight easily."

Laura snorts. "Yeah, I'm a regular on the dinner party circuit." She runs her hand over the smooth mahogany table. "It was Marge's. It didn't fit when she moved into her apartment, so I inherited it. Use this room mostly for my home office." She grins at

Austin. "But I'll be sure to let you know when I'm cooking for that dinner party."

Austin shudders. "Yeah, you do that. I'm pretty sure I'll be busy that night."

She leads them through the door at the other side of the dining room and stops at the base of the stairs. "You want to see upstairs, too?"

He eyeballs the stairs and glances back at her. "Will I be missing out on anything exciting up there?"

"Nope. Couple of bedrooms and the master bath."

"Then I think I'm good down here."

"Great," Laura says when her doorbell buzzes. "Because I think the fun is about to begin."

*
**

"So, Alice in Chains, huh?" Austin shakes his head. "I can't believe I didn't get that." He lets his eyes roam over Laura once more, his gaze stuttering over her eyebrow piercing. *Why the hell does that turn me on?*

"Yeah. What kind of sheltered childhood did you have anyway?" She shoots him a sidelong glance as they sit side by side on her oversized sofa.

"Um, one that didn't involve fictional characters crossing over into heavy metal?"

"Yeah, I think I outdid myself this year. None of the kids had a clue who I was, and I'm pretty sure the parents who got it right were over forty."

Austin leans forward, tipping the bowl on the coffee table to get a better look at its contents. "The good news is, that means more candy for us." He rifles though it and pulls out a Reese's Peanut Butter Cup. "Want anything?"

Laura flushes slightly, and she darts her glance from his face to the candy bowl. "Yeah. Any Kit Kats left?"

Tossing the requested item into her lap, he settles back on the couch, downs half of his candy in one bite, and sighs in bliss. "I love these things." He pops the other half in his mouth and lets his eyes wander around her living room. The candy bowl is nestled in amongst several trade magazines strewn across the table. A jumbled pile of shoes rests in the corner near the front door. Laura's messenger bag is propped on a table on the opposite side of the door, files and papers sticking out haphazardly.

Austin washes his candy down with a swallow of beer from the side table next to him. "I used to take Kelli Trick or Treating. I always made her give me her Peanut Butter Cups as payment for taking her out."

"Well, hopefully the poor kid will get to eat 'em this year."

His smile fades, and he exhales loudly through his nose.

"Oh, God. Sorry."

"No, it's okay. I'm pretty sure that even without this," he says, gesturing to his leg, "I wasn't getting an invite to take her out this year."

"Oh?" Laura turns herself on the couch and sits cross legged, facing him. She smooths the dress and apron over her lap, props her elbows on her knees, and rests her chin in her hands.

"Yeah, I think Matt and Monica finally got wise to me." He can feel the smile working its way back onto his face. He adjusts his position slightly to face her and lays his arm along the back of the couch. "I would always offer to take her out and tell them to use it as a night off, have a date night, whatever. Kelli and I would go out for a few hours. That kid is a candy goldmine." He shakes his head and chuckles. "She's so cute most people give her double the candy. Which meant I always got a nice little stash as well."

"Sounds like a win-win to me."

Austin gives her an incredulous look. "Have you ever seen a six-year-old on a sugar high? It's terrifying. Poor kid had to be practically peeled off the ceiling last year."

Laura laughs and bites her lip. "You want to talk terrifying? Steven and I made a kid wet himself one year."

"What? With your punny word play? Did he pee himself from laughing so hard?"

Laura glowers at him, then punches him lightly in the shoulder. "No. We toned it down a couple of years ago."

Austin bites back a smirk and waits for her to continue.

"Let's just say that Steven made a very convincing Zombie and when he lost his head, the blood spatter may have traumatized the poor kid."

Austin grimaces. "Yikes."

"Yeah." She reaches over to the coffee table, unwraps another piece of candy, and pops it in her mouth. "So we changed our MO. Nobody's wet themselves since."

"That you know of," he adds. "I'm sure someone out there tonight was traumatized by the sight of you in a dress and facial piercings." He adjusts his position when his body lets him know that 'traumatized' is definitely not the word for what her outfit is doing to him.

Laura rolls her eyes as the corners of her lips twitch. "Shut up." She runs her eyes down his body. "Not as traumatized as they would have been if you'd have been wearing tights."

Austin lets out an exaggerated sigh. "Yeah, I was only thinking of sparing the poor children when I decided to wear pants tonight."

Shifting her position, she tucks her legs to the side and lays her arm along the back of the couch. "Well, thank you for that, Supergimp."

He eyes the inches that separate their hands, his heart quickening its pace. "No problem."

The teasing glint in her eyes and the smile on her face divert additional blood flow from his brain to his lap. He swallows against the sudden dryness in his throat and clenches the hand lying next to hers. *Come on, man. You're here for moral support tonight. Keep it together.* He closes his eyes and takes a deep breath.

His eyes pop open when he feels a soft hand on his arm.

"Hey, you okay?"

Austin's eyes move from Laura's hand to her face. Her brows are furrowed and her lips are turned downward in a slight frown.

"You look a little pale."

Austin lets out a strangled laugh. *Yeah, probably because all my blood's hanging out below my waist.*

"You're not about to have a panic attack, are you?"

"No." *Not even close.*

"Then what?" Laura's eyes rove over his face. Her fingers curl around his forearm and she rubs her thumb back and forth over his wrist.

Austin drops his head and rolls his lower lip between his teeth. *I really hope I'm not reading the signals wrong.* When he looks up, Laura's eyes are fixed on his; they dart down to his mouth and then bounce back up. He moves his arm from its resting place under her hand and lifts it to her face, running his thumb alongside her piercing. Her breath hitches at his touch and her eyes widen slightly. She licks her lips and swallows.

So far, so good. He runs his finger lightly along the chain still connected to her earring, careful not to pull it, then rubs her earlobe between his fingers.

She closes her eyes and tilts her head into his hand.

The sigh that escapes her lips makes him smile. He moves his hand to the back of her neck and draws her toward him, pausing when they're inches apart. "Is it okay if I kiss you?"

His whispered question is met with Laura's barely audible groan. "Oh God, yes." She crosses the remaining distance and wraps her arms around his neck.

Their lips meet, a hesitant greeting that quickly morphs into a more urgent exploration. Her lips are soft. Inviting. Delicious. And not just because she tastes like a Kit Kat bar, although that *is* a nice bonus. He pulls her closer and lies back on the sofa, taking comfort in her weight as she shifts on top of him.

"Laura?" he says out of the side of his mouth when she takes a breath.

"Hmmm?" She doesn't glance up, just resumes their lip lock.

"Can you," *kiss*, "move," *kiss*, "my leg?"

Laura's head jerks back and her eyes widen. "Oh God. Are you okay?"

"No, no. Don't stop. I'm fine." Austin smiles. "I'm great. Just don't think the leg's in the best position is all." While most of him is stretched out on the couch, his right foot is still on the floor, knee bent at an awkward angle.

She glances at his right leg, then back up as a slow smile makes its way over her face. "No problem." She rolls off of him and gently lifts it up onto the sofa. Kneeling beside him, she runs her fingers lightly along the outside of his leg. "How's that feel?"

Austin looks down at his leg, then back at her. "Position's fine, but you know I can't feel that, right?"

She moves her fingers several inches over and tries again. "How about now?"

"Kind of."

A wicked smile overtakes her face, and she moves her hand again. She unbuttons his jeans and slips her hand inside his boxers. "What about this?

Austin's breathing hitches, and he lets out a low moan. He manages to work a strangled "oh yeah" past his lips. *No trouble there.* Any further words are cut off when Laura slides back onto the couch beside him and plants her lips on his while her hand is busy exploring his crotch. "Oh God. It's been too long."

"What did you say?" Laura asks between kisses.

"What? Nothing." Austin presses himself against Laura's hand and feverishly works to undo the knot at the back of her apron. "I didn't say anything."

She pauses and draws her head back slightly, eliciting a more disappointed groan from him this time. "Yes, you did. You said, 'It's been too long.'" Her eyes widen, and her hand stills in his boxers. "When was the last time?"

"The last time what?"

Laura keeps her eyes locked on his. "The last time you got some action with someone other than yourself."

Austin raises his head, giving her a level stare. "Seriously?"

"Yep."

He drops his head back against the sofa. "Too damn long," he mutters.

"I'm sorry, I didn't quite catch that. What did you say?"

"You know this is totally killing the mood, right?" Austin bends his right arm and tucks it behind his head so he can see her better.

Laura shrugs. "Inquiring minds want to know."

"Geez, you and Marge with your inquiries into my sex life. Apple really doesn't fall far from the tree, does it?"

Laura wrinkles her nose. "Now who's killing the mood?"

Austin rolls his eyes, a smile tugging at the corner of his mouth. "Promise you won't make a big deal out of it?"

Laura narrows her eyes and bites her lower lip, like he's seen her do when she's deep in thought, then nods.

Here goes... "So, I haven't been with anyone since my accident. Almost six months."

Her face softens, and she places a gentle kiss on the corner of his mouth. "So, you're saying I'm your first."

"Like this, yeah." Heat gathers at the base of his neck. "I don't know what I'm gonna be able to do. You know, movement-wise."

"Seemed like you were doing just fine." She runs her index finger down his chest, sending little shivers dancing along the trail, and her eyes take on a wicked gleam. "Guess you'll just have to practice, right?" She runs her fingers through his hair and plants her lips on his, deepening her kiss when he reciprocates.

Austin's never been so happy to practice anything in his life.

Laura pulls her lips away just long enough to tug his Superman shirt over his head. "Do you think we should take this party upstairs?"

"Not sure I'll make it that far." *I'd rather take my chances with the couch.*

"Well, in that case..." Laura sits up and lifts up her arms, allowing Austin to pull off her dress, then quickly divests herself of her tights, balling them up and flinging them across the room.

Austin licks his lips at the sight in front of him. Firm, small breasts and gentle curves at her waist that seem tailor-made for his hands. His gaze intensifies on her right breast. The polka dot print of her bra is marred by a dark red stain. "What is that?"

Laura looks down. "Oh, yeah. Had a little accident with a bottle of Merlot."

Austin chuckles. "Classy."

"Well, I really wasn't planning on showing my underwear to anyone tonight."

"I usually stick to beer, but I could be persuaded to try some Merlot." He encircles her wrist with his hand and gently pulls her back down, flicking his tongue over the thin wine-stained fabric. "Hmmm," he says, "tastes like it's gone rancid. I think we should get you out of this before it's too late."

"All right. But those jeans better be coming off pretty soon."

"Don't count on it." He traces Laura's bra strap with his finger. "Takes me ten minutes to get 'em on and take 'em off." *Not sure how sexy she's gonna think I am after watching that.*

Laura wiggles her fingers and grins. "Well, you know what they say—many hands make light work."

Austin can't keep the smile from creeping back onto his face. "They also say idle hands are the devil's playthings."

A look of mock horror crosses Laura's face. "Well then, what are we waiting for?"

FIFTEEN

Laura awakens slowly, a smile spreading across her face as Austin's chest rises and falls steadily. She's snuggled up next to him on the sofa, her right arm and leg draped over his still sleeping body, and she buries her head a little more into the crook of his neck. A contented sigh crosses her lips as she relives last night's "practice session." She's not sure who was the teacher and who was the student.

Her blissful existence is interrupted by a full-body shiver. She lifts her head and spies their clothing in scattered piles, none of them within easy reach. She rolls over, searching for the blanket they'd snuggled beneath after their final round of activity, but finds the floor instead. *Thank God for carpeting.*

The sofa squeaks, and Austin peeks over the edge several seconds later. "You okay down there?"

"Yeah. Great. How're things up there?"

"Give me a minute, I'll let you know."

Laura sits up and wraps the wayward fleece blanket around herself. She yawns as Austin works his way into a seated position. "Need any help?"

He hisses through clenched teeth as he moves his leg with his hands and shakes his head.

"Okay, let me know. I'm gonna go put on some coffee." She gives him one last glance, running her gaze over his naked body—his well-muscled chest, the strong arms that cradled her after they'd finally worn themselves out. *Delicious.*

She heads into the kitchen and hums softly while she measures the beans into her Grind & Brew, sniffing appreciatively as the freshly ground beans release their aroma. Waiting for the coffee to percolate, she ducks into her downstairs bathroom. A satisfied smile crosses her face as she studies herself in the mirror. *Who knew he had such a thing for piercings?*

They'd certainly put the whole "practice makes perfect" motto to good use. Despite a couple of hiccups with positioning, Austin definitely proved Marge's worries unfounded.

Her grin widens. *Nothing wrong with* that *part of him.*

She heads back into the kitchen as the coffeemaker beeps its readiness, Austin joining her. He's put on his jeans and shoes, but his upper half is still exposed. His hair is only slightly more disheveled than usual and the increased scruff covering the lower portion of his face adds an extra layer of "*Hot damn*" as far as Laura's concerned. She reluctantly turns away from him and pours two mugs of coffee; she places one at her usual spot at the small table beside the window and raises the other toward Austin, her eyebrow quirked in question.

"I think I need to stand for now, stretch out a bit." He props himself against the counter and leans his crutches next to him, then takes the coffee. "Definitely not the worst night I've ever had, but certainly not the best."

Laura freezes in place. *Did he seriously just say that?*

"Oh God, no. That's not what I meant! I meant the couch. My leg's not really happy with me right now. But believe me, every other part is ecstatic."

Laura relaxes and pulls the blanket tighter around herself as she settles into her seat. She returns his smile and takes a couple sips of her coffee, watching as he repositions himself several times; he winces with each movement. "You need anything? I might have a couple of Steven's pain pills around here somewhere. He stayed with me for a while after his accident."

"Nah. Those things make me loopy as hell. Although I have been told I'm a delight to be around when I'm high as a kite. Apparently, I let Kelli put makeup on me once. Matt has the picture proof; tried to blackmail me with it several times." He raises his coffee mug to his lips and keeps his free hand planted on the counter. "I got off the heavy stuff as soon as I could. Then they tried to give me something for nerve pain, but it didn't do anything. Besides, I only really feel it when I've done something stupid. The couch, not you," he quickly clarifies. "But I'll take some ibuprofen if you've got some. That usually takes the edge off."

"It's upstairs. Be right back." Laura takes her coffee with her, quickly locates the pills in her master bathroom, and throws on a pair of leggings and a sweatshirt while she's upstairs. Back downstairs, she sets the bottle on the counter next to Austin.

"Aw, man." Austin's shoulders slump as she takes her seat at the table.

"What, you need help with the childproof cap?"

He shoots her a disgusted look and pops three tablets into his mouth, washing them down with a gulp of coffee. "No." He runs his eyes over her, his expression turning to one of disappointment. "You put clothes on."

Laura bites her lip but can't keep the smile from working its way onto her face. "It's cold."

"I know a way to get warm."

Her cheeks heat up as his lopsided grin emerges.

"Let me know if you need another workout. I'm game if you are." He holds her gaze as he takes another sip of coffee. "Someone told me I need the practice."

Laura barks out a laugh. "Yeah. I think you're good."

Austin winks at her and his grin turns lascivious. "That's what they all say."

"Oh God," Laura moans as she looks up at the ceiling. "I've created a monster."

"Nope. Merely awoken one."

Laura's stomach gurgles loudly and she places her arm across her midsection. "Speaking of awakening monsters..." She grimaces and gives an apologetic shrug. "I'm hungry."

Austin sighs. "Yeah. Guess we worked off all of our excess candy calories last night. Tell you what.

How about we have some breakfast, then see about getting in another practice session."

Laura's barely able to the contain the "*Hell yes*" her brain is screaming. She pretends to think about it for a few seconds, taking delight in the hopeful look Austin's sending her way. "Deal." She stands up and walks over to the cabinet next to her fridge. "Which cereal do you want?"

"Ugh."

She turns to face him and sees the look of disgust on his face. "Not up to your high standards?"

He sets down his coffee mug and crutches over to her fridge. He peers inside. "You got flour, baking soda, and salt? Oh, and vinegar?"

Laura roots around in the cabinet and pulls out the requested items. "You'd better thank Marge for this. I don't think I had any of this stuff in here before she stayed with me." Laura quickly shakes her head. "On second thought, don't thank her. Don't want to give her any ideas about why we were making breakfast together."

"Oh, I'm pretty sure she can guess."

"Yeah, that's what I'm afraid of." She takes the eggs and milk Austin hands her and sets them on the counter. "So what are we making?"

"Pancakes. My specialty."

"You mean charred cakes? Burnt-to-a-crisp cakes?"

"No. I mean fluffy little pillows of heaven. Come on, I'll teach you." He nods her over to the counter next to him and requests measuring spoons, mixing bowls, and measuring cups. "And my shirt. Could you bring that in? Please?"

Laura runs her eyes over his bare chest and trails her finger along his abdominal muscles. "I don't know. I kind of like the idea of cooking with a half-naked man. Might help me learn better."

Austin shrugs. "All right. But I hope you find grease burns sexy."

Laura wrinkles her nose, leaves the kitchen, and returns seconds later with Austin's T-shirt. She sighs as she takes another look at him and holds out the requested item. *Dang it.*

"Yeah, didn't think so." Austin leans against the counter while he slips his shirt over his head. "All right. Dry ingredients in this bowl." He nudges a mixing bowl toward Laura then plants both hands back on the counter.

Laura stands still and peruses the ingredients on the counter in front of her. She chews on the inside of her cheek. *What the hell is he talking about?*

"Oh, man. It's worse than I thought." He props his arm on Laura's shoulder and flinches when she elbows him in the ribs. "So, dry ingredients would be the flour, salt, and baking soda. Versus the wet ingredients, which would be the eggs, milk, and vinegar."

"So far, so good," says Laura as she slides a glance over toward Austin. She snakes her arm around his waist and holds him steady while she stands up on tiptoe and plants a kiss on the corner of his mouth.

Austin shoots her a warning look. "Hey. Careful. If you keep that up, I can't guarantee the end product."

Laura presses her lips together and turns her attention back to the counter.

"Okay. Measure out one cup of flour, a half teaspoon of salt, and a half teaspoon of baking soda into the bowl and then stir them together. Be sure to fluff up the flour before you measure it."

"Fluff the flour? Is that a technical term?"

"No." He removes his hand from her shoulder and takes the wooden spoon from her hand. "But would you know what I meant if I said to sift it?"

"No."

"Here. Like this." Austin shows her how to stir the flour in the bag as an alternative to sifting. "Now measure it out and level off the top with the handle of the spoon." He gives the spoon back to her and places his arm back on her shoulder.

She follows his directions and gives the ingredients a few stirs.

"Good. Now in that bowl," he points to another metal mixing bowl, "measure out one cup of milk, add one teaspoon of vinegar, and beat in one egg."

Laura does as told, then combines the contents of the two bowls together.

"Just stir it a few times. Don't overdo it." Austin makes sure all of the dry ingredients have been worked in, then nods in approval. "Okay. Now we cook 'em."

"You mean burn 'em."

"Nope. There will be no burning here today." He glances at Laura. "Except maybe my leg after our next workout session. But I will definitely suffer for the cause."

"Oh, you're such a martyr."

Austin sighs and flutters his eyelashes. "I know. What can I say? That's just the type of guy I am."

Laura elbows him in the ribs again and rolls her eyes. *Dammit. So sexy.*

"Okay. Now stand here," Austin gestures her over in front of the stove, "and let's make some pancakes."

Laura shakes her head vigorously from side to side. "Uh-uh. I thought you wanted edible food."

Austin tilts his head toward the stove. "Come on. You'll be fine. Promise."

Laura shoots him a look of warning. "Don't blame me when you're trying to chisel through your pancake."

Austin's lips quirk and he bites his lower lip, nodding to the stove again.

Laura gives an exaggerated sigh. "Fine." She stands in front of the skillet and places her hands on her hips. "Happy now?"

Austin grins and carefully uses the counter and then Laura's body, along with one of his crutches, to maneuver until he's standing behind her. He props his crutch against the counter and slides his arms around her waist. "Definitely."

"Oh, you sneaky little…" His hands tighten around her waist when she begins to turn around.

"Nope. You'll make me fall."

The skin under Austin's hands warms as he gently runs his thumbs in small circles. Her nipples harden when his warm breath comes in little puffs on the back of her neck.

"Okay, turn the burner to medium heat and drizzle a little oil into the skillet."

"Now what?" Laura asks, once her next task is completed.

"Now we wait for things to heat up."

Laura can't stifle the laugh that bubbles up.

Austin leans into her and kisses the side of her neck. "What. Did I say something funny?"

Laura wraps her hands around his arms and gently strokes the fine layer of hair of his forearms. "That is one of the cheesiest double entendres I've ever heard."

"Give me time. I'm sure I can come up with worse." He rests his chin on her shoulder and readjusts his stance. "Okay. Skillet's sizzling. Now pour in a ladle-full of batter." He waits until Laura's finished with the task. "Now we wait until we see bubbles forming in the middle, then flip it."

Laura tightens her grip on Austin's arms and shifts so she can see him out of the corner of her eye. "Hope you're not expecting to teach me how to do one of those fancy flips." She can see the grimace on Austin's face as he imagines said action.

"Yeah, no. Don't think either of us need to visit the ER today."

"Ooh, look. Bubbles!" Laura uses the spatula in her hand to gesture toward the pancake.

"All right. Careful now. Don't want to spook it."

Laura bites down on her lip to keep the smile from taking over her face. "You sure you want to trust me with this?"

"Are you kidding me? You're doing fabulous. Now, just slide the spatula underneath the pancake, right under the middle, and then a quick flip of the wrist and we're on the home stretch."

"Okay." Laura recoils her head slightly and steels herself. *Here goes.* She follows Austin's instructions and within the span of two seconds she has a pancake happily sizzling away and several globs of batter on her sweatshirt.

Austin sighs, his breath puffing out against her ear. "Pity. Guess we'll just have to get you out of those clothes."

SIXTEEN

Jack finishes stretching out Austin's leg and pats his knee. "All right. Over to the parallel bars for some balance work."

"Aye aye, captain." Austin grins and follows his therapist across the room.

Jack gives him a curious look. "You're awfully chipper today."

"I had a good weekend." Austin can't fully contain the smile that works its way across his face. "Really good."

"Care to share?"

Austin settles between the bars, fighting to keep his balance while thoughts of his weekend's activities swirl through his brain. He and Laura spent the majority of Saturday together, and part of Sunday as well. While their time engaged in additional "practice sessions" had definitely been a highlight, he was just as happy with their hours on the couch watching movies. Having her curled up next to him, shushing her constant commentary, and generally enjoying each other's company.

It was one of the best weekends I've had in a long time. "Let's just say there's one more significant post-accident milestone I can cross off my list."

Jack makes a slight adjustment to the position of his leg. "If I recall, you've got a pretty long list. Want to narrow that down for me?"

"Well, I'm still not driving, haven't gone home, and I didn't miraculously go for a run..."

Understanding flashes across Jack's face. "Oh. Well then, congrats. How was it?"

Austin sends his therapist a wary look. "I know we've been through a lot together, man, but..."

Jack holds up a hand, gesturing for Austin to stop. "Not like that. I mean, how did your leg hold up?"

"Okay, I guess. Really sore, but totally worth it." His grin widens.

He'd spent part of his time on the couch alternating hot and cold packs to his hip and upper leg. A small price to pay for his weekend activities. Especially when Laura had insisted on helping him massage his leg. Her soft, skilled hands roaming his body...

"You gonna see her again?"

"What?" Austin grips the bars as his balance wavers.

"Whoever it is that put you in such a good mood. You gonna see her again? Or was it a one-time deal?"

"Definitely gonna see her again. Heading over to her office after we're done here."

"Kinky."

Austin rolls his eyes. "Not like that." *Although, on second thought...* He shakes his head. *Gonna talk to Steven. Get your mind out of the gutter.*

Jack checks his watch. "Well, whatever you are or aren't gonna do in her office, looks like you're in luck. Time's up. See you Wednesday. Don't forget you see Greg tomorrow."

"Yep. I'll be there." His previous good mood takes a bit of a downturn at the reminder of his brace fitting. He knows it's for his own good. To get him closer to whatever his new normal will be. He's just still trying to wrap his head around it. Both the brace itself and the thought that his "normal" won't be anywhere close to what it once was.

He makes his way to the end of the parallel bars and slides his backpack on, then heads to the front desk to check out.

The receptionist is on her cell phone, her urgent whispering making it clear she's trying to hurry the conversation. She gives Austin an apologetic smile. "Yes, Janie. I know, honey. We'll find it. But Mommy's got to get back to work now, okay? All right, sweetie. I'll see you later." She ends the call, shaking her head. "I'm sorry."

"No problem. Everything okay?" *Why the hell does the name Janie sound familiar?*

"Oh, yeah. Just my little girl. Lost her favorite barrette. Stupid, I know." She sighs. "But my mother-in-law gave it to her for her birthday, and she died not too long ago, so…"

Austin's mouth forms a silent O. *Right. Tell Janie it's behind the cabinet.* He racks his brain for some kind of plausible explanation. "Well, I don't know about you, but I'm always losing stuff. Usually find it somewhere later. One time when I was a kid I thought I'd lost my favorite baseball card. Turns out, it had fallen behind a cabinet and gotten stuck." He shrugs. "Maybe Janie's barrette is stuck behind a cabinet somewhere."

The receptionist smiles at him. "Thanks. I'll be sure to check it out."

"No problem." *Hope my crazy superpower helps someone out there.*

*
**

Laura checks her watch, then glances across the office at Theresa, who's sitting at her desk, typing. Her receptionist usually leaves by three. It's now three thirty. "Shouldn't you be leaving soon?" *Austin's gonna be here any minute now.*

Theresa's fingers continue to fly across the keyboard, and she maintains her focus on the computer screen. "Just a few more entries. Why, are you trying to get rid of me?"

Laura lets out a nervous laugh.

Theresa leans back in her chair and scrutinizes Laura. "What's with you, anyway? You've been acting weird all day."

Laura does her best to put on an air of innocence. "Weird? Me? How?"

Theresa taps her nails against her desk as she continues to study Laura. "I'm not sure. Can't quite put my finger on it. Just different somehow." Her face lights up and she leans forward in her chair. "Is it Marcus? Did you finally go out with him?"

Laura sends her an exasperated look. "No. I did not go out with Marcus. Now will you please drop it?"

"One of these days…"

"What? One of these days you'll stop badgering me about my love life?"

"What love life? You don't have a love life." Theresa turns back to her computer and continues typing. "My ninety-year old grandmother has more of a love life than you do."

Laura presses her lips together in an attempt to keep any further snark from escaping. *Just shut up and let her do her job so she can get the hell out of here before Austin comes.* Her hand inches toward her phone. *Maybe I can text him and ask him to wait.* Before she's able to get her message typed, however, she hears the ding of the elevator, followed by the unmistakable clicking squeak of his crutches. *Crap!*

She scrambles out of her chair, managing to get halfway to the door before Austin appears.

"Hey," he says. "You ready to try to talk to…" He trails off when he sees the look of panic on Laura's face. "You okay?"

Laura jerks her head toward Theresa.

"Well, hellooo."

Laura closes her eyes and sighs at the tone of Theresa's greeting. *Yep. Never gonna hear the end of it.* Her shoulders sag as she turns to face her receptionist. "Theresa, this is Austin. Austin, Theresa."

"Oh, hi." Austin crosses the room and shakes her hand. "I've heard a lot about you."

"Funny," Theresa says, her eyes narrowed as she turns her attention from Austin to Laura. "I can't say the same." She turns back to Austin, a wide grin on her face. "But it's nice to meet you." She looks him up and down. "*Very* nice."

Laura pointedly looks at her watch, then back to her receptionist. "You're gonna be late."

Theresa looks at the clock on the wall. "Oh, shoot." She pulls her purse out from underneath her desk and slips her coat on, then makes a few quick keystrokes and shuts down her computer. "Just when things were getting good." She hustles out the door. "We'll talk about this tomorrow!"

"I have no doubt about that," Laura mutters. She locks the door behind Theresa, then heads to her desk and plops into her chair. "So, you ready to try to talk to Steven again?"

"Umm, nice to see you too?" Austin crosses the room, lowers himself into Steven's chair and props his crutches on the desk.

Laura sighs and rubs her forehead. "Sorry. It's just been a long day. There's a set of drawings that aren't making any sense and my calculations are all screwy. Richardson keeps threatening to re-bid the project. Then you show up while Theresa's still here…"

"Yeah. Sure. No problem."

The dejection in his voice breaks her out of litany. "Hey." She stands up and crosses the room.

He raises his eyes to hers and holds her gaze. His smile has taken a downward turn, and his eyes no longer hold the same light they'd had when he'd entered the room.

She turns his chair and braces her arms on the armrests on either side of him. "Nice to see you." She brushes her lips against his, deepening her kiss when he reciprocates. He circles his arms around her neck, drawing her closer, and she straddles him on the chair. A sigh crosses her lips as she runs her fingers through his hair.

She knows exactly what Theresa meant when she said Laura was acting differently. She's been feeling like a giddy schoolgirl since her weekend with Austin. Caught herself humming when she was getting coffee from the breakroom. Daydreaming about his abs while she stared at an Excel spreadsheet. Wondering if he was thinking about her as much as she was thinking about him.

A loud thump from her right pulls Laura out of her blissful existence. Her eyes widen and she pulls her head back, turning just in time to see the top drawer of the filing cabinet creak open.

"You see that, right?" Laura whispers. She's not sure if her wild heartbeat is due to Austin or the potential supernatural activity playing out in front of her eyes.

"Uh, if you mean the filing cabinet opening by itself, then yes."

"Steven?" Laura calls out. Another thump and the drawer closing is the only response. She turns to Austin. "Is he saying anything to you?"

He closes his eyes and remains still, then opens them again and shakes his head. "Nothing." His eyes travel back over to the cabinet. "Maybe you should look in the drawer."

"Or maybe he just doesn't want us making out in the office." Laura's not sure which option would be less apt to freak her out—her brother's spirit sending messages through a filing cabinet or the knowledge that he's watching her and Austin getting hot and heavy.

She wipes her damp palms on her pants, then pushes herself off of Austin. As much as she wants to do no such thing, she inches closer to the cabinet in question. The same one that had held her phone. *You'd better not be fucking with me, Steven.* She reaches out a trembling hand and rests it on the handle of the drawer, holding her breath as she pulls it open.

There, on the bottom of the drawer, is a set of drawings. She searches her memory, unable to recall if it had been there when she'd found her phone. She pulls them out and takes them to her desk, spreading them out to get a closer look.

"Huh." *What the hell?*

"What?"

"Give me a minute." She studies a formula that runs along the side of the drawing in her brother's familiar handwriting. "Son of a..." She punches numbers into the spreadsheet on her computer at a furious pace, her eyes widening as the calculations finally work. "Thank you, Steven." *Love you, you big jerk.* A puff of cold air blows across her cheek.

She cackles in glee and kisses Austin square on the lips. "This damn thing's been driving me nuts! Don't know why I didn't think about using this formula before!" A rueful smile crosses her face. "I think I'm kind of glad you're not able to hear Steven right now."

"Oh, yeah?"

"Yeah. Pretty sure he'd be calling me a dumbass."

Austin cups her backside and pulls her toward him. "If it'll make you feel any better, I can think of several ways that describe your ass. Dumb isn't one of them."

"Thanks. I think."

SEVENTEEN

"All right, spill it."

Laura lets out an exasperated sigh as she closes the office door behind her.

Theresa's already at her desk. She folds her hands, resting them demurely in front of herself, a smug look on her face. "So, Austin, huh? I'm guessing he's the reason for your giddy schoolgirl impersonation?"

Laura pulls her messenger bag over her head and plops it on the floor beside her desk, careful to keep the coffee in her hand from spilling. "I don't know what you're talking about. We're just friends."

Theresa scoffs. "Yeah. Right."

"What? We are." *At least, I think we are.* There have been no discussions of putting any kind of label on what they're doing, and if Laura has her way, they will stay firmly rooted in the friend stage. *Even if it is Friends with Benefits. Anything more than that, and it all goes to crap.*

"We'll see about that." Theresa leans forward, a shrewd look on her face. "So. Who is he?"

"Marge's neighbor."

"He from around here?"

"Nope."

"Is he a good guy?"

Laura tries to keep her features schooled, but is unable to fully bite back her smile. "Yeah."

"Ha! I knew it! You *do* like him!"

"Well, duh. Of course, I like him. He's my friend."

Theresa huffs. "You are so stubborn. Just admit it. You like him. You want to have hot, nasty sex with him."

Laura's eyes skitter away from her receptionist and Theresa's eyes widen. "Oh, my God! You *have* had hot, nasty sex with him!"

Laura clamps her lips shut.

Theresa crows in delight. "Best. Day. Ever!"

"Oh, shut up."

Theresa rolls her eyes. "Now, while I fully support you getting out of your slump, I do have to mention the elephant in the room."

Laura crosses her arms and waits for Theresa to continue.

"The crutches. You're not on some crusade to save some stranger because you couldn't save Steven, are you?"

Laura opens her mouth, full of righteous indignation. She quickly closes it again. *Not like that thought hasn't crossed my mind, too.* While at first, it *was* the similarities between the two of the them that drew her to Austin, it's now so much more. His sense of humor. His ability to keep up with her snark. His ability to make her feel normal again.

"Maybe? At the very beginning?" *But I think now he might be saving me.*

*
**

Laura pays the delivery guy and waits at her front door as Austin climbs out of the taxi. "Come on, Supergimp. I'm starving." *And not just for dinner.*

Austin pauses at the bottom of the short flight of steps leading to her front door. "Cut me some slack here, Sasspants, I'm going as fast as I can."

"Yeah, yeah." She grins at him, then nods toward to the bags. "I ordered from an Indian place nearby. You okay with that?"

"I'm pretty sure as long as you didn't make it, it's fine."

"If that statement weren't so true, I'd be horribly offended."

In the kitchen, Laura unpacks the bags and Austin arranges the containers of curry, chana masala, chicken vindaloo, and the foil-wrapped package of naan between the two place settings already on the table.

He inhales deeply. "Oh, my God. This smells so good. Thanks for not cooking."

"My pleasure."

They dive into their food, Austin the first to come up for air. "So, how was your day?"

Laura tears off a piece of naan and sops up some of the sauce from her vindaloo. "Fine, I guess. Finally made some headway with that project I've been working on, thanks to the new formula."

"Thanks to Steven."

Laura nods in agreement. "Oh, and Theresa knows."

Austin helps himself to another helping of curry. "Knows what?"

"About you."

"Well, yeah. I did meet her yesterday. Pretty sure you were there."

Laura rolls her eyes. "About you and me."

Austin's mouth tugs into a crooked grin as he chews. "Oh yeah? There's a you and me now, huh?"

Laura's eyes widen and her fork halts its progression to her mouth. *Oh, shit.* Her brain whirls as she tries to retreat from the implication that they might be something approximating a couple. Fun, she can handle. Commitment, not so much. "No. I mean... I just..." Her lips continue to twitch even though she produces no sound. Her heart's trying to bang its way out of her chest, and she's beginning to feel a bit lightheaded. *At least if I pass out I won't have to continue this conversation.*

Austin reaches over and lays his hand on the arm not frozen in mid-air. "Hey. I'm kidding. Take a breath."

Laura pulls in a deep breath and blows it out slowly.

Austin keeps his eyes locked on hers. "Okay?"

"Yeah."

"Okay, then," he says, giving her arm a squeeze. "New topic."

Laura takes a gulp of her water. *Thank God.*

"So, I figured out who Janie is."

"Who?"

"Janie. You know, 'Tell Janie it's behind the cabinet'?" He raises his eyebrows for emphasis.

"Oh, right. Janie."

"Turns out she's the daughter of the receptionist at my therapist's office. Overheard a conversation yesterday and she confirmed it when I was there today." He smiles around his mouthful of food. "Score one for Supergimp."

"But isn't today Tuesday?"

"Yep. All day."

Laura shoots him an exasperated look. "I thought you had physical therapy on Mondays, Wednesdays, and Fridays."

"Yep. But today I had the fitting for the new leg brace."

"Oh, that's right. I totally forgot. How'd it go?"

Austin shrugs. "Okay, I guess. Weird. The orthotics guy, Greg, made a molding of my leg, so it was mostly just me sitting there trying to stay still and not go crazy." He tears off a piece of naan and rolls it between his fingers. "I'll get my new brace next week. Think maybe you'd be able to come? You know, for moral support?"

Laura remains silent. She wants to say yes, but she's not sure if she'll be able to handle it.

"It's okay. You don't have to." The smile he sends her doesn't quite reach his eyes.

She swallows, the pain and uncertainty she sees on his face canceling out her own feelings. "No. Of course, I'll come. What kind of friend would I be if I left you high and dry for something like that?" She pushes a piece of rice around her plate. "I spent a lot of time with Steven at his therapist's. Helping him learn a bunch of the same stuff you're doing. Didn't think I'd have to step foot in one again, you know?"

"Oh, shit." Austin lays his hand on hers, interlocking their fingers. "Sorry. I didn't even think about it that way."

"Why would you?" She squeezes his hand. "Okay. Enough depressing thoughts for tonight. I don't know about you, but I could use some fun."

Austin raises an eyebrow. "Depends on what kind of fun you're talking about."

"I think you know."

"I think I do."

*
**

Laura fidgets in her chair and rests her elbows on the kitchen table. "This isn't quite what I had in mind."

Austin looks up from the cards in his hand. "No?" *Just wait.* He grins at the look of disappointment on Laura's face. "You got any sevens?"

Laura rifles through her cards. "Nope. Go Fish." She waits for him to complete his turn. "Got any nines?"

"Go Fish." When Laura adds her newest card to her hand, he asks, "How about any threes?"

"Dang it." She hands over two threes, and he places all four threes down on the table.

"All right." He waves her up from the table. "Get to it."

The confusion on her face is apparent. "Get to what?"

"Oh, did I forget to mention we're playing Strip Go Fish?" He chuckles at the look that crosses her face; it's somewhere between awe and outrage.

She stands up, closes the blinds and the curtains, then maintains eye contact with him as she peels off a sock. She throws it into the living room. "Game on."

Ten minutes later, Austin's down to his jeans and boxers, having been divested of both shoes, both socks, his brace, and his shirt. Laura's only missing her socks.

"Seriously?" Austin asks, when Laura lays down all four Jacks. "Am I being hustled?"

Laura cackles and claps her hands. "Off with 'em!"

Austin winces. "Yeah, you know how unsexy watching me try to get out of my pants is."

Laura stands up and holds out her hands. "Well, then, sir. Please allow me to do the honors. Won't you accompany me to my boudoir?"

"While I fully accept your offer, I sadly need to make a few small adjustments. I swear to you they will come off again when we get upstairs." He puts on his brace and shoes, then allows her to haul him to his feet and follows her through the living room. He slings an arm around her and gives her his crutches, using her body and the railing to get upstairs quicker than he'd be able to himself. *Desperate times call for desperate measures.*

In her bedroom, Austin removes his shoes and brace, then scoots himself up onto Laura's bed. She bats his hands away when he begins to unbutton his jeans.

"Uh-uh. Please. Allow me." She climbs onto the bed and straddles him, running her index fingers lightly down his chest and stomach before her hands stop at the waist of his pants. Leaning forward, she lightly flicks her tongue against one of his nipples, then the other, trailing a line of kisses down his chest until she reaches his navel.

"Oh my God, are you trying to kill me?" he groans. "So help me, if you don't take these pants off right now…"

"You'll what?" Laura's mouth curves into a lascivious smile.

"I'll do this." He grabs hold of the bottom of her sweater and pulls it over her head, then removes her bra in a deft move he's practiced on more occasions than he can possibly remember.

Laura's mouth forms a moue of disapproval. "Hey, that's cheating."

"Pretty sure I don't care."

His hands busy themselves with working her jeans down over her hips while his mouth keeps hers from offering any further snarky retorts. He wiggles and shimmies as she works his jeans off in turn, his hormone-soaked brain not even registering the level of awkwardness caused by his leg.

By the look on Laura's face, neither does she.

EIGHTEEN

Laura glances over to her right, then quickly returns her focus to the road ahead. "You okay over there?"

A noncommittal grunt is Austin's only response.

She stops at a red light, taking the opportunity to study him more in depth. They'd spent a lot of time together this week, and she'd begun to notice a slight change the closer they'd gotten to Kelli's party. Just little things—fidgeting, more distracted than she's used to seeing him. But an hour and a half into their two-hour drive, he went from "just a little off" toward something more closely approximating "nervous wreck."

"Your leg's been bouncing at warp speed ever since we left the highway. That was fifteen minutes ago." She reaches over and places her hand on Austin's leg, which stills under her touch. "And I'm a little concerned that if you're not careful, you'll chew through your lip." She gives him a playful smile. "I might need it later."

"Yeah. Sorry."

"Want to talk about it?" She removes her hand from his leg, reaches out, and turns down the volume of the radio, not quite muting John Mellencamp's story of Jack and Diane.

"I just…" Austin repositions himself in his seat and clears his throat. "I'm nervous."

Clearly. "Okay…" Laura waits for him to continue and accelerates when the light turns green. She can hear him taking slow, deep breaths and sees him rubbing his palm on his thigh out of the corner of her eye.

"Matt and I have been best friends since grade school. My mom wasn't around a lot, so I spent a lot of time at his house. He and Monica live a couple doors down from where he grew up. I pretty much know all the neighbors. Used to mow their yards, landscaped for a few of them." Austin's leg resumes its workout. "I haven't been back since the accident."

"Oh." Laura presses her lips together, not quite sure what else to say.

"Yeah. So, not only am I pretty sure I'm gonna get crap from Matt and Monica about my disappearing act, but I'm also really looking forward to all the questions about the accident and my leg." He forces out a noisy exhalation through his nose. "If I'm lucky, I can get Kelli nice and sugared up and she can provide enough entertainment to take some of the heat off of me."

"Wow. Great game plan. Fake uncle of the year."

"Might as well make her earn her present."

"Am I gonna have to slip you something to get you to calm down?" She lays her hand on his leg again and gives it a squeeze. "Or maybe you just shouldn't have any birthday cake."

Austin sucks in a breath. "Shut your mouth, woman."

"Never." She follows Austin's directions through a confusing series of intersections, then pursues another line of questions. "So, do I need any warning about these people? Or how about some juicy secrets?"

Austin taps his fingers on his leg. "You'll probably want to steer clear of Mr. Ellis. Especially if he's hanging out near any dairy products. He's lactose intolerant, but in denial."

Laura wrinkles her nose. "What does he look like? So I can keep my distance."

"Tall string bean, early sixties, looks a little like Art Garfunkel."

Laura nods her head. "Got it. If Garfunkel's near the dairy, get the hell out of the way. What else?"

"Hmmm. Kelli's friend, Mikey, is a biter. Rumor has it, his mom is, too."

Laura snorts. "You wouldn't happen to know that from personal experience, would you?"

"Me? No."

"Uh-huh."

He raises his hand in the air. "Swear to God. I have not dated or slept with anyone who'll be at this party. Besides you." He pauses. "Of course, I did ask Monica out back before she and Matt started dating."

"And?"

"And she told me to fuck off."

Laura laughs. "Ooh, I think I'm gonna like her."

"Unfortunately, I think so, too."

*
**

Oh shit. Austin's chest constricts as Laura pulls to a stop in front of the two-story brick house with balloons tied to the mailbox. He sits in his seat, his eyes glued to Matt and Monica's house, the rise and fall of his chest the only break in the stillness as the memories come flooding over him. He and Matt riding their bikes through the neighborhood when they were kids. Learning to drive on this very street. Helping Matt and Monica move into their first home. Holding Kelli's hands while she learned to walk.

He tries to swallow past the lump of emotions lodged in his throat. *Now I'm the one who needs help walking.*

"Are we getting out or what?"

He flinches at Laura's question, having forgotten for the moment that she's sitting beside him. *Thank God she is.* He's fairly certain he would've chickened out long before now if it hadn't been for her willingness to come along and her insistence that he "suck it up" when he'd started to have second thoughts. He reaches out and intertwines his fingers with hers, a reluctant smile on his face. "Thank you. You know, for being here. With me."

She squeezes his hand and runs her thumb along his. "No problem. Glad to help. That was the deal, right?" She winks and her eyes take on a mischievous glint. "Plus, I'm hoping to get some good dirt on you."

Austin's smile fades. "You wouldn't."

"Um, do you know me at all?"

Austin drops his shoulders in resignation. "Yes."

She cackles and gets out of the car, poking her head back in and gesturing toward the overnight bags in the backseat. "Want me to bring those in?"

"Nah, leave 'em in here for now. Might not need 'em." Austin opens his door and maneuvers his right leg out onto the asphalt. He reaches over the seat and gets his crutches, then pulls himself into a standing position.

"It was nice of them to offer to let us sleep here tonight."

Austin shoots Laura a glance while he gets the cuffs of his crutches settled on his arms. "Yeah, well, I might freak out within the first hour. Might not even end up staying the whole time."

"Well, good luck getting a ride home."

Austin lowers his eyebrows and sends her a dirty look over the top of her car. "You're my ride home."

Laura grins. "Exactly."

Austin shakes his head. "Sometimes I wonder why I hang out with you."

"For my sparkling personality and my sassy candy coating."

Austin bites the inside of cheek but fails in his attempt to keep a straight face.

"Come on." Laura rounds the front of her car and beckons him toward Kelli's house.

Austin's grin falters and he tightens his grip on his crutches. He can feel the edges of panic beginning to take hold. *Oh crap.* He drops his head to his chest, takes a deep breath, and blows it out.

"Hey," Laura says softly as she walks toward him. She places a hand on his bicep and gives it a gentle squeeze. "I really think you should do this, but if you don't want to, just say the word. I'll take you back home."

Austin swallows and clenches his jaw. He raises his head and locks eyes with Laura, holding her gaze as he blows out another breath. "Thanks. But I'm okay. I can do this."

She gives his arm another squeeze. "Yeah, you can."

NINETEEN

"Uncle Austin!"

Austin tenses as Kelli makes a beeline for him, praying to God he doesn't end up on the floor if she knocks him down in her overexuberance. *Talk about making an entrance.* He relaxes when Kelli pulls up in front of him, although his relief diminishes when she looks up at him shyly.

"Is it okay if I give you a hug?"

Swallowing past the lump in his throat, he nods. "Of course it's okay, Kelli Bean. Just give me a second." He shifts his weight and holds onto the table near the front door with one hand, reaching down as far as he can and wrapping his other arm around her shoulders while she hugs his waist. *Not quite the same, but I'll take it.*

"Hi, Laura," Kelli says, peeking around Austin's hip.

"Hey, Kelli. Good to see you again. Happy birthday."

"Hey, stranger!" Monica leans against the doorway, her eyes traveling from his face down to

Kelli and back up again. "Looks like your little barnacle found you already."

"Yeah. Just can't quite seem to get rid of her." Austin tugs one of Kelli's braids.

Kelli swats his hand away with a giggle, then points to the box in Laura's arms. "Is that for me?"

"How about you take that into the living room, put it with the other presents, okay Kelli?" Monica watches to make sure her daughter does as she's told before she swings her glance to Laura. "I'm guessing you must be Laura." She shakes Laura's hand, then envelopes Austin in a hug. "Welcome back," she whispers in his ear.

Austin gives her a one-armed squeeze in return and blinks against the threat of tears. *Don't fall apart now.* "Thanks. Good to be here."

Monica releases him but keeps a hand on his arm until he has his balance. She steps back, a wry smile on her face. "Liar. Room full of sugared-up six and seven-year olds. Even *I* don't want to be here. I'm trying to keep them contained in the basement, but I don't know how long that's gonna last. Matt's mom is down there with them now. Poor woman." She glances between Austin and Laura. "You two bring stuff to stay the night? We have the spare bed in the guest room, but the couch in the living room pulls out."

Austin winces at what his leg will have to say after a night on their lumpy pull-out couch. "Yeah, our bags are in the car." He catches Laura's eye. "But the one bed's fine."

Monica's eyebrows rise, and a grin spreads slowly over her face.

Austin rolls his eyes and shifts his stance. "Shut up."

Monica lifts her hands in a defensive gesture. "I didn't say anything."

"What didn't you say?" Matt ambles into the foyer and kisses his wife on the cheek. "Glad you could make it." He takes a sip of the beer in his hand, then holds the bottle in their direction. "You guys want one?"

"God, yes," says Austin. *Anything to make this less awkward.*

"Come on." Matt nods toward the back of the house. "I've got a cooler out back. You want one, Laura?"

"Yes, please."

Monica waves off Matt's offer to Laura. "I'll get you one from the fridge. Come with me. I think we have some things to discuss."

Austin really doesn't like the glint in her eyes. "Monica…" he growls out in warning.

Laura sends a smirk over her shoulder while Monica steers her toward the kitchen. "Oh relax. I'm sure your secrets are safe."

Austin drops his head back and looks up at the ceiling. "Oh God. I'm doomed."

Matt chuckles and leads Austin toward the back of the house. He stops and turns before they reach the living room, takes a sip of his beer, and shoves his other hand in his pants pocket. He darts his eyes around the hallway, then locks eyes with Austin. "I'm really glad you're here, man. It's good to see you again."

Austin dips his head and tightens his grip around his crutches. "Yeah. Good to see you, too." He clears his throat and takes a deep breath. *Okay. You can do this.* "Matt. I'm sorry for being an ass."

"You wanna narrow that down a little bit? I've known you for twenty-five years, man. You've been an ass a lot."

Austin releases a hint of a laugh. *True.* "I'm sorry for being an ass for the past six months. But nothing before that. I wholeheartedly stand behind any assiness before the accident."

Matt's posture relaxes, and he looks down at Austin's leg. "Speaking of... Looks like you're getting around a little better."

Austin snorts. "Better than what?"

"Well, last time I saw you—before your apartment—you were in rehab." Matt's voice takes on a gravelly tone. "You were in so much pain. And I didn't know what to do."

Austin sucks in a breath and blows it out quickly. "Okay, listen up. Cause I'm gonna say it once, and then we're gonna forget about all this 'feelings' crap. Capisce?"

Matt crosses his arms, looks down at his feet, and nods.

"I'm sorry for how I treated you. Monica and Kelli, too, but it was mostly directed at you." He holds up a hand in warning when Matt opens his mouth. "I couldn't handle it. Being with you guys just reminded me how much had changed. It felt easier starting over without the constant reminders of this life. So I shut you out. And I'm sorry."

Matt scuffs his toe against the carpet. "Shit, man."

"Yeah."

"I mean, two apologies in one day? Who are you and what have you done with my best friend?"

"Shut up." Austin rolls his eyes as a smile works its way onto his face. *One down, several hundred more awkward moments to go.*

*
**

"Austin! Kelli said you were here. So good to see you!"

Austin grins as Matt's mom gives him a hug. "Hey, Linda. Good to see you, too." He repositions himself as she lets go and tries to ignore the concern on her face. "Did you make your chocolate cupcakes?"

She crosses her arms, a look of disbelief on her face. "How many birthdays have you shared with this family? What kind of question is that? What kind of grandmother would I be if I didn't bring my chocolate cupcakes to my own granddaughter's birthday?" She shakes her head and huffs. "Honestly."

"Any chance I can sneak one?"

"You and your sweet tooth." Austin can see the corner of her mouth twitching as she fights a smile. "Haven't changed a bit, have you?"

Maybe not as much as I'd thought.

She disappears for a few seconds and returns with a cupcake, casting furtive glances around the room like she's dealing in state secrets instead of baked goods. "Here. But be quiet about it."

"Hold on." He props himself against the buffet table at the side of the living room, then leans his crutches on the wall beside him and the cupcake. "Care to keep me company?"

Linda waits, grinning while he takes his first few bites of precious cupcake, then begins to pepper him with questions. "So, how are you? Really?"

He wipes a stray crumb from his lip and swallows his mouthful of chocolate memories. "Not wasting any time then, huh?" *Good ole Linda.*

"Nope."

"Well, I could tell you I'm doing fine. Getting better."

"And I could tell you to stop being a liar."

Austin chuckles. Matt's mom has always had one hell of a bullshit detector. *Matt and I sure tested it enough.* "Would you believe it if I said it sucks?"

"Now *that*, I *would* believe."

Austin finishes his cupcake, then shifts his position against the table. "But I actually do think it might be getting a little better. Not sure about this so much," he says, patting his leg, "but maybe up here." He points to his head and shrugs. "Not so many low times."

A shrewd looks crosses Linda's face. "And that woman in the kitchen with Monica wouldn't happen to have anything to do it, would she?"

"Laura?" The grin on his face betrays the nonchalance he'd been aiming for. "Maybe. We're good friends. Been through a lot together."

"Funny. I don't recall meeting any of your women friends before."

"Uhh…" *Crap.* "Laura's different."

"Uh-huh." Linda gives him a knowing look and pats him on the cheek. "Well, anyway, good to see you up and around. You gave us all quite a scare. Let me know if you need anything, okay?"

"Thanks, Linda." He glances toward the kitchen. "Depending on what Monica and Laura are talking about, I might need a second cupcake."

*
**

Monica pops the cap off a beer and hands it to Laura. "So. How do you and Austin know each other?"

Laura takes a sip and leans against the kitchen counter, running her eyes around the room. Twilight filters through the kitchen windows. A birthday cake sits on the table in the corner, roller skates and a jump rope are shoved in another corner, and an overflowing backpack sits on a bench by the back door. The comfortable mess puts her at ease. "He lives across the hall from my aunt."

"And you two are…"

"Friends?" They still haven't had any discussions about what they're doing. *Besides having a good time.* Austin seems to be perfectly happy with their casual arrangement, and Laura certainly hasn't pushed the issue.

A smile breaks over her face when she spies the refrigerator door. It's covered in photos, and the evidence points to Austin playing a significant role in

Kelli's life. She pushes off the counter and plants herself in front of the appliance, studying the little slices of life on display. Austin standing behind Kelli, helping her hit a whiffle ball on a T stand. Austin giving Kelli a piggy back ride. Kelli kneeling beside Austin in a flower garden. *Huh. He might really be fake uncle of the year.*

Monica stands beside Laura and gestures to the collage of photos. "Those two are something else."

Laura glances over and sees Monica's grin disappear; a frown takes its place.

"Is he doing okay?"

Laura takes a swallow of her beer, buying time to figure out how to answer the question.

Monica shakes her head. "He was in pretty bad shape there for a while. Laid up in the hospital for close to a month, then he was moved to a rehab center. So, the fact that he's upright and walking again is a good sign." She sighs and takes a sip of her beer. "But then he went AWOL. Had us really worried."

The concern on her face tugs at Laura's heartstrings. *What the hell was he thinking?* It's clear from what she's seen so far that he's got a good support system. People who care about him. *Why would he leave that?* Her hand tightens around her beer bottle as another thought slithers through her brain. *If we got closer, would he leave me?*

"Laura?"

Laura's eyes focus back on Monica. "What?" She works a smile onto her face. "Yeah. I think he's doing all right. Still trying to figure things out."

"Well, I hope he figures them out soon. Kelli's dying to get her Uncle Austin back."

Laura nods, studying the fridge photos again. Laughter bubbles up when she spies a photo two-thirds of the way down. "What the hell is that?" She points to an image of Austin sitting in a hospital bed with Kelli, clinking plastic tea cups. Austin's face looks like it was attacked by a drag queen with a heavy-handed tremor, he has a dopey smile on his face, and he's wearing a tiara on his head.

"Oh. You mean Prince Handsome and Charming, there?" Monica laughs. "That's the infamous pain medication tea party."

Laura smirks. "He mentioned something about this. Think he might have left a few things out, though. Prince Handsome and Charming, huh?"

Monica grins. "You gonna use this against him?"

"Oh yeah."

"Hey." Austin's eyes narrow in suspicion as Laura and Monica approach. Laura's eyes hold a glint of mischief, and Monica has a bland smile on her face. *That can't be good.* "What have you two been up to?"

"Just looking at some pictures." Laura curtsies. "Your Highness."

He glances between Matt and Monica. "I thought I asked you to get rid of that picture."

Matt grins. "You did. Unfortunately for you, it's one of Kelli's favorites."

Monica nods. "We were thinking it might work as this year's Christmas card."

He gives them disgusted looks. "I hate you both."

"Yeah, yeah. Tell me something I don't know." Matt takes a swig of his beer.

A half-smile pulls at Austin's lips. *God, it feels good to be back.*

"Uh-oh," Monica says, at the clomping of feet on the basement steps. "Looks like the Kraken's about to be unleashed." She looks at Austin. "You might want to get out of the way. Stampede of sugar-seeking missiles coming through."

Laura settles on the loveseat and pats the empty space next to her. "Come on Prince Handsome and Charming. Keep me company."

He gets himself settled, placing his crutches in the corner, out of the way of the children zipping around the room.

She gives him a bland look. "So, did you forget to tell me something?"

"What? That I'm devastatingly handsome and wickedly charming? Thought you would have figured that out on your own." He grins and slings an arm around her.

Laura rolls her eyes but snuggles closer to him. "Well, at least your ego's intact."

He runs his finger along her shoulder, eliciting a shiver. "Among other things…"

"Uncle Austin! Laura! These are for you!" Kelli carefully hands a cupcake and a napkin to each of them. She dashes away and returns several seconds later. "Here. Put these on." She holds out conical party hats with elastic chin straps; the one on top of her own head is sliding off to the right.

"Thanks Kelli." Laura snaps hers in place and slides a glance toward Austin. "But I think your Uncle Austin would rather have something with a little more... sparkle. You don't happen to have anything like that, do you?"

Kelli giggles and claps her hands. "Yep, be right back Uncle Austin!"

He narrows his eyes at Laura once Kelli is out of earshot. "I hate you so much right now."

She grins. "No you don't."

He bites the inside of his cheek to try to keep the scowl on his face. *Dammit, she's right.* Her mischievous smile. The way she teases him. *The way she treats me like a normal human being.*

Kelli returns, bouncing from foot to foot, the excitement evident on her face. "Okay, lean down." She gently places the tiara on Austin's head, dashes away again, and returns with another cupcake. "Can I sit with you?"

"Absolutely, it would be my honor, birthday girl." Austin hands his cupcake to Laura and helps Kelli scramble up onto his lap, careful to keep the majority of her weight on his left leg.

She lightly pats his injured leg. "I'm not hurting you, am I?"

"No, Kelli Bean. Not even close."

TWENTY

Monica drops onto the sofa and puts her legs up on Matt's lap. "Oh my God. Remind me never to do that again."

Matt hands his wife a beer and leans back. "She finally fall asleep?"

"Well, she's in bed. She might not sleep for days." She takes a sip and looks across the room. "Seven-year old adrenaline and sugar. If you could bottle that combo, you'd be a millionaire."

Laura grins, recalling Austin's story of Kelli and her sugar-fueled Halloweens. "Add in some caffeine and you've got a recipe for world domination." She tucks her legs underneath her and slides her arm along the back of the loveseat, coming to rest behind Austin. "Thanks again for letting us stay the night."

"Hey, no problem. You got him here." Matt gestures at Austin with his beer. "So, thanks. Although I'm seriously considering the wisdom of that invitation now." He shakes his head. "Getting Kelli that gigantic piano mat keyboard. I know you love the movie 'Big', but do you hate us that much?"

Austin chuckles. "Yeah, might not have thought that one all the way through. Sounded like a dying cow in here. Should have just gone with the ice skates, but, well…" He gestures to his leg and shrugs.

Matt keeps his eyes on Austin while he tilts his beer to his lips. His eyebrows draw together, and he clears this throat.

"What?" Austin asks after several seconds of heavy silence.

Matt and Monica share a glance, then return their attention to Austin. "So," Matt says, "how are you doing? Really?"

Laura feels Austin tense beside her and sees his knuckles whiten around his beer bottle. She moves her hand on the loveseat so it's resting on the back of his neck. *You're fine. You can do this.*

Austin looks at her out of the corner of his eye, a hint of a weary smile on his lips. He runs his fingernail over the label of his beer and teases an edge free, then turns his attention to the couple on the couch. "Okay, I guess. Mr. Henderson challenged me to a race around the block." He glances back at Laura. "He's eighty-five, has a bad hip, and walks with a cane." He turns his attention back to his beer and releases a soft laugh. "He's got a really good chance of winning."

Silence hangs over the room until Austin speaks again. "I still can't really feel my leg. Not sure if I'll get enough function back to drive with my right leg or if I'll have to use my left."

Matt gestures to the limb under discussion, a concerned look on his face. "Is it getting any better?"

Austin rolls his bottle between his hands. "Not for the past couple of weeks. Still doesn't hold my weight. Getting a full leg brace this week which should help."

"Oh, Austin..." Monica presses her hand to her chest, her face creased in a concerned frown. The sorrow in her eyes is unmistakable.

Austin flinches, his shoulders tightening under Laura's hand. He clenches his jaw and swallows several times. "Don't say it. Don't you dare say you're sorry."

Laura's chest tightens. *So much pain.* She gives Austin's neck a light squeeze and sends Monica a reassuring smile. While he's come a long way in his healing process, from what she can tell, it's been a long day. Facing his friends, remembering what he's lost, trying to figure out where he fits now. She can tell he's close to the edge. *Time to step in.*

"So," she says, careful to keep her tone light. "I've only known Austin for a couple of months. Seems he might have left a few things out." She feels his shoulders relax under her hand. "What else can you tell me about him besides the fact that he enjoys princess tea parties?"

Matt's snort breaks the tension in the room. "Prince Handsome and Charming, here? Where should I start?"

Austin groans. "Oh man, I might need some more beer for this."

*
**

Laura traces her finger along Austin's ribs. She lies on her side facing him, propped on her elbow, while he's on his back with his arms folded underneath his head. "So how come you never told me this stuff?"

He moves his hand and intertwines his fingers with hers, stilling her hand on his chest. He turns his head and sends her an innocent look. "What? You mean how I killed Mrs. Gordon's prized rhododendron by taking a leak on it when I was thirteen?"

Laura rolls her eyes. "No. I mean about this." She untangles her hand from his and waves it around the guest bedroom. "Them. Matt and Monica. Kelli." She places her hand back on his chest and gives him a gentle shake. "These people are important to you. And you to them. What the hell were you thinking?"

"Can I plead temporary insanity?"

"Probably. Especially if you mention the voices."

"Yeah, not sure I want to try to explain that one to them. Hell, I don't even know if I can explain it to myself."

Laura shifts her position and rests her head on Austin's chest, draping her arm across him. She takes comfort in the rhythmic rise and fall of his chest beneath her. "And why didn't you tell me you had an Associate's Degree in business? Or played three varsity sports in high school? And that you've dated the equivalent of a small country? Although that last one really shouldn't surprise me." Her eyes pop open when Austin moves his hand from her hair and tickles her in the sensitive spot of her lower back. She squirms in an effort to get out of his reach.

Austin rolls onto his side, then counts off his answers on his fingers. "One – it never came up. Two – it was high school. Three – what can I say?"

Laura raises a finger in warning. "Don't you dare say you're handsome and charming."

"Well then, I've got nothing." He grins at her bland stare, then reaches out and covers her hand with his. "But I *can* say I've never brought any of those women to something like *this* before."

She glances down at his hand and back up to his face. His green eyes bounce between her eyes and mouth, and she licks her bottom lip reflexively. "You mean to a seven-year-old's birthday party?"

Austin keeps his eyes locked on hers. "No. I mean to something important." He reaches up and crooks his finger under her chin, drawing her closer until their lips meet.

Wrapping her arms around Austin's neck, she moves with him as he rolls onto his back. She rubs her body against his, her lips curving upwards when she feels him come to attention against her thigh. She dips her hand into his boxers and slides it along his length, pausing when he groans. "We probably shouldn't do this in your best friend's guest room."

"The hell we shouldn't. They totally threw me under the bus. Told you all of my dirty little secrets." He stills, placing his hand on hers. "But maybe you should lock the door first. Don't want a sugared-up Kelli wandering in."

Laura scurries to the door and locks it, then jumps back into bed. "Now. Where were we?"

"About to desecrate my friends' bed." He tugs off the cotton T-shirt Laura wears to bed, kissing the curve of her breast.

Laura has to remind herself to breathe as Austin takes his time working his way from her breasts to her belly button. His lips are alternately soft and demanding, his tongue both playful and maddening.

While she's had her fair share of partners, no one has ever made her feel the way Austin does. Something that scares her as much as it excites her. At first, he'd been shy and hesitant, trying to figure out what his leg could handle. It hadn't taken long for her to see the changes, however. More confident, less apt to get frustrated by what he can't do and figure out an alternative. She is more than happy to help him on his journey toward healing. Because he is one hell of a lover.

I'm really just doing womankind a favor. Helping him get back in the game.

"Wow," Laura says several minutes later. "That was some pretty good revenge. Might want to tell them to burn these sheets." She kisses the angle of Austin's chin, then includes his neck as well. She looks up at him when she gets no response.

He's taking slow, deep breaths, his eyes closed, his fists clenching the sheets beneath him. The muscles of his upper leg jerk in an irregular rhythm.

She covers his hand with hers. "Hey, what's going on?"

He opens his eyes and sends her a tight smile. Using his hands and left leg to pull himself into a seated position, he massages his still spasming thigh. "Nothing. I'm fine."

"Obviously." Laura sits up and wraps a blanket around herself. "Anything I can do?"

He lets out a strangled laugh. "If you do anything else to me right now, I won't be able to walk for a week." He winces as he adjusts the position of his leg with his hands. "But you could distract me."

Laura raises an eyebrow.

"You got to hear lots of sordid details about me tonight. What about you?" He leans his head against the headboard and closes his eyes, inhaling and exhaling slowly. "First kiss?"

She eyes him, then adjusts the blanket. *Okay. I can do distraction.* "Jason Taylor. Spin the Bottle. Sixth grade."

"Worst date?"

"How much time you got?" She grins when the corners of Austin's lips quirk. "Let's see. Most embarrassing was probably in ninth grade. I was making out with Brian Murphy at the movies. Somehow, he cut his tongue on my braces. Had to call the paramedics to get the bleeding stopped."

"Ouch." Austin cracks one eye open and continues to knead his thigh. "So, I'm not the only one who ends up needing medical attention after he's been with you. Good to know."

"Hey!" Laura scowls and swats his shoulder.

"Kidding, kidding."

"Yeah, well, you keep kidding like that, and I'll be sure to take my skill set elsewhere."

"Uh-huh."

"What? You don't think I can find another Prince Handsome and Charming in a heartbeat?"

Austin shrugs. "Maybe. But I believe I remember Marge calling you 'perpetually single'."

"And?"

Austin tilts his head, his emerald green gaze locking with hers. "What did she mean by that?"

Laura's scowl deepens. "Can't I just get you some painkillers?"

"Nope."

She lies back and looks up at the ceiling. *Dammit, Marge. You're not even here and you're interfering.* Silence stretches between them as she weighs her need for self-preservation against her willingness to be honest. *Fuck it.* "I don't really do relationships."

"You're doing me."

"Ha ha."

"Okay," Austin says when she fails to offer further explanation, "*why* don't you do relationships?"

Laura gently nudges Austin's hands away from his thigh and takes over the duty of masseuse. A wry smile crosses her face at the thought of having to distract herself while she's supposed to be distracting him. *Yep, that's about par for the course.* She focuses on working out the knots which are still causing his leg to twitch, taking note of the gradual relaxation of his breathing.

"Because it's easier to hide behind a wall." She runs her finger along the light pink scar that runs the length of his outer thigh. "I don't have a good track record with people sticking around. Mom left. Dad died. Dated a couple of bastards; Nick decided he'd rather have my friend Zoe, and Will dropped me when I got a job promotion over him. Finally figured out people can't hurt you if you don't let them in."

Austin's hand envelopes hers and halts her continued exploration of his scar. "That seems like a very lonely existence."

"Well, it's not like I'm a nun or anything."

"Clearly."

Laura jabs him in the ribs. "So, what's your excuse?"

"For not being a nun?" He grins when Laura pokes him again. "Pretty sure my testosterone levels are way too high."

She lets out a disgusted sigh but fails in her attempt to keep her grin in check. "For having the dating attention span of a flea."

"Again, let me reference my testosterone levels."

"You're ridiculous."

"I believe the words you're looking for are 'handsome' and 'charming'."

Laura drops her head in an attempt to muffle her groan. "Oh, for Pete's sake." She adjusts her position so she can see him. "Come on. I just told you why I'm messed up. The least you can do is return the favor."

Austin runs his hand through her hair, taking his time to answer. "I guess I just never found the right woman."

"Oh, that is so cliché."

Austin shrugs. "What can I say? No one's ever held my attention long enough."

"Well, from what Matt said, that might be due to your typical choice of partner."

"Ugh, Matt. Made it seem like I only date bimbos with big boobs."

"Lucky for you, we're not dating. Because I clearly have more brain than boobs."

Austin tugs the top of her blanket. "I think I might need to check the validity of that statement one more time."

His inspection is *very* thorough.

TWENTY-ONE

"All right. You promise it won't be another two months until we see you again?" Monica's hands are on her hips, but a teasing gleam in her eye takes the sting out of her words.

Austin keeps his left crutch planted on the sidewalk in front of their house and gives her a one-armed hug. "Yes. Promise." He lets her go and regains his balance, then nods his chin at Matt. "You need a hug too?"

"Shut up." Matt grins and punches him in the shoulder.

Thank God. Not sure I would've been able to handle a hug from him.

Kelli bounces from one foot to the other. "I need a hug, Uncle Austin!"

Austin makes a show of letting his shoulders sag and dropping his head back to look up at the clear blue sky. He sighs and looks down at Kelli. "Do I have to?"

"Yes!"

He smiles at her look of determination and braces himself to take her weight. "All right. Come on." He waves her over and wraps his arm around her shoulders, disappointed when she finally lets go.

Kelli looks up at him, a concerned look on her face. "Are you gonna come back?"

"Of course, I'll come back."

She swivels her head and looks at Laura, then looks back at him. "Is Laura coming back, too?"

Austin raises his eyebrow and looks at Laura, who shrugs. He moves his eyes over to Matt and Monica, taking no comfort in their smug expressions. "Maybe?"

"Is she your girlfriend?"

Heat creeps up Austin's neck. He's not sure if it's due to the intensity of Kelli's gaze or the nature of her questioning. "What do you know about boyfriends and girlfriends?"

"Rena's brother has a girlfriend. They like to hold hands and kiss and stuff. It's gross." Kelli looks back over at Laura. "But I think you'd be okay."

"Thanks, kiddo." *I think so, too.* He glances at Laura, catching the hint of panic in her eyes. Last night's conversation rings in his ears. "But we're just friends."

The relief in Laura's eyes sends a little stab through his heart. It feels suspiciously close to disappointment. *What the hell?* Her admission of having relationship issues should put him at ease. Make it much easier to keep things casual. *My life is complicated enough already. Not looking to add more.*

Austin lowers himself into Laura's car, waving at Kelli until she's out of sight. He repositions himself in his seat, angling himself toward Laura. "So, thanks. You know, for coming. And driving. And being a friend." He runs his index finger over his leg, crossing between the areas of full sensation and no sensation. *Still can't get used to that.*

"Yeah, no problem. I had a good time." She glances over at him, then directs her gaze back to the road, a smirk on her face. "And it was very educational."

Austin leans his head against the headrest and sighs in disgust. "You're going to make me regret inviting you, aren't you?"

"Yep. Probably."

"All right. Guess I'll just have to get buddy-buddy with Marge, then."

Laura's eyes narrow, and her lips flatten. "You wouldn't."

Austin shrugs. "I've got nothing better to do. I can probably put up with her decaf coffee and desserts in return for a little intel."

"I think you're bluffing."

"Maybe. Maybe not. Guess you'll just have to wait and see." He grins at her scowl, then looks out the window. "Hey, make a right at the next light." The words pop out of his mouth before he can stop them.

"Are we going home a different way?"

Austin drums his fingers against his leg as the familiar neighborhoods pass by, the urgency behind his movements increasing as they get closer. "No. There's something I want to show you." He directs Laura down a few additional side streets. "See that house up there? The one with the For Sale sign in the front yard?" He glances over and catches her nod. "Pull up there."

Laura puts the car in park and leans forward on the steering wheel, craning her head to see out of the windshield. "Slow your roll there, Supergimp. I like you and all, but I'm not sure I'm ready to buy a house with you."

Austin releases a soft laugh but keeps his eyes locked on the old three-story Victorian house. The yard looks like it could use a mow, the flower beds need to be weeded, and there are several old, yellowed papers scattered across the front lawn. Austin closes his eyes and leans his head against the car window. *Come on. You can do this.* He looks at Laura and tilts his head toward the house. "You wanna come in?"

Laura's eyebrows inch upwards, and her eyes travel back and forth between the house and Austin. "This is your house."

Austin nods, the emotions lodged in his throat preventing any form of verbal response. He hadn't been planning to come by this weekend. He'd fully intended to leave his return to the house until another visit, to spread out his "first time since the accident" experiences over a longer period of time. He's not quite sure what changed his mind.

Steeling himself against yet another onslaught of sentiments, he works his way out of the car and leads Laura up the front walk, carefully ascending the warped stairs he hadn't yet gotten around to fixing before his accident. His hands shake as he unlocks the front door and he stands in the doorway, working to drag air into his lungs until Laura clears her throat.

"You okay?"

Her words act as a sort of reset button, allowing his breathing to return to normal. "Yeah." He steps over the threshold, stands to the side as she enters behind him, and closes the door behind her. He lets his hand rest against the metal of the old-fashioned doorknob before he turns around.

"Oh, Austin. This is beautiful." Laura runs her hands along the curved banister of the staircase, her eyes roaming around the entryway, a soft smile on her face.

Austin follows her gaze and takes in the familiar high ceilings, the refinished wood floors, and the sconces along the stairway. "Thanks. This was my grandparents' house. Gran left it to me in her will." He wrinkles his nose. "She had these horrible carpets in here. Drapes on the windows too. Matt and I spent a lot of time here together after she died, trying to fix it up." He swallows, then clears his throat. "We were about to get started with the kitchen when I had my accident. I was living upstairs at the time. Matt and Monica offered their spare room to me after rehab, but I got the apartment instead." He looks around the entryway and blinks. "I'm gonna miss this place."

I miss you, Gran.

He turns away and leads Laura into the living room; he and Matt had shared many a pizza and beer in this room after a long day of remodeling. His grandparents' old paisley sofa and his grandfather's well-worn leather recliner still take up space in one corner. A fireplace with a shoulder-high mantelpiece runs along the far wall. Bright light filters through slatted wooden shutters of windows that reach from two feet above the floor to two feet below the ceiling. *So much better than those old drapes.* "Sorry it's so cold in here. Haven't had the utilities on for a couple of months, and this place tends to be drafty."

They continue into the kitchen, and Austin leans against the island in the center of the room. He glances around and has second thoughts about the wisdom of coming here today as the memories flood over him. He nods his head toward the old stove in the corner. "The pancakes and pasta sauce? Learned how to make 'em right here. Gran taught me."

Laura leans next to him, snakes her arm around his waist, and rests her head on his shoulder. "She did a great job."

"Yeah. She always said I'd thank her when I could impress the ladies with a good meal." He turns his head and looks at Laura. "Was she right?"

"Thank you, Gran!"

Austin smiles as Laura's words echo through the room. He rests his head against hers and closes his eyes. *Yes, thank you.* Austin squeezes his eyes shut, listening intently for any signs that his grandmother's spirit is still nearby. *I could really use some of your wisdom.* Sighing when he gets no response, he opens his eyes and clears his throat of the lingering emotions. "You want to see upstairs? Third floor's got a really good view."

Laura turns and wraps her arms around neck. "I don't know, I've got a pretty good view right here." She leans in, brushing her lips against his.

"Dammit, woman." Austin pulls back, shaking his head in feigned disgust. "You're stealing all my best lines."

"What can I say? I've been hanging out with *you* too long." She laughs and tugs his shirt. "Come on. Show me the rest of the house."

"I'm not entirely sure I'll make it up both sets of stairs after last night."

She runs her hand down his chest, sliding her hand into the waistband of his jeans. "Come on, Supergimp. Let's show those stairs who's boss. Then upstairs, you can show *me* who's boss."

"You are evil."

Laura grins. "No. I just know how to motivate you."

*
**

"Son of a bitch." Austin grimaces and tries to pant through the fire burning in his leg. His hands cramp around the handle of his crutch on one side and the wooden railing on the other, and he can feel the sweat between his shoulder blades. "I forgot how steep this second set of steps is."

They're halfway up the twisting stairs to the third floor and Austin's seriously wondering if he'll be able to make it the rest of the way. The more stairs he climbs, the more fatigued his quad muscle becomes, and the harder it is for him to lift his leg. Between last night's vigorous activities and the workout of the stairs, his leg is the worst it's felt in a long time.

Despite the fact that Laura's been nothing short of encouraging, trying to keep things lighthearted, he can feel his control slipping. Can feel the edges of self-doubt beginning to take hold once again. The little fingers that dig into his brain, poking at all his most sensitive areas.

"You want to sit down?" Laura keeps one hand on his back while the other holds a crutch.

He remains silent, locked in a battle of wills with his own leg. *Come on, come on, come on, come on.* "FUCK!" His frustration bounces off the walls when he fails to gain the necessary motion to clear the top of the next step.

"Hey. It's okay."

Austin stiffens and drags in ragged breaths as he fights to keep further emotions from bubbling over. "Okay?" His breathing hitches, and tears gather at the corners of his eyes. "How is this okay?" His arms tense as he holds his crutch and the railing, turning himself enough so he can sink onto the stairs. Clamping down on his bottom lip, he repositions his leg and digs his fingers into his thigh.

"Nothing about this is okay. Matt and I were supposed to hike the Appalachian trail this summer. I'm supposed to be teaching Kelli how to ice skate. I'm supposed to be able to climb two fucking flights of stairs." He swallows several times and blinks in an effort to keep the first tear from making its escape, then feels his failure as a wet line trails down his cheek and reaches his chin. It plops onto the fabric of his jeans; several more follow suit. He props his elbows on his knees and presses the heels of his hands against his eyes. "It's not supposed to be like this."

He feels Laura's presence, even though she remains silent and still. "Can you leave me alone?"

"Austin…"

"Just go. Please." His voice holds an air of desperation, and he's torn between relief and additional dejection when she brushes past him on her way to the third floor. He flinches when her hand rests briefly on his shoulder, and he curls into himself, covering his head with his arms while the self-doubt washes over him in crushing waves. *What the hell am I gonna do? What am I good for?*

Austin's shoulders shake as he grieves for all of the things he lost that night in the accident. Saturday afternoon basketball games with Matt. Hopscotch with Kelli. Landscaping. Running. Walking. A normal life. *Oh God, I can't do this.*

Austin.

His breath catches. He holds himself still at the sound of his name, ears straining for any further words in that all too familiar voice. *Gran?*

I miss you too, Love.

The tension in his shoulders eases a bit at the soothing sound of her voice. *I need help, Gran. I don't know what to do…*

Keep fighting. You'll be fine.

He squeezes his eyes shut and takes a ragged breath, blowing it out slowly. *But I can't….*

Keep fighting. You'll be fine.

The corner of his mouth lifts. *You always were persistent.*

Had to be, to get through your thick skull.

A soft laugh escapes Austin's lips. He can almost feel her hand ruffling his hair.

Keep fighting. You'll be fine.
How do you know?
Because I know you. And you'll be fine.

Austin works on getting his breathing under control, the destructive self-doubts warring with Gran's words of encouragement. *Everything's changed. I don't know if I can handle it.*

Things change. You adapt. That's life. You'll be fine.

A peaceful calm washes over him and he blows out a deep, cleansing breath. *Thanks, Gran. You always did believe in me.*

Darn straight. Now believe in yourself.

TWENTY-TWO

Laura paces in front of the window, the breathtaking view of the rolling hills much less interesting to her than the man in the stairwell.

You stupid, stupid idiot. As if this weekend hadn't been hard enough on him already, she had to go and push him into trying to conquer yet another set of stairs. While his frustrated outburst hadn't really surprised her, his total meltdown had caught her off guard. *Me and my big mouth.* The empty placation of "it's okay" had rolled off her tongue before she'd been able to stop it.

Because he's right. *Nothing* about his situation is okay. Just like nothing she can say or do can make it better. It's up to him to figure it out. *God, I hope he figures it out.* She doesn't want to think about what might happen if he doesn't.

She stops, body tensed, at the sounds of movement in the stairwell.

"Okay," Austin calls out, "I think I'm done freaking out. You can come down now."

She pokes her head around the doorway at the top of the stairs. "Are you all right?"

Austin moves his right leg down a step with his hands and turns slightly so he's angled on the stairs. He leans his head against the wall and sends her a wobbly smile. "I think I will be."

She scrutinizes him as she descends the stairs and sits down against the opposite wall, several steps below him. Although the rims of his eyes are red and his eyelids are puffy, the tension in his shoulders has dissipated, and his hitched breathing has given way to the gentle rise and fall of his chest. "Austin, I am so sorry—"

He shakes his head. "Don't be."

"But I made you—"

Austin holds up a finger. "Stop. First off, you didn't *make* me do anything. And second, I heard Gran." He drops his hand, a wistful smile on his face. "So maybe I should actually be *thanking* you."

"Huh. What'd she say?" She relaxes against the wall, laying her hand on his leg.

"She told me to keep fighting and that I'll be fine." He releases a soft laugh. "Oh, and that I have a hard head."

"She sounds like a wise woman."

"Yeah, she was. I think you would have liked her. Always spoke her mind. Kind of bossy. A little like someone else I know."

"Hey." Laura swats his leg.

"Gran helped raise me. I never knew my dad—he died when I was really little—and my mom worked a couple of jobs to make ends meet. Gran was the one who made sure I did my homework, stayed out of trouble, did my chores." He drops his eyes while he runs his finger along his leg. "My mom died while I was in college. So, then it was just me and Gran. And now it's just me. I really miss her, you know?"

"Yeah, I do. But you have the memories." She takes Austin's hand and twines her fingers through his. "What do you remember most about her?"

Austin rolls his lower lip between his teeth, relinquishing it when he laughs softly. "There was this one time I got caught cheating on a test. Got detention, was grounded for a week, missed a big basketball tournament." He shakes his head. "But that was nothing compared to Gran's punishment. You remember those gigantic wooden shutters downstairs?" He waits for Laura's nod. "Gran made me scrub every one of them. With lemon oil and a toothbrush. There's a dozen of them. Took me forever. My arms were sore for a week."

Laura chuckles and gives Austin's hand a squeeze.

"She covered 'em up with drapes a few years later. Ugly things with ruffles. Took the drapes down after she died and thought about her the entire time I was refinishing those damn shutters."

A wistful smile plays across his lips, and Laura runs her thumb along his, offering her nonverbal support. After a few moments of silence, she asks, "Think she would have been able to teach me to cook?"

Austin gives her a level stare. "She wasn't a miracle worker."

Laura takes another swat at his leg.

He reclaims her hand and gives it a squeeze. "What about you? What do you remember most about Steven?"

Laura leans her head against the wall and closes her eyes, pushing away the still-vivid details of his suicide. "That he was a great brother. My partner in crime." She looks at Austin, her eyes locking with his. "And he always told me to be me." A smile plays at her lips as she runs a finger along her piercing. "Sure, he might have mocked me, but he told me to always listen to my instincts."

"Sounds like good advice."

She sighs. "Yeah, it was. Still is." *Just wish my instincts would've yelled a little louder that night.*

They sit in silence until Austin speaks. "I think I'm okay to head downstairs if you're ready."

Laura nods and stands up, stretching out her back.

Austin holds out his hands. "A little help?"

She braces herself, a firm grip on his hands as she hauls him upright. "You want your crutches?"

"Would you mind if I just…" He trails off as he throws one arm around her neck and grips the railing with the other hand. "I think it'll be quicker this way."

"Yeah. No problem." Laura snakes her arm around his waist and holds his crutches in her free hand. She's careful to let him set the pace as they make their way down the stairs. "But I'm on to you. Using your injury as an excuse to feel me up. Shameless."

Austin pauses and readjusts his arm around her neck. "Yep. You got me. My game plan here was to totally freak out, have my dead grandmother talk me down off the ledge, and then get handsy with you when you felt sorry for me." He slides a glance toward her, then continues down the stairs. "So far I'm two out of three."

"Yeah, well, maybe we wait until we're back on the first floor to complete the trifecta, huh?"

Austin lets out a belabored sigh. "If we must."

His words float lazily through her brain like a dandelion puff on a gust of wind. Halfway down the second flight of steps, her calculating brain kicks in.

"So, Gran had to talk you down off the ledge, huh?"

"Not one of my proudest moments, but yeah."

She can almost feel the synapses in her brain firing in rapid succession as they try to make a connection. "And when you first heard Steven, it was after your run-in with the stairs, right?"

Austin stops and looks at Laura, his eyebrows drawn together. "Yeah. Why?"

She nudges him forward. "I have a thought. But I need a pen and a piece of paper."

When they reach the bottom of the stairs, Austin settles himself on his crutches and leads them into the kitchen.

As they pass through the living room, Laura gives the wooden shutters a closer look. *Damn. Those things are huge.* "Thank God I didn't know Gran when I was a kid. With all the crap Steven and I pulled, I'd probably still be scrubbing something, somewhere."

Austin chuckles as he rifles through one of the junk drawers in the kitchen. He hands Laura a pen and a scrap piece of paper, then takes a seat at the small kitchen table.

She sits down across from him, pen poised above the paper. Her gaze is locked on Austin while her idea continues to percolate. "Do you remember each time you heard a voice?"

"Most of them. I'm not so sure about the early ones." He twirls his index finger around his ear. "Loopy on pain meds."

Laura taps the pen against her teeth. "Give me what you remember."

"Let's see." Austin narrows his eyes and begins to count off on his fingers. "There were quite a few after my surgeries. Several while I was learning how to walk. Steven, of course. Marge's apartment. At my PT appointment the other week. Gran, here."

Laura makes notes while he speaks. She looks over the list, then glances up at him. "Do you remember how you felt during each of those times?"

"What, are you my shrink now or something?"

"Just humor me. Any common emotional threads? Anger? Frustration? Fear?"

Austin's eyes widen. "Holy shit. You might be on to something." He leans forward in his seat and braces his forearms on the table. "I think the times I heard the voices were during moments of extreme frustration. Or when I was having serious doubts about my life."

"So, your emotions seem to trigger your ability to hear the supernatural frequency. Guess we don't need to send you to superpower training camp after all."

Austin shakes his head. "One of these days…"

Laura grins. "What? One of these days you'll just own the fact that you have a freaky superpower?"

The look he gives her lets her know he is not amused.

TWENTY-THREE

Austin drums his finger against the armrest console between their seats. "You sure you don't want to go talk to Steven tonight?"

Laura pulls into the parking lot of his apartment complex. "No."

"Are you sure? I still think this might be a good time for me to try."

She turns to him, an incredulous look on her face. "Are you kidding me? After what happened at your house earlier?" *Not sure I can watch him suffer like that again.*

"Exactly. I could take the stairs again. It would be like a double whammy. Might make it easier to hear him."

"Or it might kill you." Laura gets out of her car, then retrieves Austin's bag from the backseat. "I'll take this in for you. I want to stop in and say hi to Marge." *Pick her brain a little.*

"Fine. Whatever." Austin gets out of the car, freezing before he manages to get himself fully upright. His breaths come in short, little puffs and he squeezes his eyes shut. "Oh, shit."

Laura hustles to his side and puts a steadying hand on his shoulder. "Hey. What's wrong?"

"Hazards of being an overachiever." He cracks open one eyelid; the rest of his face is locked in a grimace. "Probably wasn't the best idea to have sex, climb several flights of stairs, and sit in one position for so long all in the span of twenty-four hours. My leg seized up on me."

I rest my case. Laura gives his shoulder a gentle squeeze. "Anything I can do?"

"Yeah. If I ever try to complete the gimp triathlon in the future, please talk me out of it." Austin's rigid posture gradually relaxes and he hisses as he straightens up.

Laura watches him closely. "Any better?"

"Yeah, a little. Shit."

"Come on. I'll get you tucked in with some ice and heating pads before I go over to Marge's." Laura relinquishes her grip and adjusts the bag over her shoulder, then ambles up the walkway alongside Austin.

"Dammit." He winces with each movement of his leg. "Have I told you how much this sucks?"

"I do believe you've mentioned it once or twice." Laura tries to keep her tone light, well aware of the fact that her mouth already contributed to one epic meltdown today. She pauses outside the door to his apartment and waits for him to unlock it.

"Can you do me a favor? Reach into my front pocket for my key." He gives Laura a tired half-smile. "I swear to you it's not an invitation to get in my pants. I mean, it is. But not like that. Not right now anyway. I'm pretty sure I'll fall over if I let go of either of these." His hands tighten around the handles of his crutches. "And please don't do anything except get the key. Because otherwise, you might kill me."

Laura fishes out the key and unlocks the door, then deposits Austin's bag in his bedroom. She gathers the rice-filled cloth sack he uses as a heating pad and sticks it in the microwave, then pulls out several ice packs and wraps them in kitchen towels. Once the heating pad has been sufficiently warmed, she returns to the living room to find him stretched out on his couch, arms draped over his face, sucking in deep breaths and blowing them out between pursed lips.

"You gonna be okay if I head over to Marge's? Just say the word if you want me to stay." She watches him closely for anything approximating this afternoon's level of defeat.

He takes the warm rice bag and molds it to his leg, directing her to set the ice packs down on the coffee table. "Nah. I'm good. Thanks. For everything."

She leans over and brushes her lips against his. "You're welcome, Supergimp. I'll come back over before I leave, okay?" *Definitely not leaving him alone for long.*

He gives her a tired smile. "Sounds good. I'll probably be right here."

Laura gives him one last kiss, then crosses the hall to Marge's apartment. She can hear her aunt's favorite "oldies" station playing through the door as she knocks. Her hand stills in mid-air as an unwelcome thought flits through her brain. *Please don't let there be any other "oldies" in there with her. And if there are, please let them be fully clothed.*

Marge opens the door, fully dressed, a smile breaking over her face when she sees her niece. "Laura! What a pleasant surprise! I was just about to sit down to dinner. Come on in."

"Oh. I don't want to interrupt you." Laura's mouth waters as the wafting scent of her aunt's homemade lasagna teases her nose.

"Nonsense. You can interrupt me anytime." Marge squeezes her in a hug, then ushers her into her apartment. "I have plenty." She peers into the hallway. "No Austin?"

Laura shakes her head. "He's down for the count."

Concern etches Marge's features. "Is he okay?"

"Yeah, he'll be fine." *No thanks to me.* "He has a date with his couch and a heating pad right now."

"Oh, poor thing. Any particular reason?"

Laura pulls her expression into a sympathetic wince. "He had a rough twenty-four hours. His leg's acting up." She can tell that her aunt is itching for more information, and she knows Marge is skilled in the art of interrogation, so Laura quickly moves to another topic. "But on the plus side, I think we figured out how he's able to hear things."

"Ooh, do tell. But come sit down and eat." Marge heaps Laura's plate with lasagna and green beans, then does the same with her own. "I'll fix some for Austin, too."

"Thanks, Marge. You're the best."

Marge winks. "I know, dear. Now, what is it you think you've figured out?"

Laura tucks into her food, releasing a moan of pleasure before she answers. "We think it's linked to how he's feeling—his frustration levels and self-doubt."

"Well, that could certainly make sense."

"Really?"

Marge nibbles on a green bean, then nods. "Sure. Do you remember me telling you about that time I lived on that commune out in Colorado?"

Laura nods, shoveling a forkful of lasagna into her mouth.

"Well, there was this man there, Milton, who was able to converse with the Spirit Plane when he was on the brink of orgasm."

Laura pauses mid-chew, then shakes her head. *Why does anything she says even surprise me anymore?*

Marge taps her fork against her lips. "Of course, he could have been faking. The part about talking with the spirits, not the orgasm." Marge winks at Laura. "He definitely wasn't faking about the orgasm."

The smile that spreads across the older woman's face makes Laura feel slightly dirty. "Okay, not quite sure what that has to do with Austin…"

Marge blinks and returns her gaze to Laura. "Oh, right. Well, I just meant that emotions can open us up." She gives Laura a sidelong glance. "It's not *sexual* frustration that's the issue, is it?"

Laura's careful to keep her eyes averted from her way-too-perceptive aunt.

"Because that would be a pity. I don't wish that on anyone. I went through a dry spell once. Almost drove me insane. Worst month of my life." Marge takes a bite of lasagna, then continues. "But I do believe I got a bit off-topic."

You don't say.

"Does this mean you've been able to speak with Steven?"

"No."

"Why not?"

"Because we just figured it out earlier today."

"I see." Marge's gaze intensifies. "Is that the only reason?"

Laura pokes holes in the congealed cheese on her plate. *Dammit, she's good.*

Despite the fact that she'd still like to get answers to some of her questions, she's no longer one hundred percent sure it's worth the risk. Even though the hole in her heart is still there, it's not the gaping wound it once was. She still feels his absence every day, but there are longer periods of time when she feels normal. When she doesn't feel the weight of his death crushing to soul.

And then there's her biggest fear.

"What if he tells me something I don't want to hear?"

Marge reaches over and covers Laura's hand in hers. "Like what, dear?"

Laura takes comfort in her aunt's touch—the soft hands that stroked her back while she lay sobbing on her bed; the grounding force that enabled her to get through Steven's funeral. She relinquishes the thoughts that have crossed her mind more times than she'd care to count. "Like it's my fault. Or that I should have tried harder."

"Oh, honey." Marge squeezes her hand, her voice heavy with emotion. "Nothing about this is your fault. You did everything you could. You know that. I *know* you know that."

Laura nods, afraid that if she tries to reply she'll wind up unleashing yet another tidal wave of emotions.

"And if that brother of yours says otherwise, I will reach across to the Other Side or wherever he's hanging out right now and give him a piece of my mind."

A puff of laughter escapes as Laura pictures her aunt doing just that. *Wouldn't put it past her, either; poor Steven wouldn't stand a chance.* "Thanks. I'll hold you to that." Laura gives her aunt a reassuring smile, then draws her hand away.

"Is that all that's going on in that wonderfully complex brain of yours?"

Laura bites her cheek, not wanting additional fears and insecurities to tumble from her mouth. And there are more than enough of those. *That Austin never would have given me a second look before his accident. That he'll wind up leaving me, too. That he'll end up like Steven.*

"Come on. Out with it. I can practically see the smoke signals coming out of your ears."

She clamps her lips together, giving Marge a tight smile. "I'm okay. Really." To give voice to any of those thoughts would suggest that she and Austin might be something more than friends. *Which we're definitely not.* Because crossing over into *something else* automatically sets her up for heartache and loss. Something she doesn't know if she can endure again.

"I should probably get going. It's been a long weekend. See you later this week?"

"Of course. You know I look forward to it. Oh, let me get something together for Austin."

Laura clears their settings and loads the dishwasher while Marge prepares another serving.

Laura hugs her aunt, then takes the plate prepared for Austin. "You know, you could take this over to him yourself."

Marge's eyes twinkle, a knowing smile on her face. "Oh, I know. But I think he'd rather see you."

TWENTY-FOUR

Austin clenches his jaw and grips the sides of the leg press machine. *Come on, dammit.*

"You feeling okay today?" Jack nods toward Austin's leg. "Normally takes about ten more reps before it starts to shake like that."

Austin fully extends his knee and places a hand on his quivering thigh for extra support. "Yeah, just a little tired. Overdid it this weekend." He bends his knees and braces his right leg with his hands to keep the weight on a steady trajectory back to its resting place. "Just give me a sec. I'll be fine." A smile plays on his lips as Gran's words echo through his brain. *She always did know just what to say.*

Jack studies him, then taps the machine. "I think you're done here for the day."

"You letting me go early?"

"Yeah. You wish." He helps Austin get his foot onto the floor, then beckons him over to a table at the side of the room. "Hop up."

"Oh, man." Austin eyeballs the electrical stimulation machine Jack's setting up. "You know I hate that thing."

"Yep. Tough. Gotta get those muscles firing."

Austin scoots onto the table and hikes up his pant leg. Settling back against the wall, he tries to contain his displeasure while Jack puts the sticky patches on his lower leg and foot. As Jack turns up the intensity of the signal, he begins to feel the thumping achy sensation and finally sees his foot twitch. *So weird.*

Jack watches several contractions, then nods his approval. "So, was it worth it?"

Austin winces as the next contraction flexes his entire foot. "What? Swerving to avoid the cat? Definitely not."

"No. Whatever you did this weekend. Was it worth it?"

"Yeah, I think it was. Had a great weekend. Well, *I* did. The leg, not so much. I went back home."

"Oh." Jack's face shows his surprise. "Wow. You're really crossing things off that post-accident list, huh?"

"Yeah."

"Well? Was it as bad as you thought it'd be?"

"No."

A smug look crosses Jack's face but he remains silent.

"You'd better not say 'I told you so'."

Jack holds up his hands in a defensive gesture. "Would I say that?"

Austin gives him a bland stare.

Jack chuckles and rechecks the machine and the force of Austin's muscle contractions. "You planning on going back?"

"Yeah." He watches his leg as it continues to move in response to the machine. "You remember that big old house I was telling you about?"

"The one you were redoing?"

"Yep." Austin rolls his lower lip between his teeth. *I must be nuts.* "Do you think it'd be possible for me to keep working on it?"

Jack shrugs. "I don't see why not. You said you and your friend were working together, right?"

"Yeah, Matt."

"Well, you'd probably need to get creative. Might have some really frustrating times, especially at first. But yeah, depending on what you're doing. Lifting and carrying stuff, not so much. But sitting, painting, refinishing, that sort of stuff—sure. Should be even easier with the new brace. You've still got to be careful, though. Don't want you back in here bitching and moaning because you had a setback."

"Would I do that?"

Jack's level stare makes his answer clear.

*
**

"Hi, Marge. I brought your plate back." Austin gestures to his backpack.

"Oh, thank you." Marge steps aside and beckons him into her living room. "You didn't have to do that."

"Yeah, well, you didn't have to send me Meals on Wheels, either, but you did." He grins as he props himself up against her table, slides his backpack off, and hands her the plate. "It was delicious, by the way. Thanks. I might need that recipe."

"Laura said you were a good cook." She raises an eyebrow. "A man of many talents, I dare say."

He huffs a laugh and glances at his leg. "Yeah. A few *less* these days."

"Oh, pish. You're young. You'll figure things out."

"Geez," Austin mutters, "you sound just like Gran."

"What was that, dear?"

Austin shakes his head. "Nothing."

Marge hugs the plate to her chest and runs her eyes down his body, a worried look on her face as she returns her gaze to his face. "Are you feeling better today?"

"Yeah, I'm fine. A little sore from my therapy, but much better than yesterday."

"Would you like to sit down? You could join me for my mid-afternoon kaffee klatch. Well, I guess it's really only a 'klatch' if you stay. Otherwise, it's just an old lady having coffee and talking to herself."

Austin chuckles. *She is something else.* He opens his mouth to decline, then thinks better of it. *Maybe I could make good on that threat to dig up some dirt on Laura.* "Thanks. I think I'll take you up on that offer."

"Wonderful. Be right back." She waves him into a seat and returns several moments later, a steaming cup of coffee in each hand. Setting a china cup in front of Austin, she settles herself across the table. "So, I hear you two figured out how to talk to Steven."

Damn. News travels fast. "Yeah. We think so, anyway. Haven't tried yet." Austin works to keep his face expressionless as Marge's coffee makes his taste buds weep in disappointment.

She leans forward on the table, cup held between her hands. "How did you figure it out?"

"By accident, really. I kind of lost it trying to climb a couple sets of stairs and I heard another voice." His lips curve into a smile. "It was my gran, actually. I heard her telling me I'll be okay."

Marge pats his hand. "Oh, that's nice."

"Yeah, it was actually." Austin huffs a laugh. "Well, not the freaking out part. But hearing Gran."

"So, I take it you were with Laura when it happened?"

Austin nods, then takes another sip of coffee. *Ugh.* "It was the house I was redoing before my accident. My grandparents' house."

"The one that's a couple of hours away? In the small town you mentioned?"

"Yep. That's the one. We were in the neighborhood anyway, so I had her stop on our way back."

"From?"

Austin hesitates. *Is this what Laura meant when she mentioned her aunt's sneaky interrogation methods?*

Marge gives him a reassuring smile and shakes her head. "Doesn't matter. Just trying to live vicariously through you young people."

Austin relaxes. *She's just lonely.* "Well then, don't count on living through me. Unless a birthday party for a rambunctious seven-year-old is on your Bucket List."

"Can't say that it is. Relative of yours?"

"No. Well, kind of. Honorary, I guess. Kelli, my best friend Matt's kid. Calls me Uncle Austin."

"I see." Marge taps her finger against the edge of her cup. "Did you have a good time?"

"Mostly. It was good to see Matt and Monica. And, of course, Kelli. Matt's mom, too. Lots of explanations and awkward conversations about the accident, though. Those weren't so hot." Austin shrugs. "But I think overall it was good. Especially if our hunch about Steven is right."

"Yes, about that. I had a little talk with Laura yesterday. Seems she might be a tad gun-shy about talking with him; afraid of what he might say." Marge's eyes search his face. "She's not as invincible as she pretends to be."

"Don't worry. He has to go through me first." Austin taps his temple. "First line of defense, right here." The smile he gives her belies his own misgivings.

Despite his words to Marge, he's also a little concerned about what might happen when he tries to talk to Steven. Or, more accurately, after. The thought that perhaps Laura's just been sticking close to him until she gets to talk to her brother again has crossed his mind more than once. *God, I really hope that's not the case.*

Marge tilts her head, a twinkle in her eye. "She sure is lucky to have you."

"Yeah, well, same here." *Not sure I could've gotten this far without her.* He drains his cup and lifts it toward his hostess. "Thanks for this, but I think I need to get back home." He winces as he stands up. "My leg could really use a heating pad."

"Thank *you* for keeping me company. It was a pleasure. I do hope you'll join me again. Perhaps you and Laura could come over for dinner after you've spoken with Steven. You know, give me an update?"

"Of course."

Austin sees himself out and settles back on his couch, warm bag of rice draped over his upper leg. It's not until he's dozing off that he realizes his plan to wheedle secrets out of Marge came nowhere close to being a success.

TWENTY-FIVE

Heart thumping against his ribcage, Austin wipes his sweaty palms on his pants as he eyes the entrance of his therapists' building. "Tell me again I can do this."

Laura reaches across the car and takes his hand, giving it a squeeze, then runs her thumb over his. "You can do this."

He leans his head back against the headrest, closes his eyes, and takes several deep breaths. *Okay. Suck it up. You can do this.* When the edge of panic begins to recede, he loosens his grip on her hand. "All right. Here we go. One big-ass leg brace coming up."

Laura gets out of the car and holds his crutches while he hauls himself upright. "Yep. Supergimp 2.0."

He rolls his eyes but can't keep a smile from ghosting across his face. *Just like Gran. Knows how to talk me down.*

Inside, the receptionist directs him to one of the exam rooms. Leaning his crutches against the wall, he hoists himself onto the table. He lets his legs hang off the side and leans forward, bracing his arms on the edge. "So, thanks again for coming with me today. In case you couldn't tell, I'm a little nervous."

"Yeah, just a bit." She settles onto the plastic chair next to the table and places her hand over his. "I know how big this is for you. And I know you're nervous. But you've got this. Okay?"

He stares at her hand on his. Swallows down his doubts and tries to accept the reassurance in her words and her gesture. Locking eyes with her, he nods.

She grins and winks. "Go Team."

He releases a laugh, any further response cut off by Greg's entrance.

"Wait, did I miss the team cheer?" the orthotics specialist asks. "Hey, Austin."

"Hey, Greg." Austin's eyes linger on the contraption in Greg's hand, and he can feel the queasy edges of panic sneaking into the room. He makes a concerted effort to head it off at the pass and turns his attention back to Greg. "Oh, this is my, uhhh... friend." He pauses and swallows. "Laura."

Laura gives him a questioning look, then shakes Greg's hand.

"Sorry," Austin says to no one in particular, "kind of trying not to freak out over here."

"Totally understandable," Greg says. "But hopefully you'll feel differently about this pretty soon." He raises the brace. "Shall we?"

Austin eyeballs the brace again. *Shit, that thing's huge.* He swivels on the table and guides his right leg up beside his outstretched left. His hands tremble slightly as he removes his shoe and brace. *Come on, keep it together.*

Greg slides the brace onto his leg, making sure his knee aligns with the hinge of the metal struts, then fits his foot snug against the foot plate. "All right, now you want to make sure these straps are tight, but not *too* tight." He adjusts the four thick Velcro straps over his pants, then slides Austin's shoe on.

Austin's pulse jumps when he sees his disability stretched out before him. His AFO had been bad enough, but there's no hiding from this one. *Fuck. This is it.* Eyes locked on his leg, his breathing grows rapid and shallow. The familiar pull of panic sets in— the lightheadedness, the nauseating stomach flips, the sensation that his heart will jump right out of his chest.

Laura moves her hand, resting it gently on his arm. Her touch grounds him. Brings him back from the edge. Reminds him. *Slow down. You're okay.* He tunes back in to Greg's words.

"All right," the older man says, "let's go try it out. Head on into the therapy room and get set up at the parallel bars. Don't put any weight on that right leg yet, though, not until you're at the bars."

Austin nods, working to swallow past the desert dryness of his mouth. *Here we go. You're fine. Oh God.* "Is it okay if Laura comes?"

"Yeah, sure. The more the merrier. I'll meet you in there."

Austin slides off the table, careful to keep his weight on his left leg as he gets his crutches in place. "Sorry," he says, glancing at her. "Should have asked you. You mind?"

Laura stands up and gives the back of his neck a gentle squeeze. "Of course not." She ambles down the hallway with Austin beside her. "Sasspants and Supergimp, right? Go Team."

Laura chews her thumbnail as Greg coaches Austin through the mechanics of his new brace. She knows he's concerned with whether or not he'll regain further function in his leg. How the brace will alter people's perceptions of him. What it'll allow him to do, and what it'll keep him from doing.

And I know there's absolutely nothing I can do about any of it except be there for him.

While she can handle being his cheering section, it's the literal interpretation of "being there" that's the hardest for her. Being physically present in yet another therapist's office. Watching someone else she cares about trying to get his life back.

She's trying to put on a good face, but her stomach's in knots and she's not sure if her mangled fingernails will ever recover. She reminds herself on several occasions that only one of them is allowed to freak out at a time. *And right now is not my turn.*

Sitting up straighter, she musters a smile as Greg and Austin walk toward her. *Be supportive.* "Looking good." Despite the clunkiness of the brace, it actually *does* look like walking might require a little less concentration on his part. The worry lines on his forehead are much less apparent, and the tension around has mouth has eased as well.

"Yeah, this thing takes sexy to a whole new level." Austin unlocks his brace, giving his knee more range of motion, then carefully lowers himself into the chair beside her and sets his crutches to the side.

"All right, you're done for the day," Greg says. "Good job. Looks like you're getting the hang of it. Remember, you can double your wearing time every day as long as it's feeling okay. Let me just check your skin and make sure it's not rubbing anywhere, then you're out of here." Greg undoes the straps and lifts up Austin's pant leg. "Yep. Looks good. I'll check in on you during your next couple of appointments, okay? Make sure things are going well, see if you need any fine-tuning. Call me if you need anything in the meantime."

"Hey, thanks, man." Austin shakes Greg's hand.

"No problem. And nice to meet you, Laura. Go Team."

Laura returns the man's smile, then waits until he's out of earshot. She places her hand on Austin's back and absently works her fingers into the knots created by his crutches. "So, are you feeling better now?"

"A little, I guess. Feels weird. Especially since I can really only feel part of it on my leg."

"No, I mean, do I have to worry about another freak out?"

The corner of Austin's mouth lifts. "Oh, I still reserve the right to freak out. Make no mistake about that. But I think you're safe for now." He redoes the straps of his brace, slides his jacket on, then pulls himself upright. "I don't know about you, but I'm starving. Want to grab some dinner?"

Laura's stomach lets out a ferocious growl. "Guess that's your answer." She walks beside him as they head toward the parking lot.

"Then maybe we could try to talk to Steven again? You know, since you're holding up your end of the bargain pretty well. Least I can do is return the favor."

She pulls her coat tight around herself as a gust of chilly wind blasts through the automatic doors. "Yeah, you're really slacking. Might need to think about starting to charge interest."

He casts her a sidelong glance. "Oh, I think we can work something out."

A delicious shiver of excitement races up her spine at his lascivious smile. *Pretty sure these paybacks are gonna be anything but a bitch.*

*
**

"This is a step up from our usual fare." Austin glances around the restaurant as they wait for their server. While the place isn't exactly packed, it's more crowded than he would have expected for a weekday evening. Couples and families are scattered throughout the cozy dining room, candles supplement the low lighting, and pictures of famous Italian landmarks grace the walls.

Laura looks around and shrugs. "If you mean it's not take-out, then yeah." She turns her attention back to the menu. "I come here for work sometimes. Been here with Marge, too. She likes to see if she can copy their recipes. I think her lasagna's getting pretty close."

"Your aunt is quite the character."

Laura looks up. "Oh, is that what you'd call her?"

Austin bites back a smile. "Did I tell you I had coffee with her yesterday?"

"Oh, you poor thing," Laura says, wrinkling her nose.

"Eh, it wasn't all bad. I mean, yeah, the coffee left something to be desired, but the conversation was entertaining." *Not to mention enlightening.*

"Yeah, I'll bet."

Their conversation is interrupted by the arrival of their waitress. Laura orders the chicken parmesan with a house salad, while Austin orders the manicotti and a Cesar salad.

"Oh, and a bottle of house red, too, please," Laura adds.

He continues after their waitress leaves. "Anyway, Marge said you were a little skittish about talking to Steven?"

Laura unfolds her cloth napkin, then refolds it.

He leans forward and braces his arms on the table. "And I totally get it. It's fine if you don't want to try again."

Laura acknowledges their waitress with a smile as their drinks are delivered. She unwraps her straw and pops it into her water, then twists the wrapper around her finger.

Austin reaches across the table and twines his fingers through hers. "I don't know about you, but if it were me, I'd want some closure. I can't guarantee you'll get it, but I think talking with him might be the best chance you've got."

I just hope closure with him doesn't mean closure with me, as well.

"Oh, hey, you two," a female voice says.

Laura's eyes widen and she glances down at their entwined hands, then draws hers away and shoves them under the table. Her cheeks take on a crimson stain as the woman approaches their table. "Hi, Theresa."

Theresa glances between the two of them, her mouth curving into a satisfied smile. "Hi, Laura. Austin."

Laura looks past her, waving at the man with two teenagers sitting in a booth across the room. She turns back to Theresa. "Out for a family dinner?"

"Yep. Devon's soccer team took second in States a couple weeks ago. It's been a madhouse, what with Rob's work and the kids' schedules. This was the first time we could manage to pull ourselves together for a celebration dinner."

"Well tell him congrats," Austin says.

"Will do." Theresa steps to the side as the waitress slides steaming plates onto their table.

"Can I get you two anything else?" the waitress asks.

"No, we're good. Thanks," Laura says.

"Anyway, guess I should get back. They're liable to kill each other right here in public if I don't run interference. Besides, don't want to ruin your date." A smile stretches across Theresa's face.

"We're not on a date." Laura gives Theresa a pointed stare.

"Uh-huh. Enjoy." Theresa waggles her fingers, then returns to her family.

"Ugh." Laura takes a gulp of wine. "I swear to you I did not tell her we were dating."

"I have no doubt about that," Austin mutters.

Laura has made it abundantly clear she wants nothing approximating a relationship. While that's usually his party line as well, he's been thinking it might not be such a bad thing after all. As far as he can tell, they *are* actually kind of dating. *At the very least, friends with extremely good benefits.* But given their respective track records and what he knows about Laura's skittishness regarding relationships, he figures it's safer just to keep doing whatever the hell it is they're doing and shut up about it.

Instead of pressing the issue, Austin tucks into his plate of manicotti. "Oh my God. This is fantastic. Gran would be so jealous."

Laura reaches over and spears a bite of his pasta, shoving it into her mouth before he can protest. "Oh, wow. That *is* good. Haven't had that here before."

"Hey, no fair."

"Oh, quit your pouting. Here. Have a bite of mine."

Austin leans forward and takes the bite of chicken Laura holds out to him. He chews thoughtfully, then nods. "Good, but I like mine better."

They fall into quiet contentment as they savor their food. Austin is the first to break the silence. "So, I've been thinking about going back home."

Laura coughs. Her hand shakes as she reaches for her wine, downing a decent amount in one long swallow.

"You okay over there?"

"Yep. Never better." The tight smile she sends him isn't entirely convincing.

Austin studies her, continuing when she swallows another forkful without incident. "It might be overly-optimistic on my part, but I'd like to try my hand at doing some more work on Gran's house. I have absolutely no idea what I'll be able to do, might be setting myself up for an epic fail. But I was thinking I could see if Matt's free. If he'd agree to try to work with me again, that is. And... I'm hoping you'd want to come too?"

The tension in her face and shoulders evaporates. "What brought this on?"

He shrugs. "I don't know. Several things, I guess. Felt good to be back home. Back with Matt. And seeing Gran's house again made me itch to get back to doing something productive. I'm getting antsy to do something other than rehab."

"In that case, count me in." Her hand reaches for his, but she glances at Theresa and pulls it back again. "And don't ever think your months of therapy haven't been productive. I know it's tough when you're stuck in the day-to-day, but when you take a step back at look at the big picture, you've come a long way."

He looks at the woman sitting across from him. The stranger who came into his life through dumb luck, just as broken as he was. Who's given him back some semblance of himself, while pushing him to become even better. Who doesn't seem to be weighed down by her brother's death nearly as much as when they first met. Who's become integral to his life, regardless of what they call it.

"Thanks, Sasspants. So have you."

TWENTY-SIX

"You sure you want to walk? I can drive, you know." Laura holds the front door of his apartment building for him as they head outside.

"Nah. It's all part of my plan." He winks as he passes her. "Gotta be frustrated, remember?"

She zips up her coat and falls into step beside him as they walk toward her office. They'd made a pit-stop on their way back from dinner, at his insistence. He's taken off his new brace and is wearing his old one, and the difference in his gait is readily apparent.

"I figure if we walk to your office, then I do the stairs a couple of times, that'll hopefully do the trick."

Laura balls her hands in her coat pockets. "You think it's gonna work now that we know the secret?" She's not entirely sure she wants it to. *But Austin's right. I do need closure. One way or another.*

"Won't know until we try, right?"

By the time they arrive at Laura's office, she can tell he's already beginning to flag. His steps are slower and she can see the concentration on his face as he works to move his leg. *Guess that's a good thing.* She hustles ahead and unlocks the front entrance, then locks it behind them and stands shoulder-to-shoulder with him as they gaze at the stairs. "Wish you could at least take the elevator."

"Yeah, me too. Don't think that's gonna cut it, though." He shuffles around and sinks down onto one of the bottom steps, takes off his shoe and ankle brace, then puts his sneaker back on.

"Umm, what are you —"

"I was thinking about it while we were walking. I think this'll help speed things along."

"I thought the brace kept your toes from dragging. So you don't trip."

"Well, at least if I trip, I'll get frustrated."

"And if you fall?"

"I'll get really frustrated."

Laura rolls her eyes. *Men.*

Austin hauls himself to his feet, and shuffles into place, getting a grip on the railing with his right hand while he holds both crutches in his left. "Want to head on up? This is probably gonna take a while."

"Nope." Laura picks up his brace. "Not leaving you alone *with stairs* while you're not wearing this."

"Fine. Suit yourself. But no helping."

"Can I at least call 911?"

"Shut up."

Laura watches silently as Austin struggles up the stairs. She stays two steps below him, her body tensed. Without the brace, his foot drop is very obvious. He has to hitch his right hip up higher than usual to get his leg to clear the top of the step, and it looks like it's getting harder each time.

Halfway up, he hands her the extra crutch. Grabbing hold of his pants with his left hand, he pulls his leg up to the next step while he clings tightly to the railing. As they continue up the stairs, she can see the sheen of sweat on his forehead and hear his breathing coming in faster puffs.

It's all she can do to keep her words and her hands to herself. She tucks her hands under her armpits, biting her tongue to keep any words of encouragement from accidentally leaking out. *Not helping him so he can help me. How messed up is that?*

Laura lets out a breath when they reach the top of the stairs. The trek had become more labor intensive the further he'd climbed, and Austin is practically dragging his leg by the time he lowers himself into Steven's chair.

He gives her a tight smile as he arranges his leg with his hands. "Showtime. I hope. Really don't want to have to do that again." Leaning back in the chair, he closes his eyes and takes slow, deep breaths.

She balances on the edge of her seat, body tense, and props her elbows on her desk. Fingers intertwined, she rests her head on her hands, closes her eyes, and tries to get her thoughts centered on her brother. *All right, Steven.* She pushes past her insecurities and hones in the questions that still prick at her brain. *Why'd you do it? How could you leave me alone? What the hell were you thinking?*

The ticking of the clock on the wall and the sounds of the blood pumping in her ears are the only reply for several minutes.

"He says, 'I miss you too, Sasspants.'"

Laura's eyes pop open at the sound of Austin's voice, and she glances across the room. His eyes are still closed and his eyebrows are drawn together, his expression one of deep concentration. Heart hammering in her chest, she closes her eyes again and rests her forehead on her palms.

"He says he's sorry."

Laura swallows. "For what?"

"All of it." Austin's silent for a few seconds. "He didn't mean to hurt you."

She sits up and lets her gaze travel around the room, but takes in nothing of her surroundings. "Yeah, well, you did." Her next words are just above a whisper. "Why'd you do it?"

"He says he couldn't see past the pain."

"But I was there for you. I was trying to help you." Laura's words are wobblier than she'd intended. She presses her lips together and pulls a Kleenex from the box on the corner of her desk, dashing away the tears that have made an appearance.

"He says it wasn't your job to save him. It's only your job to save yourself."

The hand with the tissue stills in midair. Her breath catches. *Save myself from what?*

Instead of the answer to that question, Austin supplies the answer to another. "He says he's still here because he doesn't want you to be alone. He knows how afraid you are that everyone will leave you. First mom, then dad; now him."

Austin moves in his chair and opens his eyes. "But you're not alone. You have Marge." He locks his gaze with hers. "You have me."

Laura's eyes well up again, unsure if it's in reaction to her brother's words or Austin's reply. *I love you, you big jerk. I'll be okay.*

A chilly gust ruffles her hair, much like Steven used to do when she'd first cut her hair, and she feels a hollowness to the room even as a swirl of warmth curls through her midsection.

I'll be okay.

For the first time in several months, Laura believes herself.

***

Laura stares up at Austin's ceiling as he lies next to her, his soft, even breathing keeping her company. Despite his attempts to make good on his promises of payback, she's still too keyed up to fall asleep. While she definitely feels a sense of closure with her brother, she feels quite the opposite with Austin.

You have me.

His words of reassurance are tempered by their dinner conversation. She can't ignore the panic she'd felt when he'd broached the subject of going home. *I don't want to lose him, too.*

To say that she's confused with what's happening between them would be a massive understatement. As much as she wants to cling to the idea that they're nothing more than friends, she has the sneaking suspicion she's deluding herself.

She's not sure when she began her slide from lustful attraction toward something more, but she knows it terrifies her. She's been so careful to keep people at arm's length. Tries to avoid letting in anyone who could potentially cause her damage when they leave. *Because they all do.* The grief counselor had tried to talk to her about her relationship issues, but she'd wanted no part of that particular discussion. Besides, her reasoning has always made perfect sense. *No relationship, no issues.*

But somehow, Austin managed to sneak past her defenses. Somewhere in the midst of healing and having fun, she might have gone and developed actual feelings for him. Something that goes against everything she's taught herself to do.

Okay. No need to freak out. Just play it cool. He doesn't want anything, either.

She rolls over to face him. Bright moonlight filters through his blinds, highlighting his face. The mesmerizing pools of green, now hidden in sleep, that have seen into her darkest corners. The full lips that delight her equally with a smile and a kiss. *Damn, Prince Handsome and Charming. Too bad. You're definitely the sexiest friend I've ever had.*

As she runs a finger along his jawline, his breathing speeds up. His eyebrows furrow, and his mouth turns down in a frown. *Uh-oh.* His legs move under the blankets, his head turns on the pillow, and he mumbles a soft but urgent "no" as his eyes dart beneath his eyelids.

She places a hand on his chest and rubs gentle circles in an effort to calm the jackhammer beating underneath her palm. "It's okay. You're fine."

He awakens with a gasp, a panicked look in his eyes, and sucks in several shaky breaths. He covers Laura's hand with his and closes his eyes. "Sorry."

"Hey, it's okay. I wasn't sleeping anyway."

He's silent for a few moments before he speaks again. "I always see the same thing. Quick flashes. The yellow center lines of the road. The cat streaking across in front of me. The tree. Then waking up with Matt at the side of my hospital bed, trying to explain what happened." He rolls his head on the pillow and locks eyes with her. "He said it took the paramedics over an hour to cut me out of my car. I don't remember any of that or the first three days in the hospital."

Laura remains quiet. *This is new.* Prior inquiries into his nightmares have been met with deflection. *Wonder why he's telling me this now.*

He grips her hand tighter. "There were times I wondered if it wouldn't have just been better if I'd died."

Laura tenses. *I don't like where this is going.* "Did you ever consider —"

"No. Never." Austin is quiet for several seconds, then clears his throat. "Sorry. I don't know why I just dumped that on you."

Laura strokes his head with her free hand. "Maybe you're ready to start letting go?" *God, I really hope he's not ready to let go of me, too.*

"Yeah. Maybe." Austin pulls Laura closer and wraps his arms around her. "Or maybe I just feel safe here. With you."

Laura relaxes and snuggles closer to him, offering her body as additional support. "Me, too."

TWENTY-SEVEN

The rest of the week passes in a blur. Laura buries herself in the Richardson job, pushing to get as much done as possible so she can spend the weekend helping at Austin's house. By the time late Friday afternoon rolls around, she's more than ready for a break. Both from her job and from Theresa.

Her receptionist took no small amount of pleasure in ribbing Laura every opportunity she got. Letting Laura know that she saw the "goo goo eyes" they'd been making at each other, saw them eating off each other's forks.

Despite Laura's insistence that they were "just friends who enjoy each other's company and looking at each other while we eat," Theresa kept hammering. Laura had come close to admitting her feelings on several occasions, but she'd managed to shove them down each and every time. She's not sure if it was more for self-preservation or to piss off Theresa.

Works for me, either way.

"Oh my God," she says as Austin gets settled in the passenger seat. "Over forty-eight hours without a spreadsheet. How sad is it that *that's* my idea of heaven right now?"

Austin buckles his seatbelt. "Do I need to look for signs of withdrawal? Like, if you start to get all twitchy, do I need to have an emergency equation available for you to work on?"

Laura wrinkles her nose and pulls out of the apartment complex. "I think alcohol would do just fine. Or sex. I'm pretty sure that would work, too."

"Oh, well in that case, how do I speed up the detox process? I do believe I still have interest to repay."

Laura smiles, the tension of the week melting away. "I missed you, too." She gets them on the highway before she continues. "Anything big happen while I was up to my neck in calculations?" *And fending off Theresa.*

"Nah. Just busy making plans for this weekend. Trying to figure out what projects I might be able to tackle and sweet-talking Matt into working with me again. And working on getting used to this thing." He pats his brace.

"How's it going?" Her busy week has precluded her from doing more than brief texts and phone calls.

"Good, I guess. So far, I've only been wearing it around the apartment and at therapy. Figuring out how to maneuver. Trying to work myself up to wearing it out in public some more."

Her heart breaks a little. *Still with so much self-doubt.* "Let me know if you need your cheering section. It took Steven a while to wear shorts with his prosthetic. But you know what? It was fine. Hardly anyone noticed. Of course, that may have been because I'd dyed my hair green." She glances at him, relieved to see a smile on his face. "I'd be more than happy to do the same for you."

"Thanks. I'll keep that in mind." He adjusts his position in his seat, angling himself toward her. "On the plus side, I think I might be able to get down to one crutch."

"Wow! That's great!"

"Yeah. No crutches would be even better, but at least having one hand free would be a huge improvement."

Laura gives him a sidelong glance. "Anything in particular you're planning to do with your free hand?"

"Oh, I have a couple of ideas. Should probably wait until you're not driving though. Not looking to get into another accident."

*
**

"Oh, man." Austin's hope of showing Laura just what he had in mind dies when he sees Matt waiting on Gran's front porch.

Laura waves at Matt. "What?"

Austin sighs. "Nothing." He hauls himself out of the car and ducks his head back in. "You coming?"

Laura has her phone pressed to her ear and holds up a finger. "Yeah, just gotta return this call." She grimaces. "I'll be quick, I swear."

"All right. But don't make me come get you." Austin turns and heads toward the house, stopping at the bottom of the steps. "Hey, man. Thanks for agreeing to this."

Matt smiles and shoves his hands in his pockets. "Yeah. I'm really glad you called. Monica and Kelli are making dinner for us tonight. Otherwise, they'd be here, too." His eyes trail down to Austin's leg. "Is that the brace you were talking about?"

Austin nods. "Thing's frickin' huge, right?" He rolls his bottom lip between his teeth, tightening his grip on the handles of his crutches as he shifts his stance. *You're fine. No one's judging you.* He nods toward the house. "Do you think I'm crazy for wanting to try to do this?"

"No crazier than some of the other stuff you've done." Matt gives him an appraising look. "Frankly, I would've been surprised if you hadn't wanted to try. Really started to wonder when I saw the For Sale sign. Thanks for the heads-up on that, by the way."

Austin winces. "Sorry. Kind of a spur-of-the-moment decision." *Not to mention drugs and self-pity.*

"I kind of figured." Matt looks out toward the front yard. "I see you took it down."

"Yeah, I called the realtor and told her I changed my mind. Haven't gotten any interest except for a couple of curious lookie-loos anyway. Can always put it back on the market come spring."

"Or you could always decide to come back," Matt says, a tinge of hope in his voice.

Laura hurries up the walkway and stops next to Austin. "Sorry. No more work this weekend. I swear."

Austin raises an eyebrow. "You'd better work this weekend. Why the hell else do you think I asked you to come?" His teasing tone is met by a challenge in her eyes.

"For my sparkling wit. And because I'm good in bed."

Dammit. The fact that she's right on both accounts does nothing to off-set the fact that he walked right into that one. Nor does Matt's laughter.

Ignoring them both, he continues. "All right. So, I figured we could just do a walk-through tonight. Get an idea of who will be doing what tomorrow." Austin unlocks the front door and leads them inside, then turns on the lights and adjusts the thermostat. "Got the utilities back on this week. Figured the weekend would go a little easier if we're not freezing to death and can actually see what we're doing."

"You mind if Monica comes?" Matt asks. "Thought an extra pair of hands would help, and Mom agreed to watch Kelli."

"Yeah, that's actually perfect." Austin leads them into the kitchen. "I know we were gonna do this room next, before, you know." He waves his hand toward his leg. "If there's four of us, then maybe it would make sense to split up. A couple people could work in here, rip out the cabinets, do some demo work."

Laura looks around the room. "Ooh, hitting things? Count me in."

"Rough week?" Matt asks.

Laura glances at Austin. "Try rough couple of months."

"All right," Austin says. "I'm not gonna be any help with lifting or carrying, but I'm pretty sure I'll be fantastic at ripping up that nasty-ass flooring in the bathrooms."

Matt wrinkles his nose. "Yeah, I volunteer Monica to help you with that." He jerks his thumb toward Laura. "I think I'm gonna work with her."

"Perfect." Laura grins. "I want more stories. The more embarrassing, the better."

Austin shakes his head. "I am *so* gonna regret letting you two work together."

Matt nods. "Challenge accepted."

*
**

"Hey. You got room for two more?" Austin grins at Monica as she opens the door.

Monica ushers them inside, then looks past Laura. "Is that husband of mine on his way?"

"Yeah," Austin says. "He made a pit stop at the hardware store."

"Likely story." Monica leads them into the kitchen. "More like he's trying to get out of helping with dinner."

Austin chuckles to himself. *That is so true.* "Hey, Kelli Bean. Told ya I'd be back."

Kelli's face lights up when she sees Austin; she jumps up from the table and makes a beeline for the newcomers. "Hi, Uncle Austin! Hi Laura!"

"Stop!" Monica calls out, her voice full of authority.

Kelli freezes.

"Do you think maybe you should wash your hands first?" Monica asks.

Kelli's pigtails bob as she nods her head. "Oh. Yeah."

Monica guides her daughter to the sink. "We're making pizzas."

"Ooh," Laura says, "I love pizza. It's one of my favorites."

Kelli dries her hands. "Mine too. Do you like mushrooms? They're a fungus. But I think they taste good. I don't like onions, though. They're too slimy. They remind me of worms. Sausage is good, but I don't like ham or bacon. Did you know they all come from pigs?"

A smile plays at Monica's lips. "She's a little excited to see you guys again, in case you couldn't tell."

"Really? I never would have guessed." Austin leans against the counter and gives Kelli a hug. *God, I missed this.* Friday nights hanging out with Matt, Monica, and Kelli. His old life.

Kelli takes a step back and studies his leg, then looks up at him, her forehead furrowed. "Is that so you can walk better?"

He adjusts the Velcro of the top strap of his brace. "Yep. Helps make my leg stronger. I'll show it to you some more after dinner, if you want."

"Okay." She leads him over to the table and scrambles into her seat, then continues painstakingly placing mushroom slices on the pizzas in a starburst pattern.

Austin lowers himself into a chair and places his crutches on the floor, then pops a mushroom slice into his mouth.

Kelli scowls at him. "Hey! Those are for the pizza."

"But we're gonna eat the pizza, right?"

Kelli tilts her head and studies him. "Yeah."

"So, if I eat it *before* you put it on the pizza, it's one less step. I'm saving you work." Austin winks at Laura and snatches another mushroom.

"Stop it!" Kelli shoos his hand away.

Monica sighs. "Why must you provoke her?"

"It's my job." Austin grins and steals a piece of sausage.

Monica rolls her eyes and turns to Laura. "Anyway, glad you could make it." Her gaze travels to the overnight bags still in Laura's hands. "Can I take those for you?"

"I can get 'em. Same room?"

Monica nods. "Third door on the left." She joins Kelli and Austin at the table and divvies up the remainder of the toppings.

"Thanks for letting us stay here again," Austin says.

"You know you're welcome anytime." Monica slides the pizzas in the oven and sets the timer.

Kelli nods, her pigtails bouncing in excitement. "Anytime."

Laura crosses the room and leans against the counter. "Anything I can do to help?"

Monica hands her a stack of plates and silverware. "If you take these over to Kelli, she can set the table." She throws a wet dishcloth at Austin. "Here, make yourself useful. Wipe the table off before Kelli sets it."

The front door slams shut as Laura, Kelli, and Austin are putting the finishing touches on the table. The ding of the timer coincides with Matt's arrival in the kitchen.

"He always seems to show up just when it's time to eat." Monica gives her husband a disgusted look. "It's amazing."

Matt grins. "It's my ESP. Extra Sense for Pizza." He kisses Monica, then kisses Kelli on the top of the head. He helps Monica carry the pizzas to the table and cuts them into slices.

Controlled chaos reigns as plates are filled, followed by the subdued sounds of chewing and appreciation for Kelli and Monica's work.

"Oh, wow, this is fantastic." Laura licks a dab of sauce off her finger.

"Thanks," says Monica. "I can give you the recipe if you want. It's easy."

Austin catches Laura's eye as he chews. "Don't bet on it."

Laura wrinkles her nose. "I'm not really the best cook."

Austin barks out a laugh. "That is the biggest understatement I have ever heard."

"I'll bet Uncle Austin could teach you," Kelli pipes up. "He's a really good teacher."

Austin keeps his eyes on the slice of pizza in his hands. "Yeah, but Uncle Austin can't perform miracles."

He grins when Laura kicks his good leg under the table. *Yep. A normal Friday night.*

TWENTY-EIGHT

"Seriously. Whoever came up with this crap should be shot." Austin teases another corner of linoleum free, muttering a curse when it breaks and flakes off.

Monica grunts as she tries to force her scraper between the layers of flooring. "I know, right? Don't know why anyone would want to cover up these hardwood floors."

The two of them have been working on the first-floor bathroom for close to two hours. They've managed to clear a depressingly small amount. *At this rate, it'll take me 'till spring just to get this floor done.* He huffs a derisive laugh. *Wouldn't make a difference if I had two good legs for this. I'd be scooting around down here on my ass anyway.*

Monica stands up and stretches. "You doing okay down there?"

"Peachy."

"I don't know about you, but I need a break." She shakes out her hand, flexing her fingers.

Austin nods. "That's probably not a bad idea." He sets down his utility blade and rolls his neck and shoulders.

"At the risk of having you bite my head off, you need any help?"

A half-smile forms on Austin's lips. "Nah. I'm okay. Gonna stay down here for now." He scoots over to the wall and leans against it. "But thanks for the offer."

Monica throws him a water bottle and takes a sip of her own.

He takes a drink, then screws the lid back on and rolls the bottle between his hands. "It's awkward as fuck, but I'm usually okay to get back up. I'll let you know if I can't."

Her eyes widen. "Did I just hear you say you'll tell me if you need help?" She looks around the room. "Am I being Punk'd?"

"Shut up." He studies his bottle, then leans his head against the wall. "And yes. I will tell you if I need help."

She slides down the wall and sits next to him. "You know that's all we wanted to do, right? Help you?"

"Yeah. I know." He takes a deep breath and lets it out slowly. "I just wasn't ready for it then."

Silence hangs between them until Monica speaks, her voice soft. "You weren't the only one affected by the accident, you know."

Austin swallows and nods, not trusting himself to speak.

"Matt lost his best friend. Kelli lost her Uncle Austin. I know we haven't always seen eye to eye, but I missed you, too."

Austin takes a sip of water. "I'm gonna remind you that you said that."

Monica wrinkles her nose. "Yeah, you would. So," she says with a grin, "Laura's still around. Is that some kind of record?"

"Shut up."

"Admit it. You like her."

"Maybe."

"You are such an ass." She pokes him in the ribs. "Just for the record, I think you make a great couple."

A wry smile crosses Austin's lips. *Me too.* "Yeah, well, don't let her hear you talking about us being a couple. She's got a thing about relationships."

"So do you. It's called fear of commitment."

"Hers is on a whole different level."

"Worse than you? I didn't think that was possible." Monica changes her position and studies Austin. "But you are a couple? Or you want to be?"

"Yeah. She's not like anyone I've ever dated." He chews on the inside of his cheek. "Scares the crap out of me."

Monica's eyes widen. "Oh my God."

"What?"

She shakes her head, a grin spreading across her face. "Nothing. Never mind."

"That wasn't very convincing, you know."

She picks up her scraper and continues working at the floor with renewed vigor. "I'm not sure you're ready for it."

*
**

"Linda, that was delicious." Austin leans back in his chair and rubs his stomach.

"Yeah, Mom. Thanks." Matt stands up and clears the dishes.

Linda waves her hand. "Oh, it was my pleasure. You all worked hard today. Least I could do was look after Kelli and get a hot meal together for you. Consider it my contribution to the 'Get Austin Home fund'."

Laura's pulse jumps. The thought of Austin moving is not a new one, but she has been finding it a more realistic possibility lately. Especially when she sees him with his friends. *He belongs here.* She shakes her head, not quite able to get rid of the thought that's been making a nuisance of itself.

"You okay?"

She starts as Austin rests his arm on hers. "Yeah. It's just been a long day."

"Ditto." He wrinkles his nose. "I need a shower. Or a bath. Don't suppose you guys installed handrails or got a shower chair since I was here last, did you?"

Matt pulls a face. "No, man. Sorry"

"It's fine. Just come get me if you hear any loud crashes. And please do not let the paramedics see me naked, okay?"

Matt's eyes widen, a look of panic crossing his face as he glances at his wife.

Austin rolls his eyes. "I'm kidding. I'll be fine."

Monica gives him a steady look. "You promise? You'll let us know if you need help?"

"I swear." Austin holds his hand up in confirmation. He gets as far as the hallway, then turns around, and catches Laura's eye. Nodding her over, he keeps his voice low. "Hey, do you think you could help me out? I'm actually not sure I'll be okay with their tub."

Laura searches his face. He's rolling his lip between his teeth like he does when he's worried, and the apprehension in his eyes is unmistakable. She pushes her own misgivings aside and gives him a reassuring smile. "Yeah, no problem."

"You know," he says, as he sits down on the side of the tub and takes off his shirt. "You could join me in here. I know there's plenty of room. I helped Matt install it. It's a pretty nice tub."

Dammit. I think he just played me. She gives him her best steely-eyed look. "You're hopeless, you know that?"

Austin takes off his shoes, then unstraps his brace and works his leg out of it. "Oh, I've got plenty of hope." He grins at Laura, then shimmies out of his pants and boxers. His grin falters as he adjusts his position on the edge of the tub. "Okay, though. Seriously. Help."

She helps him swivel around, then transfer into the tub.

He turns on the water and adjusts the temperature, then points to her. "All right, your turn."

She lets her eyes take in his naked glory, careful to keep the desire off her face. Pretending to think, she taps her finger against her lips for emphasis. "Well, I guess it would save them on their water bill."

Austin nods. "You're only thinking of them. You're a good person."

"And I guess I need to keep an eye on you. Make sure nothing happens to you."

"Yep. No telling what might happen to me in here by myself."

She holds Austin's gaze as she strips, taking pleasure in the yearning in his eyes. When she steps into the tub, she can see the evidence of his attraction in other parts, as well. A sigh escapes her lips as she sinks into the water.

"Rough day at the office?" Austin pulls her back toward him, settling her against his chest.

"Mmmmm. Used muscles today I never knew I had."

"Well, I've got to take care of my manual labor. Make sure they come back for more." He drizzles body wash onto her arms in lazy arcs. The honeysuckle scent intensifies as he massages his way up one arm and down the other, and she relaxes as his gentle hands work out the knots of tension that have been present for much longer than just this weekend. *Pretty sure some of those have Richardson's name on them. And probably Steven's, too.*

Thoughts of anybody other than Austin are quickly swept away when he turns his attention to her chest.

"Mustn't forget these lovely beauties," he says, using his hands to suds her breasts.

Her breath catches as he runs his thumbs across her nipples, and she doesn't even try to bite back her groan of pleasure. "Oh, God, you're good."

His soft laughter rumbles against her chest. "Yeah. I know."

*
**

Matt works his crowbar back and forth between the wall and the kitchen cabinet. "So there Austin and I were, buck naked with the exception of strategically-placed socks, in the grocery store parking lot just after dark. We start streaking when all of a sudden our friend, Ryan, turns on the headlights of his car and starts following us, honking his horn to draw as much attention to us as he can."

"Oh, man," Laura says, between hoots of laughter. "With friends like that..." She's cut off by a laughter-induced hiccup.

Matt chuckles. "Yeah. We did a lot of stupid stuff back then. I'm surprised we made it to adulthood. And we're actually all respectable members of society now, too." He grins. "Well, semi-respectable, at least."

They work in tandem until the cabinet gives a satisfactory crack.

"Wow, this is a good workout." Laura sets her crowbar down and wipes her face with the sleeve of her T-shirt. *Where was this kind of therapy a couple of months ago? Probably could have demolished this whole place by myself.*

"Yep. Who needs the gym when you can get exercise and a home makeover all in one easy step?" Matt leans his crowbar against the wall. "Can you help me take this cabinet out to my pickup? There's a place in town that recycles stuff like this."

Laura picks up one end and Matt hefts the other, moving in awkward stuttering steps under the bulk of the wooden structure. They hoist it into the bed of Matt's truck, and he wipes his hands on his jeans. "I've been meaning to say thank you."

"For?"

Matt pulls a couple of water bottles out of his truck, the cold November air rendering a cooler unnecessary. He hands one to Laura and takes a sip of his own. "For getting my friend back."

Laura drinks her water, keeping her eyes on Matt.

He systematically strips the label from the bottle, then tears it into shreds. "I thought I'd lost him there for a while."

Laura shrugs. "Don't know that I did much."

Matt gives her a long look. "I think you did more than you know. None of us could get through to him. He kind of shut down. Shut us all out."

"Yeah. He told me. Not that I totally understand why he did what he did, but I kind of get it. A little."

"What do you mean?"

"It's easier sometimes to just pull away. He said seeing you guys reminded him of what he'd lost. I think he needed time. And space."

"Shit." Matt kicks at a loose stone and sighs, then gives Laura a half-smile. "Well, whatever you did or didn't do—thanks." He chuckles. "And just for the record, I think you two make a great couple."

The tension Austin worked so hard to relieve creeps back in. "Oh, we're not a couple."

"Could have fooled me."

Laura shakes her head. "We've only known each other a little over two months. We're just good friends."

Matt smirks. "Yeah, nice try. The walls in our house aren't exactly soundproof, you know. And I've seen the way he acts around you; he's different. Believe me when I say I've seen him with a lot of women. You guys are really good together." Matt chuckles. "In Austin Years, you're practically engaged."

Laura lets out a strangled laugh, then clears her throat. She swallows, trying to keep the panic from rising further.

She's not all that successful.

She lets Matt carry the bulk of the conversation for the remainder of the day, her brain too busy sounding the alarm to do little more than smile and nod. She even manages to keep it together as she and Austin bid Matt, Monica, and Kelli another goodbye, although the little girl's parting words to her almost send her running for the hills.

"If you marry Uncle Austin, will that make you Aunt Laura?"

It's nothing short of a miracle that she's able to get them home safely. She lets Austin hold a one-sided conversation, reassuring him that she's just anxious about her upcoming week. When she drops him off, she doesn't even wait until he's inside before she squeals out of the parking lot.

Laura paces in her living room, her head in her hands as she tries to make sense of the confusion swirling through her brain. She knows she's being ridiculous. Knows her reactions are borne of fear and past experiences. But she also knows how comfortable Austin looked surrounded by his friends. How much he belongs there. How much better off he is with them.

Save yourself.

Her brother's words break through the surface of the maelstrom whipping through her head.

"Steven?" Even though she hasn't felt his presence since that night with Austin, she stands still, glancing around the room for any signs. *Nothing.* "What the hell did you mean? How am I supposed to save myself?"

She listens for any further insights from Steven, nodding when her own brain supplies the answer. *Trust your instincts.* Taking a deep breath, she exhales slowly.

Okay then, self-preservation it is.

TWENTY-NINE

Theresa clears her throat.

Laura's eyes remain on the spreadsheets on her computer screen. "What?"

Her terse reply garners silence from the other side of the room.

Laura heaves an exaggerated sigh and leans back in her chair, fixing Theresa with a stare. *Here we go again.* "Well?"

Theresa returns her gaze. "You know I'm gonna figure it out, right?"

Laura' eyes skitter away. *Crap.* "Figure what out?"

"What crawled up your shorts."

Laura rolls her eyes. *Aloof. Don't give anything away.*

"It's been two solid days of doom and gloom in this office. Something's up."

"I'm fine." *Maybe if I say it enough, it'll be true.*

"You know, I have two teenagers at home. I am well-versed in sarcastic eye rolls and mopey monosyllabic conversations." She gives Laura a pointed stare. "Not to mention my years of experience working with you."

Laura turns her attention back to her desk.

As much as she wants to deny Theresa's accusations of how she's acting, she knows her receptionist is right. That her resolve to keep Austin out of sight and out of mind is proving tougher than she'd thought. *Dammit. Just move on, already.*

"If it's business-related, can you at least let me know if I need to start looking for a new job?"

"The business is fine." Laura picks up a pencil and taps a rhythmless beat against her desk. "Your job's secure as long as you butt out."

"Did something happen between you and Austin?" Theresa's eyes widen. "Did you two break up?"

Laura's hand stills, and she clenches the pencil tighter in one hand, absently rubbing the sudden ache blossoming in her chest with the other. "No, we did not break up. You have to be in a relationship first before you can break up."

"Mmm hmmm."

Laura gives her receptionist a steely glare. "We were *not* dating."

"Yeah. You keep telling yourself that."

That's the plan.

*
**

Austin checks his phone again, then lays it next to him on the sofa. *Dammit.* He's left Laura several voicemails and text messages but hasn't heard back from her.

It's been three days.

She'd been fine over the weekend. A smile crosses his face as he remembers just how "fine" they'd been in Matt and Monica's tub, then again later that night. *Should probably just go ahead and buy them new sheets.*

Something changed on Sunday, however, but he's not quite sure what. She'd been her normal self when they'd headed to Gran's, but by the time they'd finished working, he could tell something was up. Her typical snark was missing, and she'd been quiet the entire ride home. If he hadn't been working with Monica the entire day, he would have sworn he'd done something wrong.

Austin drums his fingers against his leg. *Really wish I could pace right now. Or go for a run.*

He hoists himself off the sofa and decides on the next best thing—a walk to the coffee shop. Not only is it a good way to practice with his brace, but the caffeinated reward at the other end is an added bonus. The fact that he might run into Laura has nothing to do with it.

Liar.

He nods in satisfaction when he checks his watch at the door of the coffee shop. Nine minutes fifty-five seconds. *Not bad. Half a minute faster than without the brace.* It's feeling less awkward, just like Greg had predicted, and he's finding that his confidence has started to grow. He's now kicking himself for not listening to his therapists' recommendation about the KAFO earlier.

Holding the door open for a woman in business attire who has both hands filled with carry-out coffee cups, he gives her a genuine smile when she offers a harried "thanks." He steps inside and glances around. Several people are waiting in line to order, a number of tables are filled with customers holding hushed conversations or engrossed in their laptops, and the soft sounds of Sarah McLachlan filter through the overhead speakers.

A quick stab of disappointment shoots through him. *No Laura.*

He tries to tell himself she's probably buried in a work project again, but he can't shake the feeling something's different. *At least last week she returned my texts and left me funny voicemails.*

He steps up to the counter and places his order, his eyes darting to the door every time he hears it open. *Not her.*

The barista slides Austin's cup across the counter, his eyes moving to the next customer in line.

Austin clenches his jaw as he eyes his drink. *Okay. No biggie. You can do this.* "Could I get some help, please?" He gives the barista an apologetic smile and nods toward his crutches. "Got my hands full at the moment." *God, I can't wait to get rid of one of these things and have a free hand again.*

Before the barista can answer, well-manicured fingers wrap around his cup, and a velvety voice interjects. "Here, let me." A woman who appears to be in her mid-to-late twenties gives him an appraising look and gestures toward a table in the corner. "Care to join me?"

"Uh…" Austin looks around the sitting area, several open tables providing much less daunting choices. Before he can argue, however, she's turned away, her painted-on jeans emphasizing a nicely-rounded backside. *Crap.* Instead of yelling across the room, "No thanks, I'd rather sit by myself," he follows, his heart beating a mile a minute.

Prior to his accident, the woman would have been right up his alley—curly auburn shoulder-length hair, tight-fitting sweater, an ass that won't quit. The fact that she's making the first move—because he's pretty sure that's what's happening here—would have also intrigued him.

Now it scares him to death.

He gives her a tight smile as he unlocks his brace, then lowers himself into the chair and leans his crutches against the table.

She licks her lips in a move Austin's seen numerous times, a quick flick of the tongue designed to draw attention to the mouth, then gives him a smile that unleashes a set of dimples. "I'm Amber."

Of course you are. While he's known many Ambers in his lifetime, none of them have held his interest for more than a few days.

"Austin." He adjusts his leg under the table, then taps his coffee cup. "Thanks."

The corners of her kohl-rimmed eyes crinkle. "Oh, it was my pleasure." She leans forward, propping her elbows on the table, chin on her hands, revealing an impressive display of cleavage.

Eyes up. Eyes up. Despite his best attempts, his gaze dips. He's more than a little surprised to find that it doesn't hold nearly the same appeal as it would have six months ago.

"So, Austin. Do you come here often?"

He works to swallow his coffee without it ending in a spit-take, remembering back to having said the same thing to Laura. *Wow. That really is a bad pick up line.* He shrugs. "Maybe once a week."

"Huh. I've never seen you here before." Her smile becomes feral. "And I'd definitely remember you."

Oh my God. Is this how cheesy I used to sound?

Despite the fact that his palms are sweating, his jangling nerves settle down a few notches. *Just relax. You're fine.*

Her eyes dart down to his outstretched leg. "What's your story?"

Any lingering anxiety is whisked away by her question, replaced by the more familiar disgust and resignation. *Yep, that's more like it.* "Car accident."

"Oh, you poor thing." Amber reaches across the table and places a hand on his arm, gently stroking it.

Austin looks at her hand, then slides his arm out from underneath. Unlike when Laura's made similar gestures, he finds no comfort or encouragement in Amber's gesture. Just a skin-crawling sensation that makes him contemplate leaving his mostly full coffee behind.

Fine lines around her mouth mar her otherwise perfect skin as her lips form a moue. "Are you from around here?"

Wow, she is persistent. "Not really. Moved here a few months ago."

"Well, if you need a tour guide, you let me know." She scribbles on a napkin, then pushes it across the table. "Feel free to call anytime. Day or night." She gathers her belongings and stands up, slipping on her jacket. "Hope to see you around, Austin."

His eyes follow her sashaying backside out the front door, and he shakes his head when she's out of sight.

The barista passes by on his way to the storeroom. "Man, you are lucky. I've been trying to get her number for weeks, now."

Austin grins, handing him the napkin. "Here ya go. Go nuts."

"Hey, thanks, man. Next coffee's on the house."

Sipping his coffee, he people watches, trying to make sense of what just happened. On the one hand, he's flattered Amber showed interest in him. On the other, he had no interest in her. *Weird.*

Reaching the bottom of his cup, he heads outside, intent on additional practice time with his brace. He's only slightly surprised when he finds himself standing outside Laura's office building, his breath forming little clouds of condensation while he debates the wisdom of stopping by unannounced. She could be with a client. Or trying to make a deadline. *Of course, if she'd answer her damn phone, I wouldn't have to resort to this.*

He presses the elevator button. *I'm just checking to make sure she's okay.* This lie is only slightly more palatable than the one about the coffee shop.

He knocks on the open door of her office and peers inside.

Theresa looks up, her posture straightening when she sees him. "Hi, Austin."

He steps inside, his gaze roaming the small space before resting again on the only occupant in the room.

Disappointment stabs him again. "Hey, Theresa. Laura's not here?"

The receptionist shakes her head. "Sorry. She's got a bunch of meetings today. Were you supposed to meet her here?"

"Nah. Just thought I'd stop in." He rocks back and forth on his crutches and rolls his lower lip between his teeth. "Is she okay?"

Theresa barks out a laugh. "If by 'okay' you mean maddeningly stubborn, then yeah." She tilts her head and studies him, her expression softening. "Look, I don't know what's going on between you two." Her lips twitch. "I mean, I have some ideas, but Laura isn't exactly the Kiss and Tell type, you know?"

He bites back a grin. *No kidding.*

"And I have a sneaking suspicion you were responsible for getting the *Happy* Laura back. Just as much as I suspect the less appealing replacement I've been dealing with recently has something to do with you, as well." Theresa leans forward and braces herself on her desk. "Can you at least tell me what happened?"

Austin sighs. "I wish I knew."

THIRTY

Laura pulls the covers over her head and swats at the alarm clock blaring the start of a new day. *How is it morning already?*

She'd dragged herself to bed around ten thirty, but recalls the LED readings of 11:34, 2:17, and 4:53. *No wonder it feels like I haven't slept in a week.* In fact, the last good night's sleep she'd gotten was at Matt and Monica's. *Crap. It* has *almost been a week.*

When she finally makes contact with the beeping menace, she accidentally knocks it to the ground, where it continues its incessant outcry. *Wish I had a gun. I would shoot that bastard right now.* She rolls out of bed and unplugs the clock from the wall. *Problem solved.* She quickly shakes her head in an effort to dispel the memory of the last time she'd uttered similar words—at the brewery with Austin.

Dammit.

In her quest for self-preservation, she's decided the easiest thing to do is to avoid him. Which is easy in theory. Difficult in practice.

She's been trying desperately to keep her thoughts Austin-free. It's not working. She can't seem to go five minutes without his name, his face, or even his smell popping into her treacherous brain. *Damn aftershave. It's bad enough he looks good, but why the hell does he have to smell so good, too?*

In the shower, she gives her hair a brisk scrub in an effort to stimulate her lethargic brain cells. The unfortunate side effects, however, include flashbacks to the baths she's shared with Austin. His hands massaging her scalp, trailing kisses down her neck...

Her eyes fly open. She curses at the sting of the wayward shampoo, as well as Austin's inability to keep his hands to himself, even in her own damn head.

In the kitchen, she rifles through her cabinet, looking for a box of cereal with enough contents to fill a bowl. She glances toward the stove and gets a fluttering sensation in her chest as she recalls the weight of Austin's body against hers. She slams the cabinet door in an attempt to get him out of her head. It doesn't work.

Driving to the office, she casts a sidelong glance out her window at the apartment complex she's successfully avoided for almost a week. She's spoken to her aunt on the phone nearly every day, but has been making excuses to get out of her regular visits. One of these days she'll have to show her face in person to avoid Marge's suspicions. *Austin's therapy appointment is today at two; maybe I could pop in then. Wonder how he's doing with his brace?*

"Dammit!" She slaps her hand against the steering wheel at yet another invasion of Austin into her thoughts, wincing when she hits the horn by accident.

Standing in front of the elevator, she jabs the UP button several times in rapid succession. *Come on.* She's careful to avoid looking at the stairs leading up to the second floor. She'd usually forego the elevator in lieu of the exercise, but Austin's presence lingers on the steps as well.

Not that her office is any better. Despite her best attempts to keep herself on-task, her eyes constantly track over to Steven's chair. While it used to trigger thoughts of her brother, it now elicits images of an exhausted Austin, sweat-stained and in pain, putting her own well-being ahead of his own. *The ass.*

Laura lays her arms on her desk and lightly bangs her head against them when her thoughts take a more literal turn. She lets out a low groan when she can't get the vision of his backside out of her head.

The click of Theresa's heels stop in the doorway. "That good, huh?"

Laura sits up and slumps back in her chair. "I hate mornings."

Theresa takes off her jacket and hangs it on the coatrack, then heads to her desk and places her purse underneath. "Somehow I don't think it's the time of day that's the issue."

Laura gives her receptionist a long look. "What do you mean?"

Theresa turns her attention to the stack of mail on her desk and shrugs. "I just think it might be less of an issue regarding the hour and more an issue of a particular someone."

Laura shoots her receptionist a disgusted look. *I hate it that she's right.* Doodling on her desk calendar, her hand sketches something that looks suspiciously like Austin's full lips. *Oh, come on.* She throws down her pen and crosses her arms, a scowl on her face.

"Look, I don't know what the hell happened between the two of you." Theresa scrunches her forehead. "I'm not sure he knows, either, to be honest." Her gaze sharpens on Laura. "What the hell did you do?"

She's spent the past week telling herself to listen to Steven. Both his words to save herself and his previous reminders to trust her instincts. *Be strong.*

"Just what's best for both of us."

She shoos away the feeling that somehow, she's got it all wrong.

*
**

"Hi, Aunt Marge."

"Well, if it isn't my long-lost niece. Almost forgot what you looked like."

"Sorry. Got caught up in work again." The look Marge gives her makes her squirm.

"Uh-huh. You sure that's all? You've been awfully cagey lately." Her gaze travels over Laura's shoulder, then back to her niece. "You want to go see if Austin wants to join us for coffee?"

Laura gives her head an emphatic shake. "He's at physical therapy." *Or else I wouldn't be here.*

Marge studies her niece, then steps aside and waves her in. "Have a seat. I'll get the goods." She serves them both coffee and pumpkin pie, then settles in her chair. "All right. Spill it."

Laura blows on her coffee. "What? Can't I just stop in to say 'Hi'?"

"You *can*." Marge holds her gaze. "But you didn't."

Laura takes a sip of coffee; her hiss is partly due to scalding her tongue and partly due to the taste. *Or lack thereof.* Her aunt's perceptiveness adds to the reaction.

Marge leans forward on the table, her eyes searching Laura's. "You know you can tell me anything."

The concern in her aunt's voice is almost Laura's undoing. Moisture gathers in the corners of her eyes, and the lump in her throat takes up residence once again. She takes several deep breaths and blinks, willing herself to push through the emotions she thought she'd overcome. "We finally talked with Steven."

Marge raises her eyebrows but remains silent.

"Yeah. Last week. But I think he's gone now." Laura blinks again, then dashes a tear away when it escapes.

Marge lays a hand on Laura's arm. "Oh, honey. Are you okay?"

Laura nods. *Liar.*

"He didn't say anything that upset you, did he?"

Laura takes a deep breath. "No. He helped me."

"What did he say?"

Laura bides her time, crisscrossing her pie in an intricate design. She sighs and gives her aunt a weak smile. "He told me to take care of myself." *Kind of.*

"And are you?"

"Trying to."

"Good." Marge gives Laura a calculating look. "And might someone else be helping?"

Laura stiffens.

"Maybe someone who lives across the hall?"

Laura stands up and takes her plate and cup into the kitchen, scraping her half-eaten pie into the trash before loading the dishwasher. When she returns, Marge is still sitting in her seat, her eyes narrowed as she tracks Laura across the room.

"Did something happen between the two of you?"

Laura shoves her hands in her pockets, keeping her features schooled. *Don't want to give her any extra ammunition.* "No. Nothing happened."

"Do you want to talk about it?"

"Nope."

"Did he hurt you?"

"No." *And I'm not gonna give him the chance.*

"Did you hurt him?"

Laura remains quiet.

Marge's eyes widen. "He finally cracked through that wall of yours, didn't he?"

Laura presses her lips together.

"You care about him, don't you?"

Laura feels herself beginning to crumble under Marge's masterful interrogation. *Retreat! Retreat!* She gives her aunt a quick peck on the cheek, then makes a beeline for the door. "Gotta go! Bye! Call you later!"

Out in the hallway, she leans against Marge's door and closes her eyes, taking slow, deep breaths to try to keep herself under control. When she opens her eyes, however, the first thing she sees is Austin's door.

Seriously? Ugh.

She stalks out to her car, clinging tightly to the exasperation triggered by the rogue thoughts of Austin that have been peppering her days. As long as she stays angry and irritated, she knows she'll be fine. But she's afraid that if she strays off course and allows her true feelings to surface, she'll shatter into a million pieces.

She's not sure how much longer she'll be able to keep up the façade.

THIRTY-ONE

Austin hums along to the playlist on his iPod, dicing tomatoes for his homemade chili. A smile spreads across his face when Matt's name pops up on his cell phone. He lays down his knife, wiping the tomato juice and seeds off his hands, then turns down the music and swipes to answer the call. "Hey man, what's up?"

"Not much. Just checking in."

"Trying to make sure I don't go AWOL again?" *Wouldn't blame him.*

"Nah. I think you're good."

Austin hears Kelli's excited shouts in the background. "Tell Kelli I said 'Hi'."

"Will do. Although you could tell her yourself. Say… at Thanksgiving? You doing anything?"

"You mean besides my leg exercises? I think my schedule's open."

Matt huffs a laugh. "And maybe if Laura's free, you could bring her too?"

Austin sighs. "Yeah. Maybe." *If I'm lucky.*

"Uh-oh. Trouble in paradise?"

"Don't know." Austin uses his free hand to reposition himself against the counter. "Was she okay when you worked with her?"

"Yeah. We had a great time." Matt pauses. "Why? What's up?"

"I'm not sure. I haven't heard from her since that weekend."

"What'd you do?"

"Me? What makes you think I did something?"

Matt snorts. "Your history."

Austin glares at the phone. "Just so you know, I'm giving you the middle finger right now."

"I have no doubt about it." Matt's voice is muffled as he tells Kelli to put the keyboard mat away. The caterwauling in the background says she didn't listen.

A disgusted sigh crosses Austin's. *Problem is, he's kind of right.* He *has* been known to increase his jackass tendencies when he felt it was time to move on. Has gotten very good at sabotaging things and making the woman feel like it was her decision to cut things loose. *Did I do that to Laura?*

"Sorry," Matt says. "Where were we?"

"Trying to figure out why I'm friends with you?"

"Cause we know too many dirty secrets about each other."

"True. Guess neither one of us will be running for office." *Or running for anything, in my case.* He looks down at his brace, an uncomfortable thought popping out of his mouth before he can think twice. "What if my whole *situation* finally got to her?"

"What? That you're a jackass who likes to have princess tea parties?"

276

"Ha ha. No." Austin chews on his lower lip. "You know. My leg. The whole disability thing." He swallows to keep the bile from rising, still not entirely comfortable with considering himself disabled.

"I don't think so, man. I saw the two of you together. Didn't look like she had any problem with it.

He grips the counter as a thought wiggles to the forefront of his brain. *Shit. What if she's done with me now that she was able to talk to Steven?*

"Well," Matt says, "maybe she's just busy with work again. Sounds like she had a lot going on."

"Maybe."

"You sure you're okay, man? You sound kind of down right now."

"Yeah. I just… I miss her, you know? Can't stop thinking about her." Austin runs his hand through his hair, as if the action might be able to dislodge the errant thoughts. "It's kind of annoying actually."

Matt inhales sharply, his initial chuckle devolving into a full-on belly laugh. "Oh, shit," he finally says, slightly out of breath.

"What?"

"Monica was right." Matt pauses and huffs another laugh. "I told her she was wrong. Man, is she going to make me pay."

"What?"

"Seriously?"

Austin scowls. "Yes, seriously. What's the hell's so funny?"

"*Dude.* You're in *love.*"

"What? No." A cold sweat breaks out on his palms, and he wipes them on the checkered towel on the counter. *I can't be in love.*

In fact, he's had several women question if he was even *capable* of it. Usually as they were slamming a door in his face.

Matt clears his throat. "You okay?"

"Um, yeah. It's just…" He rests his elbows against the counter, not wanting the lightheadedness and buzzing in his ears to progress to something that necessitates an emergency call to pick him up off the floor.

Shit. All he'd been trying to do was get his life back together. Pick up the pieces and glue them into something resembling normalcy. *Figure out how to conquer a fucking pair of steps.*

It's no secret that Laura's been instrumental in his progress. Her no-nonsense, tough love approach was just what he needed to get his ass in gear.

But love?

She's a complicated, snarky, relationship-averse, can't-cook-to-save-her-life woman.

Who he just may have fallen for.

How the hell did that happen?

*

**

Austin can't keep Matt's words from rattling around in his head. After the initial shock had worn off, he'd noticed kind of a warm, tingly sensation. Kind of like when he came out of anesthesia, but without the groggy headache. Although the nausea was very similar.

Who knew being lovesick was an actual thing?

When he can't stand it any longer, he calls Laura, snarling when he gets her voicemail. Again. "That's it…" *Time to get some answers.* He crosses the hall and knocks on Marge's door, plastering a smile on his face. "Hi, Marge. Can I come in?"

"Austin! How lovely! Of course." She steps aside and waves him into her apartment. "To what do I owe the pleasure?"

"Can I talk to you about Laura?"

Marge gives him a broad smile. "Of course, dear. I was just about to have some coffee. Would you like some?" She leads Austin into her dining room. "Oh, and I made some brownies. I know how much you like them."

Austin barely suppresses a shudder. "Sounds great." *I'll eat the whole damn plate full of 'em if she can fill me in on what the hell's going on.* He wrinkles his nose. *On second thought…*

"Sit, sit." Marge brings them each a brownie and a cup of coffee, then takes the seat across from him. "So, how can I help you? It must be bad if you're willingly subjecting yourself to my coffee and brownies."

Austin works to keep the barely palatable liquid from sputtering out of his mouth.

Marge chuckles. "I know Laura hates them. I'm assuming you do, too. I hope you threw out that last batch of brownies I sent over with her. They were atrocious." She takes a bite of her brownie, a look of disgust crossing her face as she chews. "These aren't much better." She pushes her plate aside and takes a sip of her coffee. "So, what about my niece?"

Besides the fact that she's driving me crazy? He keeps his eyes on his cup, playing with the handle. *Be cool.* "Have you seen her recently? I haven't heard from her in a while."

"You know, now that you mention it, I haven't seen her recently either. I think it was the day you were both over here." She leans forward in her seat and rests her arms on the table, her eyes wide, a look of concern on her face. "Do you think she's okay?"

"I hope so." He traces the edge of the tablecloth he'd used for his Supergimp costume. "She seemed fine, seemed like her normal self. Then all of a sudden, she wasn't."

"Any idea why?"

"Umm..." *Wonder how much she knows.*

Marge gives him a reassuring smile and pats his arm. "You know, Laura told me about you two. So, if something happened, you can tell me."

Thank God. Trying to keep their relationship from Marge was harder than he'd expected. He leans forward, mirroring Marge's posture. "Well, I don't know how much she told you, but I thought things were going well. Kind of dating, although we never really had the conversation. We spent a couple of weekends visiting my best friend and his family; one for that birthday party I told you about and another one working on my house."

Marge nods and gives his arm a squeeze. "I'm sure she's fine." Her forehead wrinkles as she frowns. "Although..."

"What?" He tenses, breath held as he awaits further insights.

"I wonder if she might be having some trouble. Thanksgiving's coming up. First big holiday without Steven."

He slumps back in his chair. *Of course. That makes sense.* His relief takes a slight downturn, however, as he continues along that same train of thought. *Why didn't she say something?*

Marge taps her fingers on her coffee cup. "Do you have a key to her place?"

He shakes his head. *Didn't quite make it that far.*

She gets up from the table and returns shortly, laying a key in front of him. "Do me a favor, would you? Can you pop in and check on her?"

He eyes the brass key like it might bite him. "Are you sure that's a good idea?"

"Given the circumstances, I think one of us should stop in and check on her." Her face softens. "And given what I know about your relationship, I think it should be you."

I hope you're right. As he pockets Laura's key, he can't help noticing the guilt he feels at hoping Laura's absence is due to Steven's death. *Because if it's not, I might really be screwed.*

THIRTY-TWO

The taxi ride to Laura's is the longest ten minutes of Austin's life.

By the time the cab pulls up in front of her townhouse, he's managed to gnaw through several fingernails, give his leg a tremendous workout, and second-guess himself so many times he's lost count.

What the hell am I doing?

He stares at her nondescript house, one hand on the door handle of the taxi. *What if she doesn't want to see me?*

"Hey, buddy. You need help?"

Austin blinks at the cab driver's words. "What? No, I'm okay."

The cabbie gives him a long look. "You planning on getting out anytime soon?"

"Right. Yeah." Austin gives the driver a weak smile, hands over his fare and a generous tip, then gathers his crutches.

"You want me to wait for you?"

"Give me ten minutes. If I don't come out, I'm good." *Or dead. Oh, God.*

He makes his way to her front door despite his continued litany of nonhelpful internal dialogue, then rings her doorbell. "Laura?" He peers through the window when the bell goes unanswered. The lights in her living room are on, but his view is obscured by the curtains, and he doesn't see any movement inside. *Not sure if that's good or bad.*

He knocks again, then uses Marge's key to unlock the door. "Laura?" *Nothing.* The smell of burnt something-or-other accosts him as soon as he steps through the front door, and his nose wrinkles reflexively. "Laura?"

The acrid stench grows stronger as he moves through the living room and approaches the back of the house. He pauses in the doorway. The windows in the kitchen are open, and a frigid breeze gently stirs the curtains above the sink; a white smoky haze hangs in the air.

Laura sits at her kitchen table, her head buried in her arms. She's wearing a bath towel and water drips from her disheveled hair. "I burned the couscous." Her muffled words are interspersed with sobs and shuddering breaths.

Checking to make sure all the burners are off, he hazards a glance at the blackened pan next to the sink. He picks up the nearby empty box and reads the simple instructions. *She basically had to boil water, dump the contents of the box in, and let it sit.* He sets the box down and looks over at Laura; he refrains from making any comments regarding her cooking skills.

"I forgot to turn the burner off." Laura hiccups through her sobs. "I was in the shower when the smoke detector started beeping."

Austin hobbles over to the table and sits down next to her. "Hey, are you okay? You're not hurt, are you?"

Laura draws in a ragged breath and raises her head, a look of confusion on her face. Her eyelids are puffy, and tears course freely down her cheeks; she swipes a hand underneath her nose as she sniffles. "I'm fine. What the hell are you doing here?"

"Marge asked me to come. She was worried about you." *We both are.* Austin lays his hand on her shoulder and gives it a squeeze. "Is this about Steven?"

Laura shrugs off his hand, her expression transforming from confusion to indignation. "No, this is not about Steven! This is about the damn couscous!" She stands up and holds onto her towel while she glares at Austin. "It's all your fault!"

Austin's head shrinks back. "Me? What did I do?"

"You existed, that's what!" Laura jabs her finger at him, then fumbles with her towel as it tries to escape to the floor.

"Umm, sorry?" *What the hell am I missing?*

Laura jabs the ends of her towel back in place and paces in front of the doorway to her living room. She runs a hand through her hair, then dries it off on the fluffy swath of fabric around her midsection. It would be so easy to let it fall to the floor, to jump into

Austin's lap and shower him with kisses. The noise
that escapes her throat at the thought is somewhere
between a moan of desire and a grunt of displeasure.
Get it together!

She focuses on her anger, pushing away her other
conflicting emotions. "You just wouldn't leave me
alone. Kept running your hands all over me, kept
doing that thing you do with my piercing..." Laura
huffs as her skin warms to the vivid memories of
Austin's caresses. *Focus.*

"I'm still not quite sure what—" Austin stops
when Laura holds out her hand, signaling him to keep
his distance.

Her chest heaves as she tries to keep her
righteous indignation at the forefront of her thoughts.
No matter how hard she'd tried, she hadn't been able
to get him out of her head. And not just the physical
attributes. His dry sense of humor. The way he makes
her feel safe and loved.

And it was when she'd tried to envision her life
without him that she realized how screwed she really
was. Because the only thing worse than opening up
her heart again to be with him, was the thought of
being without him.

Laura glowers at Austin. "You messed things up.
Made me feel things I've never felt before. Made me
feel vulnerable. I hate that."

"I'm sorry?"

She continues to stare at him. *He doesn't look
very sorry. Looks more confused than anything.*

Austin raises a finger. "Hang on. Let me get this
straight." He climbs to his feet and holds onto the

table and chair as he faces her. "This has nothing to do with Steven?"

"No." Laura's eyes skitter away. *Well, kind of...*

"But it has something to do with your feelings for me?"

"Wait, what?" *Crap. Did I say that?* Her eyes snap back to his, and she eyes him warily as he walks toward her. Her feet stay rooted to the floor despite her best efforts. *Traitors.* She tucks her hands under her armpits and clings to her towel for dear life. *Be strong.*

He stops in front of her and holds her gaze. "I thought I'd done something to push you away. Nearly went crazy trying to figure out what." He nods down at his braced leg. "Then I thought maybe this whole thing finally freaked you out."

Laura's protective shell of anger and righteous indignation cracks. *Shit. I didn't even think about that.* "Oh, Austin. No..."

He shakes his head and shushes her. "But I don't think it's any of those things. I think it might be something even worse." A smile plays at the corners of his lips despite his serious tone. "And it freaks me out, too."

Laura tears her eyes away from Austin's mouth. *So damn kissable.* The green of his eyes is no less alluring. "What freaks you out?" She barely manages to form the words.

He locks his gaze with hers. "Falling in love with you."

She rubs her chest, her heart pounding against her ribcage. "Love?" She swallows, the effort made difficult by the fact that her mouth is as dry as her charred dinner. "Me?" *Holy crap.*

Austin's lopsided grin emerges. "Yeah. I think I might love you." He chuckles. "Believe me, it took me by surprise, too."

"Uhhh…" A nervous giggle bubbles to the surface and breaks free. The initial giggle is joined by several others, and she's powerless to stop the laughter as it continues to build. Before long, tears course down her cheeks, and her stomach begins to cramp. "Oh, shit," she gasps.

"Not quite the reaction I was hoping for."

She wipes the tears from her eyes, hiccupping as she tries to get herself under control. "Sorry." Covering her mouth with her hand, she shakes her head. "It's just…" *Crap. I don't know what to do here. I think I'm screwed either way.*

A shiver races down her spine as a blast of cold air blows through the room.

"Hey." Austin runs a hand over the goosebumps on her arm. "It's freezing in here. And you're in a towel." He runs his eyes down her body, then back up to her face. "As much as I love the sight of you nearly naked, how about you go get dressed? I'll order something for dinner, then maybe we can sit down and have a conversation?"

Laura tightens the towel around herself, a wry smile on her face. "That sounds very adult. Not sure I'll be able to handle that."

"Me neither. But we won't know until we try, right?"

"Sometimes, I really hate adulting." Laura heaves an exaggerated sigh, then wrinkles her nose.

"Fine, we'll talk. Just don't order from the Middle Eastern place, okay? I don't think I want to go anywhere near couscous for a while."

THIRTY-THREE

Austin chews his pizza, the usual blend of Italian seasonings tasting more like sawdust. He takes a swallow of beer, hoping the carbonation settles his lingering queasiness.

So far, so good. At least she didn't bolt. Yet.

She's exchanged her towel for the same oversized sweatshirt and leggings that were the casualties of her pancake flip, and while still damp, her hair's no longer in danger of forming icicles. Sitting on the far end of the sofa, her legs are curled to the side while she wolfs down her own slice. She shoves the remainder into her mouth and licks her fingers.

Dammit, even that's sexy. He lays his plate on the coffee table and angles himself toward her. "So, uh, do you think we can talk now?"

She tips her beer to her lips and takes a long swallow, then sets the bottle on the floor. Changing position on the couch, she wraps her arms around her bent knees and nods.

Austin runs his thumb through the condensation on his bottle. "Are you okay?"

Laura hugs herself tighter, nodding again.

Austin studies her, the attempt at self-protection coming through loud and clear. "That wasn't very convincing, you know."

She shrugs and chews on her lower lip.

Crap. This is like pulling teeth. "Can you at least tell me what's going on?"

She rests her forehead on her knees and takes several deep breaths, then looks up and holds his gaze. "I'm scared."

"Of?"

She presses her lips together, her eyes searching his. "You."

Austin huffs a laugh, his response dying when he realizes she's serious. *Oh.* He clears his throat. "Because?" His hands tighten around the beer bottle as he waits for her response. *Why the hell would she be scared of me?*

"Because I really like you." She balls her hands into fists and takes a deep breath. "And that other word you said? I might feel the same way about you."

"Okay. So far, so good." The weight of uncertainty lessens, and cautious optimism takes root.

Laura shakes her head, a slight frown on her face. "No, not good. Because that means you can hurt me."

Oh, shit. The weight slams back in place as the ramifications of her admission hit him head-on. *Everyone she loves leaves her.* He gives himself a mental head slap for not seeing it sooner. *Idiot.*

He scoots closer and lays a hand on her arm. "I would *never* hurt you."

"Yeah, you say that now. But what about when you lose interest in me? Or move back home?"

Austin gives her a look of disbelief. "Okay. First of all, I can't see myself losing interest in you. You're too damn complicated."

She glares at him, but the twitch at the corner of her lips lessens the effect.

"And second," he continues, "*if* I move back home, we'd talk about it. Although I don't really see that happening, either."

"But I've seen you with Matt and Monica. Kelli. You love them. And you were so excited to be working on Gran's house again."

"Well, yeah. But not without you." He squeezes her arm. "You're a big part of the reason I could even go back there in the first place. I think you kind of saved me."

"That's what Matt said, too."

He narrows his eyes. "Matt. Did he have anything to do this?"

Laura shakes her head, then wrinkles her nose, an apologetic wince on her face. "Maybe?"

"I knew it. I'm gonna kill him."

"But only a little. It was really Steven."

"What? How the hell'd you manage to talk to him without me?"

"No. It was what he said that last time. When he told me to save myself." She plays with the hem of her pants. "I figured that by pulling away I'd be protecting myself. Even convinced myself I was doing what was best for both of us."

"Come here." Austin reaches out and pulls her closer, wrapping his arms around her and tucking her into his side. "I think what's best for both of us is if you don't listen to my idiot of a best friend or your dead brother."

"Possibly. Although maybe I should listen to my instincts? Steven did tell me that."

"Depends. What are your instincts telling you about me?"

"You mean besides the fact that you're a real pain in my ass?" She gives him a sidelong glance, a smile quirking the corner of her mouth. "That you might be the best thing to happen to me. Which, by the way, scares the crap out of me."

"It's okay to be scared, you know. I, myself, am terrified."

"You are?"

"Yep. Like, pee-my-pants level of fear. I'm wearing adult diapers right now."

"Shut up." Laura rolls her eyes, but lets a laugh escape. "What the hell are *you* scared about?"

"You mean besides the thought of not having you to drag my ass around?" He squirms as she pokes him in the ribs and softens his tone. "The thought of not having you to drag my ass around." He rests his chin on her head and waits until she relaxes against him.

"You know, we are seriously messed up."

"Yep. Not fit for others. I think that's what makes us a good match."

"Wow, Prince Handsome and Charming. You really know what to say to the ladies."

"I do." He grins. "Too bad you're not a lady."

*
**

Laura shivers as Austin trails a finger down her naked back. They'd managed to make it up to her bedroom, barely, before collapsing into a tangled pile of limbs. She snuggles closer to him, a contented sigh crossing her lips as she inhales his familiar musk. *God, I love this man.* She grins at the distinct lack of panic accompanying her thought.

As her fingers dance across Austin's chest, another thought takes up residence. "Not that I really mind, but how did you get into my house?"

Austin kisses the top of her head. "Marge gave me a key. She said she hadn't seen you in a while. Said she was worried about you. Thought you might be having a hard time with Steven because of the upcoming holidays."

Laura props herself up on her elbow and gives Austin a hard stare. "She did, did she?"

"Uh, yeah. Why?"

Laura huffs. "You know she totally set us up, right?"

Austin gives her a confused look.

Laura flops back down next to him. "I was just over at her place the other day." *Ooh, she is sneaky.* "I'll bet she wasn't really worried about me." She laughs sarcastically. "Well, not about how I'm handling Steven's death, anyway."

Austin rolls toward her. "Well, what do you think she *was* worried about?"

Laura keeps her eyes on Austin's chest, following her finger's progress as it traces his rib. "Probably that I was gonna do what I usually do." She chews on her lower lip, then drags her eyes to meet Austin's. *And damn it, she was right.* "But how the hell did she know about us? I never said anything."

Austin winces. "Yeah. That might have been me. I think she tricked me into it."

Laura gives him a hard look, then sighs in disgust. "You know she's totally gonna gloat about this, right?"

Austin grins. "I think she's earned it. I, for one, am planning to send her a Thank You card."

"You're ridiculous."

"Maybe. But you love it."

Laura laces her fingers through his hair and pulls him closer, brushing her lips against his. "Yeah, I do. And you know what? I love you, too."

"There now, that wasn't so hard, was it?"

"I'll let you know when the room stops spinning." She kisses him again, deepening it at his insistence. "Speaking of hard…" She slides her hand down his belly.

"Oh, God, woman. You're gonna kill me one of these days."

She grins. "Yeah, but at least you'll go out with a bang."

*
**

"So, we're agreed?" Austin pulls himself into a seated position and rubs his thigh.

"I guess."

"Well, geez. Don't sound so excited. We decided to date. Not commit felonies."

Laura rolls toward him and props her head on her hand. "I know, I just…" She sighs, keeping her eyes on her fingers as they trace the stripes on her sheets.

"Spill it. We agreed that for this to work, we've got to be open. Even if it practically kills us." *And it very well might.*

Heaving out another sigh, she continues to keep her eyes averted. "You know I want what's best for you. Always have. I guess there's still a part of me that thinks that might not be me."

Austin's chest tightens as he reads the uncertainty on her face. He reaches out and tilts her head, locking his gaze with hers. "On the contrary. I'm pretty damn sure it *is* you."

THIRTY-FOUR

"So, what you're basically saying is that you're trying to pimp me out." Austin cocks an eyebrow at Marge, his face otherwise impassive. He slides his gaze over to Laura; the amusement dancing in her eyes is not at all reassuring.

"No, dear." Marge smooshes the crumbs of her apple pie between the tines of her fork. "Merely suggesting that you might think about getting paid for providing a special set of services."

"You know," Laura says, "you're not really helping your argument."

Austin gives an emphatic nod. "Yeah. Because you know who else gets paid for providing a special set of 'questionable services'?" He air quotes his last few words. "Hookers."

Marge gives him a narrow-eyed stare and taps her fork against her lips.

Austin groans. *I do not like that look.*

A slow smile spreads across the older woman's face. "I'll bet there's a niche market for clairvoyant gigolos."

Marge's words rip a snort from Laura while Austin drops his head back in exasperation, staring at the ceiling. "Oh my God. Shoot me now."

"Oh, come on." Marge leans forward and pushes her dessert plate away, bracing herself on the table. "You've finally figured out how to talk with Steven. How to control your new gift. Think of the possibilities." She turns her attention to her niece. "Unless there's a reason why Austin wouldn't be available?"

"Austin *is* sitting right here." His mumbled words go unnoticed.

Laura squirms in her chair, her lips pressed together, as a blush blossoms on her cheeks.

Marge's grin widens, an expectant gleam in her eyes.

Laura throws her hands in the air and slumps in her seat, arms crossed over her chest. "Fine. We're dating. Happy?"

"Wow." Austin takes a sip of coffee. "Try to contain your enthusiasm over there." His words hold no bite; he knows how significant it is that Laura can even acknowledge their relationship status. *At least she was able to admit it without having to be tied down.* He shifts in his chair as images involving furry handcuffs and Laura's naked body pop into his brain.

Marge laughs and claps her hands. "Oh, I'm so happy for you. Both of you." She stands up and gives Austin's shoulder a quick squeeze, then envelops Laura in a hug.

"Oh, for Pete's sake. You'd think I'd just announced our engagement." Laura rolls her eyes. "You gonna leave me alone now?"

Marge lets go and settles back in her seat. "Of course not, dear. What fun would that be?"

Laura shakes her head, trying to keep a stern look on her face. The smile playing at the edges of her mouth makes it less effective. "Besides, we're not sure if Austin's even able to hear things anymore."

Marge's gaze swings from her niece to Austin, a questioning look on her face.

He shrugs. "It's true. Haven't heard anything since Steven. I think I'm just too damn happy." It still surprises him how much lighter he feels since their heart-to-heart. How he feels in her presence—all giddy and sappy. *Never would have guessed I'd feel this way.*

A twinkle gleams in Marge's eye. "Well, that's too bad. Here I had your next profession all lined up for you."

"While I *kind of* appreciate the sentiment," Austin says, "I think I might have that taken care of."

"Oh?" Laura's face registers her surprise.

While his days so far have been revolving around exercise and therapy sessions, he's beginning to contemplate what he'll do with himself when they don't. He's well aware of the fact that he might not regain full use of his leg, but he just hasn't been able to shake what drew him to landscaping in the first place. The fresh air, the physical activity, design and creation.

He adjusts his leg under the table and tightens the top strap of his brace. "Yeah. I've been looking into a couple of programs for landscape design. I think it might be a good fit. Get me back into the outdoors and planning, without the physical labor."

Laura reaches across the table and squeezes his hand. "That's fantastic."

Marge gives him a genuine smile, then slides her gaze toward her niece. "Maybe you can help give the outside of her Townhouse some personality."

"Hey." Laura retracts her hand and crosses her arms, a scowl on her face. "My house has personality."

Austin stares at her in disbelief. "Please. Your yard has the personality of a wet dish rag. You have one shrub. And it's barely alive."

"Yeah, well your apartment isn't so hot, either," Laura says.

Dammit, I hate it when she's right. He'd intentionally made his apartment a memory-free zone. *Guess it's time to change that.* "All right. Guess we could both use some help."

"Truer words…" Marge murmurs.

Laura holds up a finger in warning. "Don't even get me started—"

"Moi?" Marge asks, a look of innocence on her face. "Why, whatever do you mean?"

Laura gives Marge a dirty look. "Oh, save it. I know all about your sneaky subterfuge."

"What she really means," Austin says, "is thank you." He ignores Laura's huffing eye roll. "How would you like to come with us to Matt and Monica's for Thanksgiving? It's always an entertaining time, to say the least, and the food's amazing."

Marge pats his hand. "Oh, I would love to. Unfortunately, I have to decline. I'll be away."

"Any place exciting?" he asks.

"Bare Earth." A mischievous gleam lights her eyes. "It's a nudist colony outside Santa Fe."

Laura slaps a hand over her eyes. "Oh, dear Lord. Please do *not* send me pictures."

Marge waves her hand and scoffs. "Oh, lighten up. There's something so freeing about letting the sunshine and warm breeze caress—"

Laura stands up abruptly. "Aaaand, we're done."

Marge eyes her guests, a knowing smile crossing her face. "On the contrary. I think you're just beginning."

EPILOGUE

Late May

Laura sits down next to Monica, the cold of the metal bleachers seeping through her jeans. She nods toward the clumps of seven and eight-year-olds running willy-nilly on the soccer field in front of them. "How's it going out there?"

Monica barks out a laugh. "Brutal. I think Matt's head is gonna explode pretty soon."

Laura redirects her attention to the sidelines, several yards away from where she and Monica are seated.

Matt paces, his hands on his head, yelling. "The ball! Chase the ball!" He whirls around and throws his hands in the air, giving Monica an expression that says "I give up". He nods at Laura, then turns back to the field and stands next to Austin, his hands jammed into his armpits.

Her heart does its usual two-step when Austin looks over his shoulder and gives her his lopsided grin and a wink. *How the hell did I end up here? And how did I get so lucky?*

Never in a million years would she have guessed she'd be cheering at a children's soccer game on a Saturday morning. Of course, the last few months have been full of surprises. *Never would have guessed I'd fall in love, either.*

Not that her life is all sunshine and rainbows all the time. There are still days when she misses Steven so much it hurts. Still days when she wonders why he did it. Wonders what more she could have done.

And there are days Austin drives her crazy. Makes her wonder what the hell she sees in him and why they're still together. Although deep down she knows. *We belong together.*

Overall, they've both made huge strides in their healing.

Case in point is the fact that Austin's helping Matt coach Kelli's soccer team. He still requires the use of his leg brace, but he's been able to wean himself off the crutches except for long distances.

"Thank God Austin's over there with him," Monica says, jutting her chin toward the field. "Otherwise, I think my husband would have gone postal by now."

Laura chuckles. When she'd asked Austin if he was ready to coach so soon after getting off crutches, he'd given her a bemused look. "They're seven and eight-year-olds. I basically have to keep them from chasing butterflies."

She follows Monica's gaze. The kid who's supposed to be playing goalie is chasing a squirrel across the field.

"Hey!" Austin barks. "Mason! Leave the poor squirrel alone! Get back in goal!"

Mason looks back and forth between the squirrel and his coach, then sticks his finger up his nose and watches the ball as it rolls past him into the goal.

The referee blows his whistle to signal the end of the game, and Matt sinks to his knees. Austin palms his face, shaking his head.

"Ugh." Monica rolls her eyes. "He's gonna be a pill the rest of today."

Laura bites her lip to contain her amusement. She's come to learn just how ultra-competitive Matt is. And how much more so Austin used to be. *Not anymore.* Now he takes losing with a grain of salt. Shrugs it off and says there are much more important things in life. *So true.*

Monica plasters a smile on her face as Kelli runs toward them, and she envelops her daughter in a hug. "Hey, Kell. Great job out there today."

Kelli beams at her mom, then at Laura. "Hi, Laura! Did you see? I scored a goal!"

Laura ruffles the little girl's hair. "You did? Shoot, I missed it."

Austin limps over and plants a kiss on Laura's lips, then tugs Kelli's pig tail. "She sure did. It was an own goal, but hey, you've gotta start somewhere, right? So, are we gonna go get some ice cream?"

Laura taps her watch. "Can't. No time."

"But that's the only reason I took this gig," Austin says, a whiny edge to his voice. "For the ice cream."

Kelli puts her hands on her hips. "Hey."

Austin gives her a considering look. "Weeelll. Maybe I took it for you, too." He watches as Matt approaches. "I definitely didn't take it to spend time with your father."

Matt gives him a hard look and continues on to the parking lot. "Shut it."

Laura snakes an arm around Austin's waist and gives him another kiss. "Sorry. You're out of luck today. Us girls have better things to do."

"Better than ice cream?" Austin asks, a doubtful look on his face.

"Yep," Laura says. "We've got Maid of Honor and Flower Girl dresses to find."

Kelli twirls around and chants in a sing-song voice, "I'm gonna be a Flower Girl. I'm gonna be a Flower Girl."

Austin pulls Laura closer. "I don't know who's happier we're getting married. Us, or her."

Monica laughs and steers her daughter toward their car. "Come on Little Miss Flower Girl. Let's get you cleaned up a bit."

Kelli changes her chant as she prances away. "Laura and Austin, sittin' in a tree. K-I-S-S-I-N-G."

Austin grins. "Good idea, Kelli." He wraps his arms around Laura's waist and brings her body flush against his.

Laura relaxes into his hold and encircles his neck with her arms, staring into the captivating gaze which has seen the best and the worst of her. *And still came back for more.* "What is?"

"Kissing you." He brushes his lips lightly against hers. "Such a good idea."

Her nerve endings tingle as he deepens the kiss, his touch sending jolts of pleasure through every cell in her body. She sighs as he breaks away. "What did I ever do to deserve you?"

He rests his forehead against hers. "You believed in me."

THE END

SNEAK PEEK: TURN THE PAIGE

Hunched over the steering wheel, I peer out my windshield. Nana's yellow one-story bungalow stares back at me.

"Alright Nana," I mutter. "I'm here. Let's get this show on the road."

Not that I actually have any idea what this "show" really involves. Nor am I super thrilled to be here in the first place. But Nana always did march to the beat of her own drummer when she was alive. Why would I expect that to change when she died?

It doesn't look like Nana's house has changed all that much, either. I haven't been here in years, but the twilight-hued hydrangeas flanking the steps that lead to her front porch look exactly the same, and the same welcoming aisle of tulips lines the brick walkway.

Nana always was big on hospitality.

One of those types who's never met a stranger. Always taking people in under her wing.

As opposed to me. Not that I'm a hermit, but I figure I give all day at the office. By the time I'm done seeing patients, I just want my condo to myself. I put out enough fires in my job—I'm not looking to add any extra-curricular activities in my down time.

Not that there's much of that, either.

Between my full-time position as a Family Medicine physician and my moonlighting shifts at the Urgent Care, my free time is limited.

Nana used to harp on me about slowing down and being sure to take time for myself. I think she kind of gave up, though. Either that, or I just got better at tuning her out.

Although I guess she got the last laugh. Because here I am, at the behest of her Last Will and Testament, for two weeks, reluctantly playing along with whatever weird little parting shot she's got going on.

Two whole weeks.

How the hell am I supposed to go that long without working?

Rooting through my messenger bag, I pull out the key from Nana's attorney and get out of my car. As I drape the bag across my body, I let my eyes wander to the well-kept Cape Cod next door.

A man who appears to be in his mid-thirties mows his postage stamp-sized lawn with an old-fashioned reel mower. He takes a break and swipes a lock of wavy black hair off his forehead, then lifts his shirt and wipes his face. The flat stomach and tattoos on his arms pique my interest.

Thank you, Nana. Maybe my time here won't be so bad after all.

Tearing my gaze away from Nana's hunky neighbor, I pull the rest of my suitcases out of the car, then head up her walkway. The small suitcase with the wonky wheel gets caught on an uneven brick, and I have to yank and work double-time to keep it from flipping.

"Need some help, Princess?"

Princess?

I whip my head around to find Mr. Hot Stuff leaning on his mower, a smirk on his face, looking for all the world like he has no intentions of actually coming over to help.

My eyes narrow, and I blow a strand of loose hair out of my eyes. "I've got it. Thanks."

I pull the suitcases up the steps with a bit more force than absolutely necessary and jam the key into Nana's front door.

Princess.

Haven't heard that nickname for years. But apparently, it still sticks in my craw. I shoot the guy another dirty look, only to see that same stupid smirk on his face.

And then he has the gall to wink.

TURN THE PAIGE now available!

AUTHOR BIO & WHERE TO FIND ME

Roseanne Beck is a lover of laughter. A writer of romance. And a conjurer of crazy characters.

It is her greatest hope that the people in her head entertain you as much as they do her.

She's a physician who enjoys unleashing her creativity in her off-hours.

She loves college basketball and hates Christian Laettner.

She has way too many song lyrics rattling around in her brain. It's a wonder there's room for anything else.

She would love to hear from you if you've enjoyed her stories. If you have a spare moment, she would also love for you to leave a review, so new readers can find them!

Find her at

Facebook: RoseanneBeckWrites

Twitter: RBWrites

Or sign up for her newsletter at

https://roseannebeckwrites.com

ALSO BY ROSEANNE BECK

TURN THE PAIGE
SINGLE BY DESIGN
MEDITATE ON THIS

Printed in Great Britain
by Amazon

86849096R00185